Praise for *New Yor...*
Chris...

Prince Charming Doesn't Live Here

"Christine Warren's The Others novels are known for their humorous twists and turns of otherworldly creatures. Like her other Others novels, *Prince Charming Doesn't Live Here* is an excellently delicious story with great characterization."   —*Fresh Fiction*

Born to Be Wild

"Warren packs in lots of action and sexy sizzle."
—*Romantic Times BOOKreviews*

"Incredible."   —*All About Romance*

"Warren takes readers for a wild ride."
—*Night Owl Romance*

"Another good addition to The Others series."
—*Romance Junkies*

"[A] sexy, engaging world...will leave you begging for more!"   —*New York Times* bestselling author
Cheyenne McCray

MORE...

Big Bad Wolf

"In this world…there's no shortage of sexy sizzle."
—*Romantic Times BOOKreviews*

"Another hot and spicy novel from a master of paranormal romance."
—*Night Owl Romance*

"Ms. Warren gives readers action and danger around each turn, sizzling romance, and humor to lighten each scene. *Big Bad Wolf* is a must-read."
—*Darque Reviews*

You're So Vein

"Filled with supernatural danger, excitement, and sarcastic humor."
—*Darque Reviews*

"Five stars. This is an exciting, sexy book."
—*Affaire de Coeur*

"The sparks do fly!"   —*Romantic Times BOOKreviews*

One Bite with a Stranger

"Christine Warren has masterfully pulled together vampires, shapeshifters, demons, and many 'Others' to create a tantalizing world of dark fantasies come to life. Way to go, Warren!"
—*Night Owl Romance*

"A sinful treat."   —*Romance Junkies*

"Hot fun and great sizzle."
                    —*Romantic Times BOOKreviews*

"A hot, hot novel."   —*A Romance Review*

Walk on the Wild Side

"A seductive tale with strong chemistry, roiling emotions, steamy romance, and supernatural action. The fast-moving plot…will keep the readers' attention riveted through every page, and have them eagerly watching for the next installment."   —*Darque Reviews*

Howl at the Moon

"*Howl at the Moon* will tug at a wide range of emotions from beginning to end…Engaging banter, a strong emotional connection, and steamy love scenes. This talented author delivers real emotion which results in delightful interactions…and the realistic dialogue is stimulating. Christine Warren knows how to write a winner!"   —*Romance Junkies*

She's No Faerie Princess

"Christine Warren has penned a story rich in fantastic characters and spellbinding plots."
                         —*Fallen Angel Reviews*

Not Your Ordinary
Faerie Tale

CHRISTINE WARREN

St. Martin's Paperbacks

This is a work of fiction. All of the characters, organizations, and events portrayed in this novel are either products of the author's imagination or are used fictitiously.

NOT YOUR ORDINARY FAERIE TALE

Copyright © 2011 by Christine Warren.

For information address St. Martin's Press, 175 Fifth Avenue, New York, NY 10010.

ISBN: 978-0-312-35722-1

Printed in the United States of America

St. Martin's Paperbacks edition / November 2011

St. Martin's Paperbacks are published by St. Martin's Press, 175 Fifth Avenue, New York, NY 10010.

10   9   8   7   6   5   4   3   2   1

Not Your Ordinary
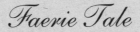

One

Metal struck metal, sparks fizzing and shooting,
scenting the air with fire and electricity. Clangs and
grunts echoed off the smooth stone of the walls,
bouncing down from the high vaults of the ceiling.
Sweat beaded on brows and coated tense ropes of
muscle with the sheen of exertion. Two forms, one
tall and lean and elegant, the other huge and thick
and powerful, stood locked in fierce battle, expressions grim, arms straining against each other's
strength. Neither made a move to end the struggle;
neither possessed a mien suited to surrender. They
had engaged, two warriors fit and fierce, dedicated
to honor and to victory.

But one had just realized that the tip of his nose
itched like a son of a bitch.

Shit.

"I can see it in your eyes, Luc," the slender one
taunted, even as strands of auburn hair slipped
loose of their confining braid and clung to his damp
face. "You're wavering. Maybe your skill becomes
rusty, old friend. Too much time sitting at the
Queen's feet; not enough on the front lines."

"Shut it, Fergus," his opponent growled, his twitching nose rather spoiling the effect of his fierce scowl. His dark hair and hard, chiseled features usually made the expression more than a bit effective against his enemies. "I'd not comment on seating arrangements if I were you. Your place seems to set your lips right at a level with the royal arse these days, doesn't it? Though I suppose all that puckering is at least some exercise for you."

Silver scraped and hissed as Fergus swept his sword arm down, dragging Luc's blade with his. A quick step and turn and metal clanged again with hollow thunder.

"Aye," shouted one of the guardsmen ranging about the open space of the practice hall. "And you need all of that you can get, Fergus, seeing how fond I've seen you grow of the Queen's honey-cakes."

Fergus parried a coming blow and stepped back to circle again, searching for a better opening. Luc breathed a profane thanks and seized the opportunity to swipe the back of his non-sword hand across his nose. Much better.

"Better to eat a few cakes than drink myself stupid like some others," the redhead retorted, his eyes never straying from his opponent. His lips curved in a sharp grin. "Or did you think no one had noticed you facedown in your wine the other night, Hamish?"

The blond guardsman colored slightly but did

his best to look superior. "I was merely admiring the fine bouquet."

Luc lifted an eyebrow. "And that requires snoring these days, does it, Hamish?"

The seven men assembled in the hall guffawed, elbows nudging Hamish's sides good-naturedly. The sight gave Luc, as captain of the Guard, a deep sense of satisfaction. The warriors in this room were his men, and he held responsibility for both their prowess with a sword and their cohesion as a unit. In Luc's mind, each of them reflected on him, testament to his leadership and his loyalty. All of them, himself included, existed to serve the Queen. And the stars knew she didn't suffer fools lightly.

Well, at least none who weren't related to her by blood.

Blowing out a breath, Luc shoved the fleeting thought of that particular bundle of annoyance from his mind and took a step back. No sense borrowing worry when he suspected it would be handed to him on a platter soon enough. It was time to get back to work.

"Good match, Fergus." He lowered his sword arm and nodded to his lieutenant, stepping out of the bounds of the designated sparring circle. "Lead the others through their exercises. I've business to see to before we meet for assignments."

Fergus's muscles tensed momentarily, as if the command needed an extra heartbeat to travel from brain to body. Then the tension bled out of him and he sheathed his sword, casting Luc a bland look. "Queen's business?"

Luc snorted. "Is there any other kind?"

Fergus's grin flashed. "Does that mean today's assignments will feature tasks a bit more exciting than patrolling for boggarts around the castle walls or protecting Her Majesty from assault by the brownie emissary? Heaven forbid the little bastard should get out of hand and attempt to clean the throne room without leave."

"Getting bored, Fergus?" Luc adjusted the strap of his own weapons harness across his chest. "I'm sure I could find a garderobe for you to clean if you so long for variety in your work."

"And I'm sure I could drop you into one, if you've such a nose for shit—"

"Children, please. You know I deplore squabbles among my Guard."

The voice from the doorway drew the pair up short. Being overheard didn't surprise Luc, not here in the palace. After all, the Summer Court ran on the power of intrigue. Survival relied on assuming that someone was always listening. Fergus, though, looked as if he might have forgotten. Luc saw a small twitch in his jaw before he gathered himself to make his bow to their sovereign.

She stood in the archway at the entrance to the room, flanked as always by the busy, buzzing swarm of her attendants. Ladies-in-waiting, advisers, entertainers, and supplicants followed in her train, elbowing and maneuvering for the privilege of adjusting the hem of her royal gown. It wouldn't have mattered if that hem swept atop a dung heap. Wherever she went, the toadies followed, and wherever she went, she might as well have sat in state upon her gleaming marble dais of power. There, atop the silver throne sculpted in the shape of a breaking wave, ruled Mab of the Silver Bells, Lady of Many Blessings, Huntress of Spirits, and Queen of the Summer Court.

Now she stood on plain, porous stone before an audience of rough, sweaty warriors, looking not an inch less regal, nor a shadow less powerful. As if she ever could. Only a fool underestimated Queen Mab, and fools died quickly in Faerie.

She wore a diadem of gleaming silver in the shape of a wreath of apple blossoms perched on her bright red-gold hair. A surcoat of russet velvet topped her gown of amber silk, each shot through with silver thread. Cunningly woven, the rich fabrics seemed to spark with every subtle movement. Her pale, slender feet peeked from beneath her hem, toes adorned with silver bells, and her graceful, ringed fingers moved unconsciously and restlessly at her sides. Luc noted the hint of impatience and braced himself.

"You become slow to answer your Queen, my Lucifer." Mab's voice, low and musical, displayed a hint of petulance that made Luc wary. A petulant Queen was a dangerous Queen. Well, more dangerous than usual. "We might be tempted to interpret such a thing as a reluctance to serve us."

Beside him, Fergus moved as if to step forward and offer reassurance, but Luc kept his gaze firmly on the changeable green eyes of his sovereign. They shifted as restlessly as the sea and could be just as deadly.

"Never think it, my Queen," he said, bowing before her. "I am ever at your command, as are all of your Guard. We answer always to Your Majesty's whim."

The formal language of court sometimes had a soothing effect on Mab. Even when it didn't, it was always safer to treat the Queen with kid gloves. Her temper made her unpredictable; her power made her deadly.

Mab shifted, her brows rising. "Is that so?" Her gaze turned to Fergus and sharpened. "Does the captain of my Guard speak true, my Fergus? Are all of the Seven as loyal to us as he would make them sound?"

Fergus bowed low again, his gray eyes warming with mischief and flirtation. Of all the Guards, he liked to think of himself as Her Majesty's favorite. Luc liked to think of him as her fool, since flirting with the Queen possessed the same inherent risks as poking a nightmare in the side—you might get away with it a thousand times, but sooner or later the creature would decide to take your head off. Fergus, though, seemed to think himself invulnerable.

"Without question, my lady. To serve in the Queen's Guard is an honor of which we Seven are well aware." Fergus straightened and placed his hand above his heart in a salute of fealty, but his gaze remained teasing. "Your safety and the rule of your word are our only concerns."

Luc fought back the urge to groan. Talking to the Queen required one to walk a thin line, one Fergus seemed hellbound to test. If Mab perceived any insult as more severe than failing to flatter her, it was flattering her insincerely. When she paused for a moment and pursed her lips, the captain concealed a wince.

Then her expression softened, and Luc felt the tension drain from his men like ale from the barrel.

"Is that so, my Fergus?" She smiled. "Your devotion is ever a comfort to us. We appreciate the reassurance now more than ever, for a disturbing piece of news has come to our attention, and we fear we must turn to our Guard for assistance."

Lucifer maintained a bland expression even as he swore silently. This was it, the trouble he had sensed coming. But maybe fate would be kind and dump it on Fergus's head rather than his own. A man could dream, couldn't he?

"Any manner of service to our Queen honors us," Fergus said, drawing his shoulders back into a swaggering posture Luc had seen him use more than once on an unsuspecting Fae maiden. He probably thought it made him look strong and confident; it made Luc liken him to a rooster courting the female birdbrains in his yard. "I personally await your orders and will see them executed with all speed and diligence."

The royal lips curved slightly, accompanied by the lifting of her chin and an easing of the tightness around her eyes. Once again, the Queen had been appeased by Fergus's nonsense. Luc might not understand, but he could be grateful. Especially if the fawning performance landed Fergus with whatever problem instinct told Luc he wanted no part of.

Abruptly, the Queen moved, sweeping her robes behind her as she entered and began to pace around the large room.

"My advisers have brought word of a small problem in *Ithir* that must be attended to." With everyone reminded of his or her place in the hierarchy of Faerie, Mab dispensed with the royal *we* and continued with a slight bend in her formality. "My Guard, of course, are the only ones I would trust to deal with such a delicate situation."

Foreboding tickled its way down Luc's spine. *Ithir* was the Fae word for the human world, which made the Queen's statement more than a little remarkable. Mostly because the Fae kept so much distance between themselves and humans that one might be surprised they even had a word for the neighboring realm. His sense of unease only grew when Mab turned her gaze on him again, clearly waiting for some kind of response from the captain of said Guard.

"Of course," he managed, willing his jaw to

unlock enough to speak. "It is our duty and privilege to serve in any way Your Majesty requires."

"I would be honored to deal personally with anyone foolish enough to disturb my Queen," Fergus offered, stepping forward with another bow. "I would indeed consider it a privilege."

Mab's face softened, and she lifted a hand to the warrior's face. "You are good to me, my Fergus. Good and true. But there is more to the story you have yet to hear. You and my captain."

Her gaze flicked to Luc. He nodded grimly. He had the worst feeling he knew what she was going to reveal. Lately, all the trouble to be had at the Summer Court seemed to emanate from a single, senseless source. A source the Queen held close to her royal heart.

"I have kept a closer eye on the mortal world since news reached me of the . . . incident in Dionnu's court earlier this year," Mab continued. "The indiscriminate use of gates into our realm by humans is something that I, of course, cannot allow."

Luc nodded sharply. He, too, had heard about the trouble the Queen referred to. The details were sketchy—unsurprising given the intense antipathy Mab held for Dionnu, King of the Winter Court, the man she considered her archenemy. And ex-husband. The situation made the flow of information between the two courts somewhat shaky.

Still, the story suggested that two human women had made it through a gate near the Winter Palace, one of whom had wandered undetected and unsupervised around Faerie for days before being discovered and returned to *Ithir*. The other human woman had at least reportedly been accompanied by a changeling with ties to one of Dionnu's attendants. They had all returned to the human realm, but whispers of troubles quickly covered up continued to circulate. At both courts.

The Queen might refer to the whole thing as an *incident*, but Luc took his defense of the Queen seriously. To him, it represented a security nightmare.

"I can only repeat my earlier advice, my Queen," he said, taking care to keep any hint of impatience or I-told-you-so out of his voice. "If we were to seal the gates, I could arrange for patrols to keep them secure. Use could then be monitored and regulated for your safety and that of your people."

She slanted him a narrow look. "I believe my people would dislike the feeling of being jailed, Lucifer, no matter how pretty the prison. I won't take such a step unless I have no other choice. But at the moment, the security of the gates is not my concern. Rather, it is what I have seen on the other side of them that disturbs me."

To Luc's knowledge the Queen hadn't traveled to *Ithir* since before the mortals had concluded it to be round, but he could guess where she'd come by her information. She had looked into her scrying pool, and he had served her long enough to know that this alone usually spelled trouble.

"Surely whatever mess the humans have made for themselves this time is no problem of ours, Your Majesty," Fergus put in, his expression a well-thought-out balance of concern and charm. "They're such troublesome creatures, after all. You yourself have always said that if we stepped in to save them once, they'd never leave us alone. They'd be popping up looking for our aid for every little thing they could think of."

Mab's glance both measured and indulged. "I should hardly like to disagree with my own words of wisdom, but in this case they remain beside the point. Of course the problems of the mortals don't concern me. What does is the knowledge that one of my own dear hearts has left my court, and I have reason to believe he has crossed over to their world."

And there it was, the sucker punch Luc had been waiting for. There was only one group of Fae whom Mab referred to as her "dear hearts"—her family. Specifically her nieces and nephews, the ones who lived in the hope of one day being proclaimed her heir and who therefore made it their lives' work to ingratiate themselves deeply within her favor. Where the hopefuls went, trouble followed, but Luc knew that it rode particularly hard on one set of heels in particular.

"Seoc," he growled.

Mab sent him a frosty look. "We dislike such hasty assumptions, Lucifer, son of Annwn. It becomes you ill to think so poorly of others."

He murmured an apology but noticed that her scolding offered nothing like a denial of the charge. He also noticed he'd annoyed her enough that she reverted to her royal *we*. His hands clenched at his sides.

Fergus warned him with a glance and shifted forward to draw the Queen's attention. "Youth often is accompanied by a certain rashness, Your Majesty. It's not surprising that a young Fae looking for adventure might decide to visit *Ithir* on a whim, but I'm certain there would be no danger. The Others know it would be folly to cause any harm or distress to a member of your court."

What the Others knew and what they would feel justified in doing, Luc reflected, might be two very different things. While the Fae had abandoned the mortal realm centuries ago, some supernatural races had stayed behind to live secretly among the humans, calling themselves the Others. Immortals such as the vampires and non-humans like the were-folk still roamed throughout the human world, keeping their identities carefully guarded secrets. Their ruling body, the Council of Others, still kept in contact with the Fae court and would have every right to dislike the thought of an unauthorized Fae visitor wandering about and causing trouble.

"Of course they know it is folly," Mab snapped. "Not even a demon would be so foolish. But there are other reasons to desire my nephew's swift return home. In our position, we must think of more than life and death at times. There is diplomacy to consider, both between our court and the Others' Council and within the court itself."

It was the use of *my nephew* that sealed it for Luc. Despite the dozens of such relatives Mab could claim, the implication of troublemaking and possible diplomatic incidents pointed at only one of the many suspects—Seoc nic Saoirse, son of the Queen's deceased youngest sister. Even though his gut had told Luc that Seoc was the source of whatever trouble the Queen had detected in *Ithir*, there had remained the slim possibility that the other budding troublemaker at court could have been responsible. Fiona might be young, a veritable teenager in Fae terms, but she was showing a gift for mischief even Seoc could not outdo. Thankfully, she seemed to have a brighter head on her shoulders than her cousin, so Luc had moved her down the list in terms of likely culprits. The list of two. Which left him with only one name.

Seoc.

Some days he hated being right.

"What has Seoc done?"

Mab pursed her lips, but she could hardly dress him down for drawing the correct conclusion. "As we said, we have reason to believe he has chosen to take himself into *Ithir* without our knowledge or approval. While boys will be boys and all young men deserve the chance to sow some wild oats, as the mortals term it, we fear Seoc might have stepped a hair over the line. We think he may have been . . . indiscreet."

Since he could think of no response that would not sink him even lower in the Queen's favor, Luc kept his mouth shut. Of course Seoc had been indiscreet. Indiscreet was his middle name. One of his middle names. Along with reckless, foolish, idiotic, and generally irritating.

"I am sure any small ripples in the Other community can be smoothed over, my Queen," Fergus said, his tone deliberately even and reasonable. All the things Luc couldn't quite manage at that point. "It is hardly the first time one of our people has had a run-in with one of theirs."

"If only my concern was for something so inconsequential, Fergus. But I fear there is more to it." The Queen paused, her stormy green eyes locking on a point somewhere just to the left of Luc's temple, as if he were unworthy of her gaze. "Unfortunately, it seems that our dear Seoc has not confined his associations to the Other-folk in *Ithir*, but has allowed his presence to be noted by the mortals as well."

Concealing his intense un-surprise, Luc acknowledged the disclosure with an impassive stare and an internal oath. Part of him had still held out some hope that Seoc might have used what little brainpower he possessed to keep himself confined in the Other society of *Ithir*. He'd known it was an unfounded hope—he'd never seen any evidence that Seoc possessed a functioning brain to begin with—but it had been deep and instinctive. The man should have known the risks of being seen by humans while the Others remained hidden among them. Whether or not to reveal their presence to humans had been a subject of intense debate among the Others for decades now, intense enough to threaten to erupt into serious political infighting from time to time; but it ultimately belonged to their Council to decide. And the Council would not like the threat of having their hand forced by sightings of a "fairy" in central Manhattan.

Luc knew better than to express disbelief or condemnation for the royal nephew's actions. Only the Queen was allowed to speak ill of the worthless dung beetle, even though it had become a larger and larger part of Luc's job recently to drag the fool back home with his tail between his legs. Such was life at court and service in the Queen's Guard.

"Seoc means no harm, I am certain," Mab proclaimed, lifting her chin and firming her lips the way she always did when she said something she knew to be not entirely accurate. "But our nephew must learn that his antics reflect on more than himself. Even our indulgence cannot shield him forever from the consequences of his actions. Especially not as we must begin to think of the matter of our succession."

Luc felt his eyebrows climb toward his hairline, but he kept his mouth shut. If Mab had any intention of naming Seoc the heir to her throne, he'd eat his own sword. Sure, as her nephew he had as great a claim to the title as any number of other relatives, but Luc doubted the Queen intended to turn her throne over to a complete imbecile.

Actually, Luc doubted she planned to turn her throne over to anyone short of her own death, and given the immortal life span of the Fae, that should occur sometime after the Fifth of Never. Unless, of course, she were to be killed, but it was Luc's job to ensure that that didn't happen. He took his job very seriously.

Even if sometimes he wanted to kill her himself. Like now.

"In Faerie we can keep his mischief contained," the Queen continued, "but we have no such control in *Ithir*. The human world chooses not to bow to our authority, and therefore is a place too treacherous to allow him free rein. And so we must ask our Guard to go after our nephew and return him to court. His presence begins to disturb the flow of human reality, and the Others have sent word they are anxious to have him gone."

Too bad no one but the Queen is anxious to have him back, Luc thought.

"Can they not return him themselves?" Fergus suggested. "The Others may not have our powers, but they are not without resources."

"The Others may be superior to the mortals they live among, but they can hardly be considered our equals, my Fergus." The Queen shook her head. "Seoc could elude them forever if he so chose. While they know of his presence in their realm, we do not think they have learned the extent of his indiscretion, which is fortunate for us. The Others still harbor a great fear of their secret being revealed to the mortal world. They believe the humans are not ready to acknowledge the truth of their existence, and we must agree on that point. The inability of mortals to accept the magic before them is the reason we abandoned their realm so many years ago. It is doubtful they have progressed so far in the time since. No, it must be a Fae to catch a Fae."

Luc fought the urge to roll his shoulders against the growing tension, caused almost entirely by irritation. "I understand, Your Majesty. I will find Seoc and return him to you with all speed, and the mortals will be none the wiser."

"I'll go," Fergus said, turning to Luc. "It's a simple enough task. There's no reason for you to do it yourself. You've duties here. You keep the Guard running, and I'll go fetch Seoc."

"Believe me, I'd like nothing more," Luc said with regret, "but it will be faster if I go. I've gone after him before. I know more of his habits. And the quicker he returns, the better for everyone. I'll leave immediately." He nodded to the Queen. "With your permission."

"You have it." The Queen shifted to smile at Fergus, lifting a bejeweled hand to his face. "I could not spare you, my Fergus. Someone must stay and see to us here at court.

"This task I have set you to is important for

many reasons." She addressed Luc more seriously. "More than my nephew's safety is at stake here. If the existence of the Others becomes common knowledge to the mortals, it will not be long before they find their way to even our realm. You must not allow this to happen."

Luc set his jaw and nodded once, curtly. "I understand," he repeated. "I will do all in my power and use all resources at hand, my lady."

Mab reached up, her cool, pale fingers cupping his stubble-roughened face, and the smile she gave him reminded him why human and Fae alike still wrote odes to her beauty, even after so many endless centuries.

"If you do all in your power, my Lucifer, then I know well you cannot fail me." Leaning up, she brushed a kiss against his cheek and stepped back, raising her hands before her and waving them in an intricate pattern that dripped trails of light from her fingertips. As the guardsmen watched, the light wove itself together into a shimmering doorway, expanding until it was large enough to accommodate even Luc's height.

Blowing out a deep breath, Luc stepped forward into the Faerie door and felt the warmth of the Queen's magic surround him. As reality bent and reshaped itself, her voice reached him on a silver whisper. "Go safely, my Lucifer, and may what you find to please you, ever be yours."

Two

A woman could only take so much, Corinne D'Alessandro decided as she looked down at the assignment sheet her editor had just handed to her. In the past year or so, she'd taken a lot: learning about the existence of vampires, watching her best friend become a vampire; learning about the existence of werewolves, watching her other best friend marry a werewolf. All in all, an eventful few months had just passed. Corinne figured it was a testament to her inner strength and resilience that she'd taken all this news without ending up in a padded room at Bellevue, contemplating her navel and holding conversations with her big toes.

But this, she thought, staring at the black print on the page before her, this just might be the last straw.

"Elves," she said with admirable calm.

"Well, maybe pixies. Reports vary."

Corinne couldn't decide if she wanted to run screaming from the office, past her curious colleagues and out onto the streets of Manhattan, or if she wanted to bang her head against the wall a few times before she buried it in her hands and whimpered. What in God's name had she done to deserve this? What sin could she possibly have committed that would justify this sort of vengeance from an angry deity? Was it the premarital-sex thing? Because a lifetime of Catholicism aside, she'd long ago come to the conclusion that Jesus had better things to worry about than her active social life. So how in the name of all that was holy had hell found a way to drag her into the fiery pit of fucktardedness that was the only way to describe being caught between her job's rock and the hard place of her unspoken promise to keep the Others' secret?

To say nothing of her very firm desire to keep herself from looking like a flaming lunatic to everyday outside observers.

A bluff. Maybe she could bluff. After all, no one knew that she knew what she knew, so maybe she could just pretend not to know.

Struggling to appear the way she would have just six months earlier, Corinne pushed her chair back from her paper-strewn desk and summoned up a baleful stare for her editor's benefit. "Elf or pixie, it doesn't matter, Hank. I can tell you right now that I don't need to do an investigation. Because mythical creatures don't exist," she lied, practically biting her own tongue. "That's why they call them myths."

Hank Buckley shifted the toothpick he was chewing from one side of his mouth to the other and shrugged. "People say UFOs are a myth, too, and I got a whole file cabinet full of statements from people who've seen 'em."

Corinne felt herself blanch and hoped like hell that Hank, with the typical male's lack of perception, wouldn't notice. Christ on a cracker, she'd barely gotten over finding out about the Others; if she had to start believing aliens were real, too, she was finished. She'd stab herself in the heart with a blue pencil, just see if she didn't.

"The difference between UFOs and elves is that we don't know what's out there in the rest of the universe. We know what's here on earth," she argued, thinking at least that much was true. She, for instance, knew more about what was on earth than she'd ever wanted to. "I think if there were elves running around the globe, someone would have stumbled over one before now. The only file you should put this in is the circular file. The one the janitors empty out every evening."

Hank shook his head. "No can do, toots. This one's hot. Even the TV stations are starting to pick it up. Don't want us to get left in the dust."

Creamed Christ on toast. The TV stations? The Others whom Corinne had gotten to know recently weren't going to like that one bit. Her friends' husbands, Dmitri Vidâme and Graham Winters, had impressed upon her from the very beginning the importance of keeping the existence of the Others a secret. Given the many pitchfork-, wooden-stake-, funeral-pyre-, and silver-bullet-wielding examples dotting human history when it came to supernatural creatures, Corinne couldn't say she blamed them. If she were a werewolf, she doubted she'd want anyone to know, either. Misha and Graham had told her the Others worked pretty damned hard to stay under the radar of their human neighbors, but if the TV stations started reporting on a story about elf sightings in Manhattan, secrecy would go right out a thirty-story window.

Provided, of course, that the thing being sighted was actually an elf, and Corinne had no idea if elves existed in the Others community. At the moment, she'd have preferred it if she didn't know about the Other community, period.

Her head began to pound and she wished for once that she was the sort of hard-bitten, steely-eyed reporter from an old film noir. She could use a bottle of bourbon in her bottom desk drawer right about now.

"C'mon, D," Hank cajoled, taking her silence for continued protest, which she supposed it sort of was. "You'll want to get on this before some other print outlet beats you to it. You want this going under someone else's byline?"

Corinne wished, she really wished, she could just tell Hank to go to hell and take his damned story lead with him, but there were two obstacles standing in her way. First, she needed her job. The *New York Chronicle* might not have been a Pulitzer-winning operation, but it paid steadily and it had hired Corinne when all the more respectable papers in town had told her she lacked experience, didn't have the right connections, and wrote with a shade too much dramatic flair. Even the *Daily News* had suggested she ought to go into fiction. The *Chronicle* had told her to use spell-check and to start in the morning. She had. Seven years ago.

The second obstacle had to do with the most misguided sense of loyalty a woman could possibly experience. A part of her wished—a really, really big part with a very fervent wish—that she could just turn her back on the Others and let them cover their own damned asses. After all, it was no skin off her butt if the Others made the front page. She was human. No one would be coming after her with a sharpened stick or a silver bullet. She could go on her merry little way with no interference and the added bonus of not having to keep a secret bigger than anything the CIA might have tucked up in the attic. She'd be footloose and fancy free.

But three of her closest friends would not.

That was where her rebellious little fantasy hit a brick wall. Corinne might not be bothered by the world discovering the existence of the Others, but Reggie certainly would. Not only had Regina McNeill, one of Corinne's closest friends, married a vampire earlier that year, she'd let him turn her into one herself. Somehow Corinne didn't think the folks with the crucifixes and stakes would make much of a distinction between Misha, who'd been a vampire for around a thousand years, and Reggie, who hadn't even been one for that many days. Bloodsuckers, Corinne was guessing, would be bloodsuckers as far as they were concerned.

And would Missy or Danice really fare any better? They might both still be human, but each of them had married a man who wasn't. Missy Roper Winters, kindergarten teacher, had married a frickin' werewolf, for God's sake. The chief werewolf in the city. She had a little baby werewolf bun in her oven right this minute. And as for Danice . . . hell, Danice was still off somewhere on her honeymoon with a half-human, half-Faerie private investigator. Would anyone care that the two woman had stayed human, or would they be tarred and feathered like Union sympathizers in 1863 Atlanta? Either way, was Corinne willing to take that risk?

Of course, if she wasn't, what the hell was she supposed to do about it?

"I'd like it under someone else's zip code," Corinne said as she reached up to rub her temple in ineffectively soothing circles. "Besides, what does it matter if someone else gets it? It's a non-story. It's fiction. And it's not like we're scooping the *Times* on a regular basis here."

"Maybe not, but we gotta give it a shot, right? Prove we're not some sort of fly-by-night tabloid operation."

She raised an eyebrow. "And doing a story the worst rag in print would think twice about running is supposed to boost our credibility factor? What'd they put in your coffee this morning? 'Cause you're seriously high."

"Only on the excitement of actually talking to you, instead of sending yet another email for you to ignore, sweetie. It's the kind of thing that goes to my head."

"Your sarcasm fails to make me laugh. As does this stupid-ass story. What are you thinking?" Reason didn't appear to be swaying her boss, so maybe it was time to pull out a little righteous indignation. She waved the note he'd handed her under his bulbous nose and upped her stare to a glare. "I'm a reporter, not a sci-fi novelist, and I'm supposed to do a story on elf sightings in Manhattan? For a Christmas season spoof, I might just down enough rum-spiked eggnog to play along, but it's August, Hank! You don't even have the Macy's parade and Salvation Army Santas on every corner to tie in to. You're a freak."

"Actually, I'm the boss, but I can see where the similarities could get confusing for you." Hank rocked back on his heels and drummed his hands in his pockets, making his loose change jingle. "Maybe you can do a write-up on the rise of insanity among the editors of small, urban newspapers. Right after you turn in the elf story."

Okay, so much for the indignation angle. Corinne was starting to get the feeling she wasn't going to be able to bury this story, but that didn't mean she wanted to write it. She knew too damned much. She couldn't take the chance that she might slip up and put something in the article that actually gave the thing some credibility. If she couldn't bury it, then, she could at least see that it got the lowest amount of traction possible.

Corinne ran a hand through her dark hair and gave a pained sigh. "Look, Hank, if we're slow for news, and you really want to run with this one, why don't you hand it to Shawn? You know what a geek he is. I think he still plays D and D with his buddies every weekend. He'd probably eat this shit up." And since he had about as much skill at uncovering facts as your average tub of mayonnaise, he was pretty damned unlikely to make it interesting enough for anyone to pay attention to the finished article. "That way, you'll get your story and I can get to go back to my feature on the student protest arrests at Columbia."

Hank shook his head. "No can do. Shawn is already on the tech show over at the Javits. It's gotta be you, kid. Besides"—he grinned, his toothpick bobbing—"you're the one who went to all those Goth clubs a few months ago. I figured this supernatural crap would be right up your alley."

"Well, you figured wrong. Supernatural, my ass. There are no such things as elves. Just like there are no such things as flying reindeer, or men who break into houses to *leave* stuff under the Christmas tree. Now give the damned story to someone else."

She was going to have to spend a month on her knees saying rosaries to make up for all the whopping lies coming out of her mouth. But maybe God gave credit for extenuating circumstances?

"I gave it to you." Hank gave a pointed look to the assignment sheet. "Ironically enough, that means I want you to have it. Now, do you want me to fill you in on the particulars, or do you want to go it alone and get me ticked when you come back with a lousy article?"

Closing her eyes on a sigh, Corinne laid the sheet down on top of a teetering pile of manila folders, yanked open her desk drawer, and dug out a bottle of extra-strength aspirin. Shaking three little white tablets onto her palm, she slammed them into the back of her throat and washed them down with a few gulps of cold coffee. Then she turned back to the man standing beside her desk and picked up a pencil.

"All right. Fine. Fill me in. But I won't pretend to be happy about it." She also wouldn't pretend to do more than a half-assed job. Quarter-assed, if she could get away with it.

"I don't need you to be happy. Besides, they say hardship builds character." Hitching up his battered khaki trousers, Hank perched one hip on the edge of her desk and folded his arms across his chest. "Okay, first off, you got the first sighting back in May. Sort of an isolated incident, that one. Easy to write off. But then around the second week in June, you start to hear stories from sources all over Manhattan that pretty much corroborate one another. All witnesses saw the same thing, and none of them knew one another before they made their reports."

Corinne looked up from the notes she'd been jotting down. "What did they see? A little man in a red-and-white suit with a pointy hat and a sack full of presents?"

Hank ignored her. "Witnesses reported seeing an extremely fair blond man, about six feet tall, with hair almost down to his butt and pointy ears."

Corinne latched onto that with all thirty-two teeth. Maybe she could still play this off?

She rolled her eyes with exaggerated flair. "Oh, for God's sake, Hank. That's not a believable elf sighting. That's just an escapee from a *Lord of the Rings* convention. Some teenage geek with way too much time on his hands dressed himself up like Orlando Bloom and paraded down Fifth thinking he was the shit. Case solved. Can I go home now?"

Hank shook his head. "Not so fast, kid. I'm not done yet." He shifted his shoulders and continued. "Now, the man in and of himself wouldn't have raised so much as an eyebrow under normal circumstances. This is Manhattan, after all." Corinne grumbled under her breath, but she didn't interrupt. "So almost universally, the witnesses initially dismissed the weird guy as just that—a weird guy. But that was before he started doing magic."

Corinne sighed. Damn his persistence. She tried to match it. "Okay, forget the convention. He was an escapee from a Dungeons and Dragons tournament. Did the 'magic' involve dice rolls and phrases like, *My wizard calls on the House of Illusion to summon forth a seventh-level Temporal Distortion plus three?*"

"From what I hear, it just involved a temporal distortion. Would the plus-three thing have been more impressive?"

Her pencil paused over her notepad, and Corinne looked up. Christ, did someone have *evidence* on this guy? "What did you say?"

"Would the plus-three thing have been—"

"Not that," she growled, her eyes narrowing. "Before that. The part where you said it did involve a temporal distortion."

"That's what the witnesses say."

Corinne looked longingly at the aspirin and debated pretending she hadn't read the warning label about permanent liver damage. "You're telling me Orlando waved his magic wand and opened a rift in the time–space continuum?"

"Get real," he scoffed. "You're just mixing metaphors. Magic wands and time–space continuums are two totally different animals. Besides, no one mentioned anything about a wand."

Her hand inched toward the aspirin. Who really needed a liver anyway?

"Forget the wand," she snarled. "I think the rift is the material question here, no?"

Hank shrugged. "Whatever. It's your story."

"Are you trying to kill me?"

Hank ignored her, or maybe he just didn't hear the question, since her face was buried in her arms and smushed up against the surface of her desk. It muffled the whimpering. "The witnesses claim that the man in question walked up to the wall of an abandoned building, and the bricks slid apart to let him through."

Corinne turned her head just enough to glare at her boss through one narrowed eye. "Meaning that Orlando Bloom took a trip to Neverland. Did he fly away on a tornado or take a trip through an enchanted wardrobe while he was at it?"

"They said the air around the wall seemed to shimmer, but after he went through, it looked totally normal, as if nothing had ever happened. The same sort of story has been reported by individuals uptown, downtown, and midtown, and that's why I want you checking out if it's true."

"I can answer that for you right now," she said, lifting her head and grabbing the assignment sheet to wad it up into a little, crumpled ball. "It's not true. Now can we talk about that proposal I sent you on the Columbia students arrested during the animal rights protest?"

"Looks good. I'll look forward to reading it. Right after you turn in the elf article."

"Someday you'll pay for this, Hank. I hope you realize that."

He shrugged and looked remarkably unconcerned. "I'll live in fear." His weathered face wrinkled into a grin, and he clamped the toothpick between his molars, chuckling. "Look at it this way. I didn't make you check out the lead this spring when that cabdriver said he picked up two were-wolves outside Central Park. I know when a story's complete crap." Then he turned and ambled back to his office, chortling to himself all the way.

Corinne soothed her temper by making an obscene gesture at Hank's back with one hand, while she used the other to rub the elbow she'd smashed on the desk when he'd made the werewolf comment. For God's sake, those werewolves had been her friends. Well, her friend and her friend's furry husband-to-be.

Throwing caution and the potential for irreversible liver damage to the wind, Corinne popped another two aspirin and slugged back the last of her cold coffee. Staring at the dregs left behind in her cup, she realized her need for caffeine superseded any attempt to appear to be starting work on her new assignment. Without a new dose of her drug of choice, she wouldn't be able to so much as lift a pencil, let alone figure out what she was going to do about the impending collapse of reality as she knew it.

Hell, as *everyone* knew it.

Grabbing a handful of change from the bottom of her purse, she shoved herself to her feet and headed for the door. Weaving her way among the desks of her colleagues, she ignored their absent greetings as easily as she ignored the ringing of telephones and the clacking of computer keyboards. All her attention remained focused on the front doors to the *Chronicle*'s office suite and the elevators just beyond. Those elevators were her ticket to the basement of the building and the vending machines that stood there, patiently waiting to dispense the sweet, dark nectar of the gods.

She tapped her foot impatiently while she waited for the car, punched the button marked B a dozen times in rapid succession as soon as she stepped inside, and stared at the digital floor indicator as it counted down. Just as the thick metal doors slid open, her pocket started to trill the opening bars to Bach's Toccata and Fugue. She cursed and debated whether or not to answer the call. On the one hand, the person on the other end was usually at least as much trouble as she was worth and was distressingly good at detecting when something was bothering Corinne and then metaphorically beating out the truth. On the other, Corinne couldn't think of a time in her life when she'd more needed a distraction.

Sighing, she dug out her cell phone and flipped it open. "Yeah?"

"I give up. I surrender. This is the official white flag I'm waving in your ear right now."

Corinne fed six quarters into the vending machine and scowled. "Ava, what the hell are you babbling about?"

"I am not babbling," the other woman snapped, her voice crackling over the line even though the cell signal came in clear as glass. "I am informing you in perfectly rational and reasonable terms that I am throwing in the towel and washing my hands of the whole mess. I may decide to take religious orders."

The machine button protested the amount of force Corinne used to punch it, but it yielded an icy can of soda with a reluctant *thump*. "Yeah, right. Sister Ava Immaculata. I can see it now." She pinned the phone between ear and shoulder so she could lift the metal tab. "Mind telling me why you're in such a tizzy?"

"This is no tizzy, Corinne Magdalena. This is utter exhaustion and despair. I give up on the whole lot. I just needed to call and wish you a nice life before I leave for the nunnery."

Corinne raised the can to her lips and leaned against the clean-ish white wall beside the snack machine. "Same to you. Leave an address, though, or you won't get a Christmas card."

The curse Ava muttered managed to retain an unexpected air of grace and elegance solely due to its manner of delivery. It had certainly never sounded the same on the lips of the dockworkers who more frequently used it. "You fail to amuse me, Corinne, darling. But then, most things fail to amuse me when so many people I've tried to care for turn their backs on me within the space of six months."

Corinne swallowed fast to keep from choking on her drink. "Turn their backs on you? Going for the melodrama here?"

"What would you call it when people ignore everything you try to do for them and shun the perfectly lovely dates you slave to fix them up with, only to end up making horrible decisions on their own?"

"Reality?"

Ava never raised her voice, but Corinne still had to fight the urge to pull the phone away from her ear and wince. "I can see I'll get no support from you. And why I should have thought I might is beyond me. After all, weren't you the first rat to desert my ship?"

"Okay, first of all, get control of the metaphors, Av." Corinne stabbed the elevator button, since she couldn't stab her friend. "Second, I did not 'desert' any ships. It's not like the fixes were working out anyway."

"They would have, if Regina and Melissa had done as they were told. I found them perfectly nice men, but no—"

"Ava, you're gonna have to let that one go. They managed to find their own men. We might see their choices as somewhat . . . unfortunate, but—"

"Unfortunate? Corinne, they married outside their species! That is not something that a person just 'lets go.' That's . . . that's . . . well, it's just un-natural. And more than that, it forces us—and by us, I mean me—to talk about characters from the late, late, late movie as if they were real. It's al-tered the entire fabric of my reality, and I have to say that I am less than pleased."

"Yeah, Av, I think we all got that memo, but there's not a whole lot anyone can do about it,"

Corinne snapped. God, she was sick of this entire topic. Could she please just go five minutes without talking about the Others? "The 'creatures,' as you call them, *are* real. Dmitri is really a vampire and Graham is really a werewolf. And now Reggie is a vampire as well, and Missy is pregnant with another werewolf-to-be. This is the new reality. Grasp it and move on."

"How can you possibly sound so casual about it?" Ava demanded in a petulant voice. "Aren't you the least little bit freaked out by having your entire notion of life, the universe, and everything suddenly flip on its axis? Doesn't that give you the least littlest wiggins?"

Corrine laughed, but honestly, it sounded more like a bark. Not really surprising, given how completely unamused she felt at the moment. "Believe me, casual is the last thing I feel at the moment. I just think the ship for getting upset about the demise of the fantasy fix-ups has pretty much sailed. We all have bigger things to worry about now."

She heard Ava sigh and imagined the other woman giving one of her vaguely Gallic shrugs. "I suppose it's an ever-changing world. One must find ways to adapt."

Which was exactly what she had just spent the last few minutes saying. Corinne seriously debated making an extremely obscene gesture, but figured the effort would be lost since Ava wasn't around to see it. So she just pictured it in vivid Technicolor as she pushed away from the wall and punched the call button for the elevator again. "Yeah, right. Well, it's been nice talking to you, Av, but I've got a pretty busy schedu—"

"Oh, no you don't. Honestly, Rinne, did I tell you I was finished with this conversation? Did your mother teach you no manners whatsoever?"

Corinne pictured her staunchly Italian Catholic mother—who had been known to slap the backs of her children's heads for slouching at the dinner table—and clenched her jaw. "I'm not in the mood to listen to you talk about my mother, Ava, so watch it."

"My, my, it sounds like someone neglected to eat her Wheaties this morning," Ava purred. "What's the matter, darling? Come on, you can tell me all about it."

"Wow, that is such an unappealing offer. Thanks." Frankly, Corinne wasn't certain she had the strength to think about the problem at hand at the moment, let alone hash it all out for an audience. The restorative powers of Coca-Cola were legendary, but even it could only do so much. Since the damned elevator seemed determined never to arrive, she'd need everything she had to climb back up to the office. She turned toward the stairwell.

"Your sarcasm is noted and frowned upon."

"Look, Ava, I don't know what happened today to stir this all up for you again, but now is not a good time. You can't wish things back to the way they were, and neither can I. All you can do is deal. Regina and Missy are happy with their impossible men. We can either be happy for them, or we can sit around and moan about how the world isn't what we thought it was. I barely have time to waste on the first one, let alone the second."

"Oh, I know," Ava pouted. She could actually do that—pout with her voice as well as her face. "Different strokes, love makes the world go round, to each her own, Ava is a bitch, yadda yadda yadda."

"Correction—Ava is *the* bitch."

"Darling, I think I'm flattered."

"Don't be, because I'm totally about to hang up on you." Corinne went ahead and tucked her soda against her side so she'd have a hand free to make that obscene gesture after all. "But because you are, inexplicably, my friend, I am first going to give you twenty seconds to tell me why the hell you called me today to bitch about how Reggie and Missy abandoned your fantasy fix plan. Like I said, that boat's already sunk."

"You said it had already sailed."

"Ten seconds, Ava."

"Well, of course I didn't call about the fixes. I'm so over that."

Corinne turned to jog up her second flight and frowned. "Stop. Rewind. Slo-mo playback. Say huh? If you didn't call about the fixes, why were you accusing me of deserting you?"

"Are you not the woman who bailed on a modeling gig booked by her struggling young agent friend, forcing the agent to scrape up an appropriate substitute just fifteen minutes before the shoot started?"

Corinne nearly tripped over a riser. "Ava, that was seven years ago!"

"There's no statute of limitations on betrayal, now, is there?"

"Okay, hanging up now."

"Wait. Not so fast. I called for a reason."

"Oh, you mean a reason other than to bitch and moan at me?"

"Clearly," Ava said, her tone changing from melodramatic to business-like in a heartbeat. "I wanted to ask you about something."

"No, Ava, I will not ask the editor to do a full-color spread on the Markham Agency. Bye."

"Will you stop jumping to conclusions? This is another matter entirely. A matter I thought my friend, the talented investigative reporter, could help me with."

Corinne lowered the now half-empty soda can and made a face. "No, I won't rewrite all your press releases this month, either."

"Then will you tell me if there's some sort of weird serial killer running around Manhattan looking like a wet dream and pretending to be the guy on the Lucky Charms box?"

Corinne froze right there in the *Chronicle*'s doorway. "What did you ask me?"

"You heard me. Four of my models have bailed on bookings in the last six weeks because they said they were being stalked by an elf. So either they're insane, the coke has melted their brains, or there's some freak who thinks Christmas-themed slave laborers in August is the perfect cover for a crime spree. Or they've actually stumbled on to something they really shouldn't know about. Have you heard about any of your fellow media types sniffing around something like this?"

Corinne's response was very pithy and, she thought, entirely appropriate. She cursed like a dockhand, hung up on Ava, and slugged back what was left of her soda. Then she shouldered her way through the fire door to the hall outside the office. She needed to get back to her desk and the bottle of little white pills waiting inside. To hell with her liver. If even Ava's bubble-headed models had sighted this "elf" bumbling his way around Manhattan, there was no way Corinne would be the only one on the story. Something was going to break, and the annoying niggle of her conscience told her that she wouldn't be able to live with herself if she didn't give the appropriate Others a heads-up.

Picturing what she had to do next, Corinne groaned. To hell with the aspirin. What she needed was vodka. Maybe there would be a bar on the way.

Three

"Shit. I need a drink."

Luc cocked one eyebrow and tried not to look too smug, but he was glad to see someone else react to his mission the same way he had. "I brought a flask of Faerie wine, if you'd like a belt of that."

His companion scowled at him and opened a cabinet door to retrieve a graceful glass decanter of amber fluid. "Thank you, my friend, but as much as I would like to pass out and forget what you told me, I don't think it would help your cause. The Council and I had hoped that we could resolve this issue before we reached this point. We had not yet confirmed that Seoc had begun to mingle with the humans." He poured two glasses of brandy, the red-gold color less exotic than the crimson of Faerie wine, but also less likely to knock a grown Other on his ass.

Luc's host, and his first stop on his trip through *Ithir*, happened to be one of the few inhabitants of the mortal world who would neither attack, nor be particularly surprised when a Faerie portal opened up in the middle of his office. As the head of the Council of Others, Rafael De Santos had grown used to unusual occurrences.

"I think that's what we all would have preferred," Luc said, accepting the snifter Rafe handed him. "As it is, I'm beginning to think getting seriously drunk might be the only thing that can help. At least if we're shit-faced, we won't realize how much this sucks."

The Feline shifter looked at him over the rim of his glass. "Even dead, this would suck, my friend."

"True. Speaking of dead and sucking, though, how's Dmitri doing? I heard he got married. And I think someone said his bride was mortal."

Rafe grinned and nodded. "He did indeed marry, earlier this spring. And *was* remains the operative word. He wed a charming young woman, who can now discard any worries over encroaching crow's-feet and age spots. They had a lovely ceremony. Great caterer. Even better scenery."

"Scenery?"

The grin widened. "The bride has some remarkably attractive friends. One of whom is currently expecting the Silverback Alpha's first cub."

Luc felt his eyes widen. "Graham bit it, too? With another mortal?" He shook his head and downed a gulp of his brandy. "What is this human world coming to?"

"Mating season, apparently."

"Does that mean you're feeling the call of the wild yourself?"

Rafe shrugged. "We cats are more solitary than

the Lupines, and the jaguar is more solitary than most cats. The wild only calls us for short stays, not permanent ones."

Luc stifled a chuckle. "Yeah, so I've noticed. But I admit that's a relief for me. I know you want Seoc returned to Faerie with all possible haste. Which means I can use all the help I can get finding the bastard. The last thing I need is for you to go off after some cute little furry thing and leave me to do this on my own. Or worse yet, some cute little mortal thing."

"Be careful, my friend. Your arrogance and Fae-centrism are showing."

Luc shifted in his seat. It wasn't that he disliked humans, precisely, but he couldn't understand how an Other like Dmitri or Graham could possibly have a lasting relationship with such a . . . such a mundane creature as a human. What could they possibly have in common?

"But you needn't worry," Rafe continued, twirling his snifter. "The Council will, of course, completely support your mission. We want nothing to happen to the Queen's nephew, especially not while he is on our turf, as they say. Now that Mab has sent you after him, I'm certain he will be easily found."

"You obviously don't know the Queen's nephew."

"I have not had that pleasure, no. But if he is moving among the humans now, as you say, I have a feeling an introduction will be inevitable." His eyes firmed, even as his mouth remained in its customary subtle curve. "Rest assured that if you have trouble with your mission, I will step in on behalf of the Council and see to his removal myself. The situation appears to be reaching a flash point. Since we had not yet heard of Seoc moving among the humans, we can still hope his presence has gone unremarked. If they begin to take note of him, our secret will be in jeopardy. No matter how many among the Council talk of the necessity of Unveiling ourselves to the humans, Luc, I shouldn't have to tell you that the Council would look very unfavorably on having such a monumental decision forced upon it prematurely."

Luc could hardly miss the underlying message there. "If you were all so anxious to have him back in our hands, why didn't you do something about it?"

Rafe's shoulders lifted in a lazy, boneless shrug. "We discussed the problem at length, but we believed we still had time to deliberate. Plus, we agreed that things would go much more smoothly if we didn't try to handle this ourselves. The last thing we want is to have an interdimensional incident on our hands."

Luc frowned.

"Like the kind we'd get if reports reached Mab that her nephew was being returned in a bucket," Rafe explained with a pointed look. "Some of our people have difficulty remembering their manners during a good game of chase, Luc. Even a Fae prince can look like prey if he's running fast enough."

"Great." Luc drained his brandy and set the glass aside. "So because you can't manage to keep your fangs to yourselves, I'm on my own until I fail miserably?"

"Of course not. As I said, we will assist gladly in whatever way we can. The Council simply feels we should not be handling such a potentially delicate matter on our own. Dmitri, damn his pale, chilly hide, has also volunteered his assistance. Which is the least he could do, considering he left his position as head of the Council to me when he married." Rafe rose, crossed to a heavy, mahogany desk, and rifled through a drawer. "Of course, his idea of 'assistance' and mine do not exactly match. Now that he has the distraction of a new bride, he often takes a kind of hands-off approach to assisting."

"That doesn't sound very helpful."

Rafe's teeth flashed, white and sharp, as he handed over a small, white card. "Feel free to point that out to him. His number is on the back."

"Thanks. I'm overwhelmed."

Luc was spared a response to his sarcasm by a throat being carefully cleared in the doorway of the large office. Rafe turned to acknowledge the intrusion.

"Forgive me, Mr. De Santos," one of the uniformed club staff said quietly. "I was unaware you had company, but I'm afraid there is someone else here asking to see you."

The Felix frowned. "I had no appointments this

evening. In fact, I told no one I would be spending any time here at all. Did this person give you a name?"

"She did not, sir, but she seemed insistent. She did inform me that it was Council business."

Luc sipped his brandy and watched his host's face. The other man's expression remained impassive, but Luc could see impatience turn to curiosity in his cat-like yellow eyes.

"Forgive me," Rafe said, nodding to Luc. "The head of the Council's time is rarely his own. Please enjoy your drink while I step out and deal with my unexpected visitor. I'm certain I won't be long."

Luc grinned. "And I'm certain how long will depend entirely on how attractive this 'she' turns out to be."

"Actually, it won't," a decidedly female voice retorted from over the footman's shoulder. "Because she isn't here for a game of touchy-feely. She is doing her good deed for the century, and then she is going to go the hell home before she catches anything in this . . . ridiculous place."

Luc stood even as Rafe turned to face the newcomer. The footman spent a split second looking mortified before he spun and made a grab for the intruder. The woman stepped sideways and knocked his hands away with a clenched fist.

"Watch it, grabby," she growled. "I don't know where you've been lately."

"At the front door, I expect. You may return to your post, Jameson," Rafe said smoothly, nodding at the still-mortified and now disgruntled servant. He stepped forward with an outstretched hand and smiled at the latest visitor. "Corinne, what a pleasant surprise. I hardly expected to see you here at Vircolac tonight. What could have brought you to our little club?"

"Nothing short of a loaded handgun or a conscience full of misplaced loyalty," the woman said. Or, more accurately, grumbled. She shot Rafe a suspicious look, then spared a glare for Luc. "I didn't know you'd be in some kind of meeting, like a normal person."

Luc raised a brow and indulged himself with a quick study of the bad-tempered female. That she was human was obvious, almost as obvious as the crushing weight of discomfort that radiated from her. She looked less than pleased by her surroundings, and equally un-enamored of her present company. Behind the scowls, though, Luc saw something that caught him off guard.

He knew Rafe had said that Regina's friends all seemed to be remarkably attractive for humans, but for Lady's sake, Luc was Fae. He lived among the most beautiful females in creation, served as elite guardsman to one who probably reigned as *the* most beautiful, so he certainly shouldn't be feeling this surge of lust for a human.

Besides which, humans were just so . . . human. They had nothing special, not compared with an Other or a Fae or any of the other legions of creatures living in the worlds. No powers, no gifts, not

even any real talent to speak of. Like many in Faerie, Luc had always thought of them as being a
bit primitive and undeveloped. So why the hell
did the sight of this woman to go directly to his
groin?

She didn't so much surpass the normal notions
of human female beauty as expand them. She had
warm, slightly olive skin and thick, dark hair the
color of the onyx Mab wove into her crown every
Samhain. She was taller than the average human
woman, too, though still a good foot shorter than
he, and she had the sort of solid, human figure
many Fae thought of as coarse and common. Luc
found it tempting. Her curves made his hands itch
to trace them, and her very substantiality seemed
to call to him, made him ache to feel her press
against him, heavy and warm and real. He wanted
to hold her, to taste the curves and angles of her
clear, classical features, to learn the earthy truth of
her scent and the richness of her flavor.

What in the Lady's name was wrong with him?

Luc tore his eyes from temptation and struggled
to regain the distant amusement he'd felt when
he'd first heard her voice, before her appearance
had distracted him. He glanced at his host. "So,
Rafe, is this a friend of yours?"

The woman stiffened, but Rafe merely smiled
and drew her carefully into the office. "Come," he
told her, in a soothing, faintly cajoling tone Luc
guessed was lost on her. "You must allow me to in-

troduce you, and then you will sit comfortably and tell me what troubles you."

Luc watched her step forward, her reluctance obvious. He half expected to see her look over her shoulder to be sure nothing intended to jump out at her and begin tearing her to pieces. Briefly, he considered being insulted on his host's behalf. It appeared their guest clung to some unflattering suspicions about the Others. But, he concluded, he was neither Other nor her host, so he decided not to muster up the energy. Especially since he could barely stand to look at her without his palms itching.

"Luc, this is Corinne D'Alessandro. She is a very dear friend of Graham's and Dmitri's wives, which, of course, makes her a very dear friend of mine," Rafe continued, ignoring the look of surprise his guest gave him at hearing his introductory words. "Corinne, please meet Lucifer. Luc, as we call him, is here . . . on business, but we've known each other for a number of years. He's perfectly harmless."

Luc tried to decide if that assessment amused or insulted him. No man liked to be thought of as harmless, especially not when he made his living with a sword in his hand. He didn't think this woman was buying it anyway. Her gaze sized him up suspiciously, and she made no move to shake his hand. Maybe her attitude would do something to cool his ardor.

"Lucifer?" she repeated, still looking quite uncomfortable.

"Luc," he corrected brusquely, barely softening the syllable with a small nod. "Luc Macanaw. It's a—" He broke off. "It is interesting to meet you."

Her brows flew up and a wry sort of amusement joined the unease in her expression. "Yeah, the, uh, interest is all mine," she said. She turned back to Rafe, giving Luc her shoulder and a vague sense of annoyance at being so easily dismissed.

"Look, I'm sorry to just barge in like this, in the middle of your meeting or whatever, but I thought you might want a heads-up about this, so you could . . ." She guestured vaguely, then let her hand fall back to her side. "Anyway, I just thought you should know, since it's got to be one of you guys, right?"

"Think nothing of it," Rafe dismissed, easing her smoothly toward a large armchair. "What has to be, er, one of us?"

"The elf everyone is talking about."

Luc, who had just begun contemplating how best to remove both himself and his unfinished brandy from the room for the duration of this conversation, tuned right back in. "Elf?" he repeated, glancing at the Felix.

Rafe seated himself across from the woman and leaned forward. "I'm afraid you've caught us off guard, Corinne. I'm not sure I follow. Who, exactly, has been talking? And about what?"

"The elf," Corinne repeated impatiently. She searched their faces for a moment, then seemed to read in their carefully controlled expressions that she needed to give them more. Luc watched her take a deep breath, then start again. "Look, I definitely don't want to get involved in any kind of . . . issue you people have among yourselves, but Reggie and Missy made it pretty clear when they spilled the truth about this whole Others business to me that you guys consider it pretty damned important that no one knows about you. So when my boss handed me this assignment today, I thought it was weird. And I thought someone should let you guys know."

She paused and made a face. "Unfortunately, I was the only someone I could think of."

Luc struggled to follow the woman's garbled explanation and discovered she might as well have been speaking a foreign language for all the sense he could make of it. Hell, she might as well have been waving semaphore flags; and normally, he wouldn't have cared, but her mention of an "elf" when he was here in *Ithir* looking for a missing Fae had definitely piqued his interest. So he could admit later that he may have been a bit brusque when he snapped, "For the stars' sake, woman, you're making no sense. At all. Do you need smelling salts or something, or can you maybe pull yourself together and let us know what the hell you're babbling about?"

Rafe shot him a speaking glance, but the woman seemed to have no need for anyone else to defend her. She swept him an utterly dismissive look, then turned fully away from him to face Rafe alone.

"I know from meeting you guys that the Others don't want humans to know you really exist," she continued, speaking directly to the Felix. It didn't take a genius, though, to realize the frigid tone of her voice was aimed at someone else entirely. "Aside from people like Reggie and Missy. And the rest of our little circle now, I guess. But I know it's not supposed to be common knowledge. Reggie made us all swear an oath when we first found out. And I know that an occasional article in the tabloids about Dracula attacking a hiker in Romania or a werewolf impregnating a housewife in Arkansas doesn't concern you. Which it shouldn't, because people can make fun of those, and when they make fun of them, that means they don't suspect anything. But this isn't like that. This is bigger."

She paused for another deep breath, blew it out slowly. "Today my boss asked me to look into half a dozen reported elf sightings here in Manhattan. None of the witnesses was an obvious crackpot, all of them are willing to swear on a Bible about what they saw, and all of them apparently have pretty big mouths. Now, if it were just my boss looking into it, I wouldn't have freaked, and I probably wouldn't be talking to you. Well, I definitely wouldn't be talking to you, but the word is that we're not the only ones on the story, and that's . . . unusual."

"Your boss asked you to look into it?" Luc demanded. "Are you with the police?"

Rafe looked up. "Corinne is a reporter."

Luc felt himself blanch. "A reporter. Wait, does that mean these sightings will be announced on your television sets? That the entire human world will hear of it?"

Corinne deigned to reply frostily over her shoulder. "Not yet. Maybe. I'm a print reporter. I work for a small local newspaper. But like I said, I'm not the only one on the story. There are other papers snooping around, and my boss thinks the TV stations might be getting curious."

The curses Luc let fly stretched the bounds of legality and creativity, but fortunately he retained enough presence of mind to utter them in his native tongue. This wasn't good news.

"While I may not understand the sentiment, I'm afraid I likely agree with it," Rafe said grimly, standing to thrust his hands in the pockets of his tailored trousers. "This is . . . distressing."

"I'm guessing from your reactions that you haven't heard about this before. Which means I was probably right to come here and warn you. Yay for me." Corinne stood as well and shouldered the battered leather backpack she'd carried with her. "Anyway, I'm sorry if this is trouble for you guys, but at least you know. So, you know, good luck and everything. I hope you . . . do whatever you need to do with the . . . whatever it is."

She turned toward the door but didn't manage a single step. Instinctively, Luc reached out to stop her. She'd just given him his first lead in discovering

Seoc's whereabouts. Right now he needed her, and he didn't intend to let her go until she gave him everything she had.

He just didn't expect that to include a punch straight to his chest.

Not literally, of course. She didn't raise a hand to him. She just arched one dark, curving eyebrow and let her gaze trail slowly from his face to the hand he had wrapped around her upper arm. She stared at it as if it were covered in leprous black spots.

"Excuse me?" Her voice sliced into him with excruciating politeness.

He made no move to release her. He doubted he'd be able to if he tried. Grabbing her arm had been like grabbing on to a live electrical cable; his entire body had clenched with the strange and powerful current that coursed through him. The hair on his arms and legs stood up and vibrated to an unheard frequency. He wouldn't have been surprised if the hair on his head did the same. He was frozen, paralyzed by some force greater than himself, something he had never seen coming, and he couldn't have chosen a less appropriate time for it if he'd charted the stars and consulted a damned oracle beforehand.

Shit, just when he'd thought her attitude had dampened that initial burst of attraction, he'd had to go and touch her. What the hell had he been thinking?

Corinne did not appear similarly moved. If she

had been, he doubted she would have yanked her arm out of his grasp with such obvious ease. Not to mention relish.

"I'm going to pretend that didn't happen, because if I didn't, I'd feel obliged to deck you for it," she said tightly, "and frankly, I'd rather just be on my way. So, toodles."

Rafe stepped forward, holding his hands up near his shoulders, palms out, when she turned her snarl on him. Luc seized the opportunity to try to get control of himself.

"Please, Corinne. Don't leave yet. We could use your help," the head of the Council admitted. "I—*we*—certainly appreciate the favor you've done us by alerting us to this issue. Clearly, you were under no obligation to do so."

She crossed her arms over her chest, but she stopped heading for the door. "Have you actually met Reggie and Missy?" she grumbled.

The Felix offered a wry smile. "You did it out of loyalty to your friends. I understand that, and I still owe you thanks, no matter your motivation. We knew that there was a . . . visitor to the city at present, but we were not aware before now that he'd been spotted by the human media. The information you've given us is not what one would call welcome news, but it *is* valuable to us."

"Valuable? Look, I'm definitely not asking anyone for some kind of reward—"

"I never thought you might be. I only mention it because we would find it equally valuable if you could stay a few more minutes and answer one or two questions for us."

In other circumstances, Luc might have laughed at the expression of horror that suggestion evoked. Unfortunately, in the present circumstances, he couldn't afford to be amused. Nor could he afford to be feeling the gut-deep, elemental attraction that had flared between them the moment he touched the bare skin beneath the arm of her short-sleeved top. Too bad no one had asked him about it first.

He cleared his throat and hoped he'd tamped down his reaction to her sufficiently for his words not to spew out like liquid idiocy before he spoke. "Rafe, I think we need to explain to her what's going on before we ask her for any more help. It's the least she deserves."

She looked a bit surprised that he'd suggested such a thing, but she nodded at Rafe anyway. "I think that might be a good idea. Especially since my editor is determined to get this story. I suppose if I know what's really going on, I can make sure the article I turn in is far enough from the actual truth to be safe."

"You're right." Rafe nodded and waved her back to her seat. "It is senseless not to fill you in when you already know almost as much as we do." He waited for her to sit, then settled himself back into his lazy pose, but his fingers beat restlessly against the arms of his chair. "The problem you've brought to us this evening is the very reason for Luc's visit to our city."

Corinne glanced at him. "You're not from around here?"

Luc shook his head.

"Luc is Fae," Rafe informed her.

Corinne just stared at him. Then she turned her head and stared at Luc. She looked back and forth between them at least half a dozen times, but her blank expression never changed.

"I'm Fae," Luc repeated, then sighed. "As in Faerie."

The blankness dissolved beneath a surprised laugh. "You're a fairy? Sure, Tinker Bell. Pull the other leg while you're at it."

Luc scowled at Rafe. "You see? That's the problem with mortals. We leave your world for a couple of thousand years and everyone either forgets all about us, or they reduce us to little glowing balls of tutu-clad good cheer."

Corinne continued to chuckle. Even Rafe had caught the bug. He met Luc's glare and shrugged. "You have to admit, the mental image of you in such a costume is amusing."

"Fuck you."

Corinne watched the interchange and managed to stifle her laughter, but she couldn't quite wipe the grin off her face. Luc tried not to notice how it made her mouth look wide and mobile and wholly inviting.

"You're serious?" she said, shaking her head. "You two honestly want me to believe Luc's a fairy?"

"No, I want you to believe I'm Fae," he said firmly. "Faerie is where I come from, but it was the most convenient word I could use to make you understand. *Faerie* is a place. *Fae* means a being from Faerie. Calling someone a Faerie is like calling someone a France."

Corinne nodded, then shook her head, then nodded again. Then she just sat there and looked confused. "So you're trying to tell me that fairies are real. Does that make the elf a fairy?"

Rafe must have seen the irritation in Luc's face, because he cleared his throat and jumped into the fray. "*Fairy* is considered a bit of a derogatory term by the people of, erm, Faerie," he explained. "They really prefer being called Fae."

Her shock faded enough for her to roll her eyes. "Okay, so is this elf a *Fae*?"

"Seoc is not an elf, but yes"—Luc nodded—"he's Fae, and he's the reason why I'm here. I was sent to return him to Faerie."

"Sent? By whom?"

"By the Queen of Faerie."

Four

Corinne couldn't quite figure out how it had happened, but at some point in the last hour she had obviously stepped off the train at the Crazyville station. Either that, or all those aspirin she'd swallowed had damaged her brain instead of her liver. How else could she explain how she'd gone from waking up in the world as she knew it, to sitting in the office of a werejaguar having a conversation with a fairy—sorry, a Fae—about why he was worried that another Fae had been sighted around New York City?

There was no other explanation. She had clearly—and likely irrevocably—lost her mind.

"The Queen of Faerie," she repeated slowly, feeling the words roll around in her mouth and deciding they really didn't fit well at all. "The Queen of Faerie sent you to bring some guy named 'Shock' back to . . . Faerie with you. Do I have that right?"

The enormous man with the pointy ears nodded. "Close enough."

It was too bad about the ears, really. In the

instant when she'd first laid eyes on Lucifer call-me-
Luc Macanaw, every cell in her body had sat up to
attention and cried, *Hello there, big boy!* The man
was just too gorgeous to be real. Which, of course,
he'd turned out to be. Not really human, anyway.
At least six-five or six-sex—er, six-six—the man
towered over not only her, but also every other
man she'd ever dated, including the oh-so-elegant
Rafael De Santos and the six-foot-two construc-
tion worker Corinne had drooled over for most of
last summer. This guy wasn't just tall, though; he
had brawn to back up his height, with the kind of
muscle definition most men would kill for.

His skin had a luminous golden cast to it, and his
eyelashes were thicker and darker than any man's
had a right to be. They made his crystal-green eyes
stand out and emphasized the dark, rich coffee color
of his hair, which was at least long enough to be
clubbed back into a ponytail. She couldn't see how
long it was, but her fingers already itched to run
through it.

Long hair on a man pushed all her buttons, especially when it was that particular shade, that
brown so dark it looked black until the light hit it
just right and pulled out those rich, chocolate high-
lights. She wanted to feel that hair wrapped around
her while she climbed on top and rode him straight
on till morning—

Holy shit! What is God's name was she thinking? This man couldn't possibly be her type; he
wasn't even her species!

She shook her head to clear out the unexpected and unwelcome fog of lust and drew a deep breath. "Okay," she said, "but I still feel like I stepped into this movie twenty minutes past the opening credits. Can one of you maybe fill me in? From the beginning?"

The story wasn't that long, but it still left Corinne with the same feeling she'd had after reading *War and Peace*—the one that went something like, *Du-huh?* She understood the part about Luc's reasons for coming to . . . well, he kept calling it *Ithir*, but since she wasn't quite ready to deal with any "alternate realities" stuff, she'd just stick to saying Manhattan. The part about him being a personal guard to the Faerie Queen made a sort of fantasy-novel sense, but after that, he lost her.

"Okay," she said again, the word drawn out the way she might have said it if she'd been attempting to placate an ax-wielding maniac. "Um, I think I understand what you're after, but I'm having a little bit of trouble with the why part."

"The 'why part'?" Luc repeated.

"Yeah. Why does everyone seem to assume he'll need to be dragged back by his hair like a runaway cave-wife? Can't you just call and tell him the Queen wants him home?"

Luc and Rafe exchanged what Corinne would have called a manly look, the kind that implied they were trying to be patient with her feeble feminine understanding.

"He didn't exactly leave us an itinerary," Luc

said in that really annoying tone. "He's not supposed to be here at all. He never received permission from the Queen."

Corinne felt her eyes widen at that. "Permission? What, like a visa? Why would he need permission to *leave* Faerie? I understand needing something like a passport to enter a place, but to leave? Is Faerie some kind of giant prison compound?"

"Don't be ridiculous."

She glared at him. "Oh, you need permission from Mom to cross your own borders, but I'm the one who's being ridiculous?"

Rafe shifted in his seat and cleared his throat. "Moving between here and Faerie isn't like driving across the Canadian border," he said, almost apologetically. "Faerie occupies its own dimension, for lack of a better word, and the only way to travel between worlds like that is through the use of magic. In this case, magical portals, or doorways."

"And the doors are tightly controlled," Luc added. "For several reasons."

"Such as?"

The Fae guardsman looked at her like he'd rather shake her than answer her question, but he managed to maintain his grip on sanity long enough to answer. And save himself a swift kick to the balls.

"First, because the Others here prefer it that way," he said. "You mentioned it yourself earlier—the Others in this world work very hard to keep ordinary mortals from learning they exist."

"Yeah, because they're afraid of how we'd react, that'd we'd try to exterminate them or put them in a lab and study them or something," Corinne agreed. "But how does that relate to visitors from Faerie?"

Rafe spoke up. "Right now, the Council of Others believes that humans are neither ready nor willing to acknowledge that what they think of as the supernatural—as magic—exists."

Corinne had heard of the Council from Reggie, whose husband, Dmitri, once headed it; now, apparently, Rafe had that pleasure. "Yeah, I know. Because you think we're primitive morons."

Luc nodded. "Compared with most other species, you are. Primitive, not morons," he hurried to add when she turned to glare at him. "Look at it from the Others' point of view. Werefolk were around for millennia before humans evolved much past the Cro-Magnon stage on *Ithir*, and even though vampires were once human, they have a much deeper connection to magic than their human cousins ever did. And Fae . . . well, we left *Ithir* about the same time humans started realizing that round things made nifty accessories for the bottoms of their sleds. In relative terms, humans are like infants to us."

Corinne couldn't decide if she should be confused or just insulted. Or maybe both. "Right. We're the cosmic equivalent of amoebae. Great. But that doesn't explain why it's so important to interrupt this Seoc guy's tour of *Ithir*."

"Actually, it does," Rafe said. "One of the primary reasons for the regulation of travel from Faerie into *Ithir* is to keep the Others' secret safe. You've seen what happens when someone comes through the door with the wrong intentions, or with no intentions at all. If people in this city are catching sight of Seoc, the chances of his identity being discovered increase by the minute, and once people know who and what he is, the veil of secrecy that protects us from discovery gets that much thinner. Break the barrier of disbelief in supernatural beings by once acknowledging there's a race of non-humans out there and people become much more likely to believe in all the races out there. In other words, it's a short step from a Fae visitor to a resident pack of werewolves."

"You're right," she acknowledged, pursing her lips. She might have to say it, but she didn't have to like it. As a reporter, she had a core-deep antipathy toward secrets. "But you said there was another reason."

"I'll admit the second reason might sound a bit self-serving," Luc said, and shifted uncomfortably. "By controlling the door into and out of Faerie, we can control who knows about our existence and who can find their way into our realm. Faerie can be a dangerous place for those who aren't Fae, partly because it's home to very powerful magic, but that magic can also be a powerful lure for those who think they can use it for themselves. The Fae left *Ithir* because humans either feared our magic or wanted it for themselves. Rather than hide in plain sight, like the Others, we removed ourselves from this world and closed the doors after us. But what do you think would happen if someone found the doors and showed everyone where they were?"

Put like that, the idea made Corinne pause. She could imagine what would happen—the same thing that would happen if the truth about the Others came out, only in this case human beings would take the show on the road. People would be either frightened or fascinated. The frightened ones would try to destroy what they didn't understand, and the fascinated ones would trample it in their eagerness to experience it for themselves. They'd pour through the doors like shoppers at a one-day sale.

"A person can learn to cope with a shift in his reality," Rafe said gently, "but people, as a group, are a different story. If Seoc keeps this up, he's going to open those doors. Then *Ithir* and Faerie will both suffer."

Luc agreed. "Faerie would be overrun by humans. Some of them would be honestly curious, but some of them would be afraid or greedy or malicious and would destroy the world we've spent centuries building for ourselves."

Yeah, she could see where that would suck. As much as she wanted to defend her fellow humans, people did tend to be a hell of a lot stupider and more selfish than individuals could ever be. As a reporter, she'd seen enough of the destruction people could create to know that.

"Then there's the fact that if the balance between *Ithir* and Faerie shifts, all the creatures we took with us when we left would come pouring back into your world. When was the last time you saw a real live nightmare?"

"Do you count?" she muttered under her breath, then hurried to cover it up. "Point taken. If Faerie is full of all the fairy-tale bogeymen they talked about in the kids' stories, then I agree that it would be better if they stayed there. So how do you plan to make that happen?"

The men exchanged glances again, and Corinne stifled the urge to smack them both upside the head. Did they think she couldn't see their little moments of silent communication?

"I think we need to concentrate on finding Seoc," Rafe finally said, nodding at Luc. "Not only is that the reason Luc came here, but if we remove him from the city, we remove the threat of anyone discovering his true identity. That is the ultimate goal."

"What about the people who've already seen him?"

"Do you know who they are?"

She nodded. "I have names and contact info, since I'm supposed to start interviewing them."

"If you will share that information with me, the Council will take care of it," Rafe said.

Corinne thought about that for a second and eyed him suspiciously. "Take care of it how?"

"Relax." The Felix flashed her a grin. "No one will so much as nibble on a single one of them, I promise. We do occasionally have to deal with situations like this, when one of our kind is seen by an outsider. Usually we can find a way to . . . alter such recollections. Convince them they have seen a stray dog instead of a wolf, and so on. Painlessly, of course. So long as we keep the number of witnesses down, we should be able to deal with it easily enough."

The idea of anyone playing around with someone else's memories didn't exactly have Corinne doing cartwheels, but she supposed it was the most practical solution. And at least they wouldn't be messing around in her mind.

"All right," she agreed. "I'll make you a copy of the info, but before you go and do whatever it is you're going to do, I still need to interview these people." She pulled her backpack onto her lap and opened the buckles to rummage inside. Digging out her notebook, she flipped open to the section marked WHAT DID I DO TO DESERVE THIS? and skimmed through her notes. "None of the initial reports was much help. They all saw basically the same thing: tall blond guy, brick walls, bright lights, disappearing trick. Of course, the initial reports are more like thirdhand scuttlebutt, since the police weren't exactly interested in filing reports on the ravings of folks they assumed should be in Bellevue."

"Did the witnesses talk to anyone other than the police?" Rafe asked.

"A couple of tabloids, a PI or two. Those reports aren't much better, though." She snapped her notebook shut. "That's why I had intended to start redoing interviews myself. I need to talk to the witnesses firsthand if I'm going to get to the bottom of anything."

Luc nodded. "Great. Then that's what I will do."

"Um, excuse me?" Corinne looked at him dubiously. "What do you mean what *you'll* do?"

"Agreeing to share your contact information is helpful to the Council's efforts to contain the story, but I need to be the one interviewing these witnesses. I must be able to follow every trail before it goes cold if I'm going to find Seoc and drag him back to Faerie."

"You know, enough with the talk about dragging. Have you ever considered just telling the guy what you're worried about and *asking* him to head back home?"

"Seoc knew he wasn't supposed to be here when he slipped through a door that he'd been forbidden to use. He knew he was supposed to return to Faerie when the Queen commanded him to do so. He's not late for his curfew, for Lady's sake, he's sparking an interdimensional incident of epic proportions!"

Corinne drew back from Luc's vehement roar

and glanced over at Rafe to see if he'd noticed the little display of temper, but Mr. Cowardly Lion had decided to examine his manicure.

"All right. Sheesh. No need to go ballistic. It was just a question."

"You have no idea how badly I wish I could just put you under a sleep spell," he said, his hands clenching into fists at his sides. "It would make my life so much easier."

"Except, of course, that it would make it very difficult for her to help us find the Queen's nephew," Rafe cautioned, giving Luc a firm look.

Corinne blinked. The idea that the Fae warrior could cast spells had never occurred to her. Of course, she'd never known anyone from Faerie before, so she really didn't know what they could or couldn't do. "You could do that? Just put someone to sleep?"

"Not you, unfortunately," he grumbled.

"But you can do it to other people."

"To some other people, but to humans, absolutely. Which is one of the reasons why I need to conduct these interviews. I'll be able to tell if the witnesses are lying. I might even be able to help them with details they can't consciously recall."

"I can see where that would come in handy." She shoved her notebook back into her satchel and stood. "I guess you can come along, then."

"Come along?" Luc shook his head. "You misunderstand. I will take the contact information you provide and do the interviews myself. Alone."

"No, you won't." Seeing him about to howl a protest, Corinne held up a hand. God, men could be so stubborn. "Look, whether or not you get any useful information from these people, I still need to talk to them to do my story. My editor gave me the assignment, and he'll know something's wrong if I suddenly do a shitty job as a reporter. I'm not saying I'll put anything I learn in the article I turn in, but I have to do my due diligence. Don't you think it will stir up a lot less interest in this whole story if we do the interviews together instead of separately?"

She saw that Luc wanted to argue the point with her, just as she saw that he could find no good reason to do so. Satisfied, she reached into her pocket and pulled out a business card. Scribbling the address of interview number one on the back, she held it out to him. "This is the first place I'll be going tomorrow. Meet me there at ten AM, and we'll see what we can find out."

He glanced down at the address and his eyes narrowed. "This is where we're going to find someone who spotted Seoc?"

"Yeah, why?"

Luc passed the card to Rafe, whose eyes widened considerably. "Who did you say these witnesses are?"

"A rabbi, three models, a sex shop owner, and a bartender."

Rafe snorted. "Walk into a bar, or are stranded on a desert island?"

Corinne rolled her eyes. "I know it sounds like the setup to a bad joke, but I'm totally serious. Those are the witnesses of record to the elf sightings. Although one of them did call him a leprechaun. I'm not sure who, though. Probably not the bartender."

Luc snorted. "Someone thought he was a leprechaun?"

"What?" she asked. "Is that one imaginary creature that really is imaginary?"

"No, they're real," Luc assured her, "but they're short, ugly, foul-tempered little bastards. You can't mistake one for Fae."

"Yeah, well, the witness must have missed that day of Things That Don't Exist One-Oh-One."

Rafe cleared his throat and handed the card back to Luc. "So tomorrow the two of you will be hitting The Pink Pillow?"

Corinne tried very hard not to think about the way that sounded. She also tried very hard to push away the images it conjured of her and the Faerie prince over there tangled up on rose-colored bedsheets.

"Yes, I agree that it's a ridiculous name," she managed, after a small cough, "but that's where our first witness is. He's the owner."

"Ah, the sex shop owner. I'm really glad it isn't the rabbi."

Corinne refused to laugh.

"Ten o'clock," she repeated, moving back toward the office door.

Luc blocked her way. "Why wait until tomorrow? It's a sex shop. They must have evening hours. Why don't we go tonight?"

Corinne lifted her chin and met his gaze defiantly. "Because I have other plans for tonight. I'm sure no one will be fleeing town before sunrise. We can start tomorrow."

He scowled down at her. "You think a date is more important than these interviews? Didn't we just go over what's at stake if we don't find Seoc as soon as possible?"

"I didn't say I had a date," she snapped, refusing to be intimidated by the sheer bulk of him looming over her. Corinne had never considered herself short, but this guy made her feel tiny. "I have some more background research to do, and I thought it would be smart to get it out of the way before we start in on the witnesses. Not that I think I need to explain to you how I do my job."

"You do if you're doing it stupidly."

Rafe stood and looked very much as if he'd rather be somewhere else. "Ah, children—"

"Not now."

"Sod off."

The Felix nodded. "Right. I'll just head home then. I'm certain the two of you can find your own way out."

Neither of them noticed him leave or the door clicking shut behind him.

"Men don't get to call me stupid," Corinne growled, poking a finger into the layer of granite muscle over Luc's sternum. "And you sure as hell don't get to call me anything on the basis of a twenty-minute acquaintance. Don't they teach kids growing up in Faerie not piss off people they need in order to accomplish their goals?"

"Don't they teach little girls in *Ithir* not to pull on the tiger's tail?"

She didn't get to answer. Instead, she got a mouthful of hot, angry, aroused man.

Luc grabbed and lifted her before she could so much as squeak in protest, and forget squeaking once his mouth slammed down on hers, punishing, devouring, claiming, and cherishing in an unfathomable deluge of sensation. Hell, forget thinking. All Corinne could do was feel, and she felt things for this aggravating, non-human warrior that she'd never felt for another man in her life.

Electricity seemed to arc between them, surging through her body in a current that could have resurrected Frankenstein's monster. A force this intense could power a star, not to mention start a heart beating. Corinne feared it might have stopped her own.

She couldn't catch her breath. She could only breathe in Luc, the heat and strength and musk of him. He filled her head until she forgot all about being called stupid, forgot what they had been fighting about, forgot her own damned name. All she could remember was that male and female bodies fit together like puzzle pieces and she wanted this man's to fit to hers. Right now.

She wrapped her arms around him, would have wrapped her legs around him, too, she was so far gone with lust, but Luc tore his mouth from hers and set her down, holding her at arm's length and shaking her until she opened her eyes. Damn it, she didn't even remember closing them.

"Now," he growled, staring down at her with green eyes that seemed to glow with intensity. "Tell me where *we* are going tonight."

Five

Corinne grumbled something about how it was unfair to pump her for information while she was clearly not thinking straight, but Luc ignored it. Partly because he couldn't regret a tactic that had yielded the desired result, but mostly because if she thought he'd had an unfair advantage after that kiss, she was out of her mind. She had gone to his head faster than Faerie wine. Faster than moonlight. The woman had nearly brought him to his knees. But he saw absolutely no good reason why he should tell her that.

In exchange, he had to tolerate her not-so-subtle grousing about unfair tactics and arrogant bastards while they walked from Vircolac to the appointment Corinne hadn't wanted to admit having at her friend Ava's apartment a few blocks away in Yorkville. He could only hope that the relatively cooler night air would help blow away the inconvenient remnants of lust that still thrummed through him.

That kiss might have gotten Corinne to stop arguing and take him along on her research trip, but in the grander scheme of things it might still turn out to be a very big mistake. Luc had a job to do. He had no time to waste getting involved with a woman, especially not a human woman.

No matter how good she tasted.

Corinne finally deigned to speak to him again as she paused before a large old mansion just on the edge of the neighborhood at the border of the Upper East Side.

"Ava lives inside," she informed him, crossing her arms over her chest to favor him with a challenging look. "I'll admit you made it through seven blocks without anyone wondering why you have that thing strapped to your back, but I have a feeling the doorman is going to want to know about it. He doesn't know you from Adam, and he might know me, but I don't usually come here armed. So before we go in, you're going to have to do something about that."

She gestured impatiently to his shoulder, where the hilt of his sword poked out from behind him. Only she shouldn't have been able to see it.

Luc froze, tearing his gaze from its idle inspection of the facade of the converted old home and turning it with new intensity onto his companion. There was no way she knew he was carrying a sword. Before they had left Vircolac, he had cast a glamour over himself and his weapon. All Fae possessed glamour before all other magics, the simplest and yet most potent power they wielded. By casting a glamour on himself, a Fae could alter his appearance in the eyes of any living being—even other Fae if he had particularly strong talents.

Luc hadn't used a glamour to enhance his looks, just to disguise them. Knowing what a stir Seoc's appearances had caused among humanity, Lac hadn't wanted to take the chance of being seen as Other out on the streets of the city. He hadn't used a big spell, just a few simple incantations that re-shaped his ears into a less pointed form, softened some of the sharper angles of his features, and disguised the glow of enchantment all Fae wore like a visible aura. And, of course, he'd bespelled his weapon to make it invisible to human eyes. He hadn't been about to leave it at the club; a guards-man never went about unarmed. But as far as any human was concerned—and most Others, too, in-cidentally—he wore nothing on his back beyond the thin fabric of a close-fitting black T-shirt. Only another Fae or one of a very select handful of other beings should have known the sword even existed. Corinne D'Alessandro could not possibly have numbered among those exceptions.

"Do something about what?" he asked care-fully.

She looked at him as if he were a drooling idiot. "About the three-foot sword strapped to your back, Einstein. I didn't say anything about it be-fore, because . . ." She trailed off, blushing, and he felt a moment of satisfaction that the kiss had shaken her up so much, even if the moment had apparently passed. "Well, because I wasn't thinking.

Clearly. But even if everyone else we passed assumed you were an extra in some kind of movie or on your way to a costume party, I can guarantee you that Ava Markham is not going to make the same mistake. Provided the doorman doesn't call the cops before you make it to the elevators. Which I sincerely doubt is going to happen."

"What makes you think I'm carrying a sword?"

"Duh! I can see it, asshole. And so will Bruno, the doorman, as soon as we walk up those steps."

"Describe it to me."

"What?"

Her expression went from telling Luc he was an idiot to telling him to go commit anatomically impossible acts in his own company, but he persisted. The human woman could *not* be seeing through his glamour. It wasn't possible.

"Describe it to me," he repeated forcefully.

"Fuck you," she bit out. "It's a sword. It's long and pointy and metal. And I can't describe it, because you've got it in some kind of harness contraption that covers at least half the damned thing. I'm assuming the sheath thingy has that cutout in front so it doesn't get hung up when you pull it out over your shoulder."

Luc shook his head, but his denial held no force of conviction. Her description was entirely accurate, and not something she should know. He couldn't deny its significance, no matter how much he wished to. And no matter how hard he tried to push the word from his mind, it swooped in and rooted there, bright and glowing like a blinking neon sign:

Heartmate.

Corinne appeared unfazed by his dazed reaction. She kept right on snarling at him. "I'll bet that's what it's for, too. You're in the Queen's Guard. You probably think that makes you some kind of medieval action hero. But who the hell thinks about that kind of thing? And who the hell do you think you are, telling me what to do? I don't take orders from you, and if we're going to do these interviews together, that's something you're going to have to understand. Clearly."

Luc understood only too well. In fact he understood things Corinne knew nothing about, and damned if this wasn't the worst of all possibilities. The last thing he wanted—or needed—while he was stuck in *Ithir* looking for the Queen's nephew was to find his heartmate. But here she was, and apparently no happier about it than him.

It didn't help that she had no idea what was going on, and he didn't have the time to explain.

Hell, he didn't have the energy to explain, either, not when the entire thing had broadsided him out of nowhere. Finding a heartmate didn't exactly happen every day. As far as he knew, it didn't even happen every lifetime, so how was he supposed to explain to a human that Fate had determined they were meant to be together for all eternity? The mind boggled.

He could understand her feeling that everything

had changed, though, because it had. The minute she had looked at him and seen through his glamour, reality had reshaped itself: an ordinary stroll with a human had become the first time he'd ever spent alone with his heartmate. Just like that.

There was no other way she could have seen through the magic. Glamours didn't fade in a couple of hours, and they didn't require maintenance. Once cast, they just existed, for weeks or even years until the Fae who cast them called them back. No one was able to see Luc's real appearance—not even another Fae—once the magic had been cast. Except for a heartmate.

The gods definitely appreciated a little irony.

Anu had. According to legend, the Great Goddess of the Fae had created heartmating.

Disappointed by her Fae children and their tendency to hide behind pretty masks and to shape the appearance of things to suit themselves, she had placed them under an enchantment of sorts. According to Anu's wishes, while the Fae might continue as masters of Illusions, that great power would be balanced by a great vulnerability: Love's Truth. From the day she first commanded it, each Fae had to recognize that at the moment he found his true love, their hearts would be irrevocably bound, and the Fae's power of Illusion would never again deceive his heartmate. Even if all the rest of the world believed in the Fae's spells, his heartmate would see through the magic to the truth.

It made a romantic story to tell the little ones,

but it wreaked havoc on Luc's plans. If Corinne was his heartmate, he wouldn't be able to manipulate this investigation to suit his own intentions; nor was the affair he'd been contemplating from the first moment he'd touched her still a possibility. He could never have an affair with her now—at least, not the kind that ended with a peck and a thank-you as he hied himself back to Faerie. This woman was his now, and leaving her—ever—had ceased to be an option.

Even if she still stood on the sidewalk and glared at him as if she'd like to rip the sword off his back and beat him with it.

Luc held up a hand and willed it not to tremble. "I'm sorry," he said in a voice much calmer than he should have managed. "I didn't mean to be insulting. I just—I needed to know what you saw so I could deal with the situation. I can use magic to hide the sword. I can't leave it behind—a guardsman never travels without his weapon—but I can make it so that no one else will be able to see it. Call it a compromise."

She eyed him for another moment, her mouth set in a firm and decidedly unhappy line. Then she gave a short nod. "Fine. Go ahead. Make it disappear."

He really wished she hadn't made it sound like a challenge. Since he'd already cast the glamour she'd just dared him to perform, he now had to think of a way to explain to her why it was already done but she was somehow seeing through it.

Now, he judged, was not the time for that particular conversation. He'd always hoped his heartmate would at least like him a little before learning she was stuck with him.

Closing his eyes, Luc drew a deep breath and hoped Corinne would see it as a signal of intense concentration. He waited for several heartbeats before lifting his lids and offering her a weak smile. "All right, then. Ready to go up?"

Corinne made an is-that-it? gesture with one hand and shot her chin forward belligerently. "What about this spell of yours?"

"Already done."

"Really?"

He nodded.

"So how come I can still see the sword?"

Luc shifted slightly. "The intention is to hide it from other people," he hedged. "You already know it's there, so I don't need to hide it from you. Right?"

"I guess," she said, clearly unconvinced. "So you're telling me that no one else can see your huge, honkin' sword at the moment, but I can?"

"Yes."

Corinne snorted and turned to the front steps with an amused shake of her head. "Fine. It's your felony conviction. Let's go say hello to Bruno."

The multipaned art deco doors swung open before they reached the top step. An older man, stocky but impeccably groomed in a plain black suit, stood back to invite them in with a wide smile. "Good evening, Miss Corinne. Is it Ms. Markham's turn to host your Girls' Night festivities?"

Corinne smiled back and stopped in the foyer—deliberately, Luc had no doubt—to give the man a good look at both of them. "Hey, Bruno. No, actually, it's just me tonight. Well, me and my . . . friend. We stopped by to talk to Ava for a bit. Luc, this is Bruno Mueller. Bruno, Luci—"

"Luc Macanaw." Luc stepped forward before she could finish and took the older fellow's hand, shaking it firmly. "How are you, Mr. Mueller?"

"Oh, not so bad," Bruno said. He wore a pleasant smile on his creased and jowled face, but his black eyes were sharp and piercing as they sized him up. "So you're a friend of Miss Corinne's, eh? I haven't seen you with her before."

"I'm not from around here." Luc deliberately gave the doorman a good look at his left shoulder and side where the un-glamoured sword would have been easily visible. It also had the advantage of placing him partially in front of Corinne, making it difficult for her to answer Bruno's questions on Luc's behalf. She'd wanted the doorman to get a good look at Luc. Luc had no problem with that, but he saw no need to allow the little troublemaker to throw gasoline on the fire.

Bruno didn't blink, just nodded, his smile widening and his stance subtly relaxing. He never took a second look at the visitor's shoulder. Luc know he'd been approved. At least conditionally.

"A visitor, huh?" The doorman shook his head. "Me, I was born and raised not ten blocks from here. Never understood why anyone would want to live anywhere else." He gestured to the gated elevator at the rear of the foyer. "Well, you kids didn't stop by to talk to me. You know Ms. Markham's apartment. Give her my regards."

Luc murmured his thanks and guided Corinne to the back of the building with a hand at her waist. She looked over her shoulder to see Bruno resettling himself at his desk beside the door, then turned back to glare at Luc.

"How did you do that?" she demanded.

He pulled the elevator gate shut behind them and gestured for her to choose the floor. "I told you. Magic."

"Right. Magic that can make things selectively invisible."

Luc hoped his face conveyed more exasperation and less desperation. He was not ready to have this talk. "Did you pursue a degree in advanced physics before deciding to give it a go in the exciting world of print journalism?"

"No—"

"Then it would be pretty pointless for me to try to explain how magic works before we get to your friend's front door." The elevator slid to a stop, and he reached out to open the gate to the fourth floor. "You're just going to have to trust me on this."

Corinne paused on the way down the carpeted

hall to shoot him a meaningful glance over her shoulder. "I'm not the kind of girl who trusts easily."

If Corinne had held out any hopes of Ava taking Luc in hand and bending him to her will the way she seemed to manage with every other living thing in the universe, she was doomed to disappointment. The other woman answered the doorbell, took one look at the tall, formidable package of manhood outside her peephole, and whisked the door open before Corinne could get two words out of her mouth.

"—me," she finished lamely, her hair stirring in the breeze created by the swiftly moving panels of wood. She quirked an eyebrow at her friend. "Have you got a few minutes to talk?" she asked drily.

"Of course, Corinne darling," Ava purred, never taking her eyes off Luc. "Anything for you. Right after you introduce me to your new friend."

Of course. The femme fatale routine. Corinne didn't think Ava normally went in for the bulky-with-muscle type, but obviously she'd taken one look at Lucifer Macanaw's breathtaking features and gorgeous body and decided to make an exception. And what Ava wanted, Ava always got.

Corinne fought back a wave of irritation. It shouldn't bother her any if her friend had set her sights on Luc. It wasn't like he was Corinne's boyfriend, or even a man she was interested in. *Remotely* interested in. He was barely one step removed from a complete stranger. He meant nothing to her, absolutely nothing.

But that kiss had certainly felt like something.

It felt like trouble, she told herself sternly, despite the warmth that brewed in the pit of her stomach every time she thought about the way he tasted—all heat and spice and magic—or when she took too deep a breath standing beside him. The man smelled almost as good as he tasted, and that, for God's sake, should be a sin. If she carried a rosary with her like her nana did, she'd be tempted to whip it out and say a decade every time the man so much as looked at her.

Like right now, which after a second she realized he was doing, because Ava had just asked her to introduce them.

"Ah, right. Sorry," she said, feeling her cheeks go red. "Um, Luc this is my friend Ava Markham. Av, this is Luc Macanaw. He's . . . well, he's interested in your models."

"And I'm sure my models will be more than interested in him," Ava said with a sly smile and a coquettish wave into her apartment. "Please come in and make yourself comfortable. Are you a photographer, Mr. Macanaw? You can't live in New York, or I'm certain I would have heard about you a long, long time ago."

"Ah, no. I'm from out of town," Corinne heard him answer as she stalked ahead of them toward her friend's ridiculously white-on-white living room. "And actually, I'm in, er, private security."

Corinne threw herself onto the snowy, over-stuffed sofa with a distinct huff. Private security? She supposed that was one way to explain wearing a broadsword to conduct a simple witness interview.

"Security? How fascinating. Please have a seat. Make yourself comfortable." Ava gestured toward the sofa, all hostessly concern. "Can I offer you something to drink? I have wine, or I've been known to mix a mean martini. Unless you'd prefer something hot? Coffee? Tea?"

Or me? Corinne snarked in her head. She didn't know why she hadn't anticipated Ava making a play for Luc when she'd been walking him over here. Ava never missed an opportunity to put the moves on a man this good looking, unless he spoiled it with his attitude before she managed her patented I'm-too-good-for-you-but-I'll-do-you-anyway come-on.

And who could blame Luc for being drawn in? Ava was, quite simply, a stunningly beautiful woman. She'd been a frickin' supermodel during her teen years, before she'd decided she'd rather spend her life using her brains instead of her looks. Now she managed models, but that didn't mean she couldn't have passed for one of her own clients. From the top of her sleek, dark head to the tips of her red-polished toes, she displayed not a single excess millimeter of fat, not a single pimple, not a single hair out of place. She wore what she probably considered a casual lounging-around outfit of flowing, black silk trousers and an equally silky knit wrap-top in pale blue. She looked like an ad from a "celebrities at home" magazine.

If Corinne hadn't already loved her like a sister, she would have hated her like the clap.

"Nothing, thanks," Luc said, shaking his head but smiling. Of course he was smiling. Ava's top showed enough cleavage to make your average lawn jockey grin.

He shifted, the movement bringing him closer to Corinne. Probably so he could ask her to pinch him to show him he hadn't dreamed up Ava's spectacular looks.

"Actually, Corinne told me you might be able to answer a few questions for me," he continued. "For us, really. I'm interested in the same thing her paper has asked her to look into. Apparently a few of your models have reported a couple of odd occurrences lately."

Ava's dark, carefully arched brows flew toward her hairline and she straightened from her seductively languid posture to give her guests a closer second look. She gazed from one to the other, her eyes lingering on Luc's face, then dropping to the space between her guests. For a minute she said nothing, and when she spoke again, the purr in her voice had subsided.

"She told you that, did she?" Ava nodded and stepped around an armchair to settle herself in the wide seat. "I'm assuming, since they're the ones we talked about earlier today, that Corinne was referring to the three young women I just booked to work an outdoor runway show in Buffalo. This November."

Despite her irritation, Corinne snorted at that. "Christ, you're cold, Av. If that's the revenge you have planned for your models for missing one shoot, it's just been confirmed for me that I don't ever want to get on your bad side."

"You've been on my bad side before," Ava informed her, her dark eyes glinting. "You survived, relatively unscathed. Though I do reserve the right to inflict further revenge should it become necessary." She tucked her bare feet up under her and rested her forearms on one arm of the chair. "Actually, April missed one shoot, but Leena and Marlie have each missed two now, which not only puts them on my shit list but also qualifies them for a lower step on my pay scale. I don't dick around when it comes to business."

As she always did when she visited Ava's apartment, Corinne moved to swing her feet up onto the antique coffee table and had to catch herself at the last minute. No matter how many times she came here, the flawlessly decorated, spotlessly white surroundings always managed to make her feel like she'd just been rolling around in a mud pit. Which made her want to actually go roll around in a mud pit and track it all over the apartment, but only because she was spiteful. Tonight the urge seemed particularly strong.

"You'd think anyone you represent would know

that," she said, crossing her legs instead and grabbing for her backpack and the notebook inside. "You said before that these are the same girls who reported being stalked by—er, by the . . ."

"By 'Legolas of the Woodland Realm'?" Ava quoted. "Yes. They each made that reference, as if he'd just stepped out of the movies."

Luc leaned forward, his attention obviously captured, whether by Ava or her story, Corinne preferred not to guess.

"Were these among the witnesses who filed police reports?" he asked.

"Hardly," Ava said. "That would have required brainpower and clear thinking, which none of these girls possesses. Besides, the police couldn't do anything if they had filed reports. No one committed any crimes. Looking weird in public? Please, two of these sightings were on St. Mark's Place. It's looking normal that's the crime down there."

Luc frowned. "Yet you called Corinne. Why do that? If there was no crime, no trouble caused, why did you even mention it to her?"

"Because she's a reporter. And because she's my friend. The day after I learned of the incidents, I saw Mindy Daniels, from Channel Seven, at the Four Seasons. She said their program director is thinking of putting someone on it. I couldn't let a cheap barracuda like that Daniels woman scoop my best friend."

Corinne tried not to be touched by that, but Ava was not what one would call a demonstrative friend; more like a demonic one. She was ruthless, demanding, controlling, and occasionally rude. Her friends jokingly referred to her as the Bitch Goddess of the Universe, only they didn't always mean it as a joke. But Ava had a gift. Just when she'd gone and done something one of them thought was unforgivable, she would turn right around and do something so sweet and generous and incredibly thoughtful that you couldn't stay mad at her even if you wanted to.

More surprising, though, were the times like this, when she did or said something lovely out of the blue, unprompted, for no other reason than that she meant it.

Corinne cleared her throat. "Well, uh, thanks, then."

Predictably, Ava waved it away like a gnat. "Believe me, I can't stand Mindy Daniels. She's like the Yorkshire terrier of the New York news market—all hair and attitude and not two brain cells to rub together. I'd rather give a lead to my Vietnamese pedicurist than to her, and Tuyet doesn't even speak English."

Mushy as a sponge cake, that one.

"I doubt I can answer any of your questions, though," Ava continued. "I didn't see the mystery elf on any of the occasions we're talking about. You'd have to go straight to my models for the details."

"That's why we came," Corinne said. "We need their contact info, names, phones, addresses. We need to get their firsthand accounts to move ahead with the story. Can you give us those?"

"Sure. Just let me get my BlackBerry." She stood and moved toward the sofa table behind them. "I'll give you everything I have and wish you good luck. None of them is returning my messages."

"Do they usually?"

"If they want to get paid." Ava copied the information onto a sheet of notepaper and handed it to Corinne. Then she turned to Luc. "Now, I understand why Rinne wants to interview the girls. She needs them to write her story and scoop that Daniels bitch. But what exactly is it that makes you so interested in meeting three attractive but dimwitted women? Looking for a date?"

Corinne heard the challenge in her friend's voice and braced herself for Ava to swoop in for the kill. She felt Luc tense. Maybe she should check her backpack for a tissue. He'd probably need something to wipe away the drool.

"No, actually," she heard him answer, yanking her shocked gaze back to his face. "I'm just looking for the man we think the models may have spotted. He's . . . a concern to, ah, a client of mine."

"Really? Well, I hope you find him, then." Ava extended her hand to him, her fingers clinging to his for a moment while she searched his face. "I hope you find any number of things during your stay here."

"I think I'm already on the right track."

Corinne watched the exchange through narrowed eyes, waiting for the inevitable exchange of phone numbers, or, God forbid, for them to just get it over with and kiss. Only it didn't look like that was a danger. The predatory female vibe Ava had put on the second she spotted Luc through her peephole had disappeared. Now she looked, well, almost businesslike. And Luc just looked . . . resolved.

Corinne frowned in confusion. Was there any chance this day could start making sense?

Six

Corinne seemed distracted as they left her friend's apartment, Luc noted. The tiniest little furrow had taken up residence between her brows, making him want to smooth it away with his thumb. Or his tongue. She'd barely said good-bye to Ava, and she responded to Bruno's cheerful address by murmuring a distracted "Have a good night." Clearly, she had something on her mind. For some reason, he didn't think it was the models they needed to interview.

"Where to now?" he asked as they stepped out into the night air, less because he thought she had an answer and more because he wanted to remind her that he still existed. She appeared to have forgotten that between Ava's living room and the front stoop.

"What? Oh," Corinne blinked and frowned at him. "Um, nowhere. I mean, it's getting late, so I think we should just leave this until tomorrow. It's after ten, so it would be really rude to start making phone calls or knocking on people's doors. Let's just meet at The Pink Pillow tomorrow morning like I originally suggested."

"And in the meantime?"

"In what meantime? We go home. To our respective homes," she added hastily. "I go to my apartment to get some sleep, and you go to wherever it is you're staying and, er, do whatever it is that you, uh, do."

Oh, but he had some suggestions for her about what he did. Or at least, about what he wanted to do. To her, specifically.

"Fine." He could bide his time. If he really had to. He couldn't help but notice, though, that Corinne appeared a little jumpy. He wondered what could be causing that. Deliberately, his arm bumped her shoulder. "I'll walk you home, then."

She nearly jumped out of her skin. Interesting.

"No! I mean, that's not necessary. Really," she said, stumbling over her own words. "Really. I won't even be walking. I mean, I live downtown. I'll have to take the subway, or something. Maybe I'll just head up to the avenue and take a cab. So I won't be walking. So you won't need to walk with me. I mean, you won't need to walk me home. I can do it. Get there myself, that is. Safely."

Luc watched her fingers clench on the strap of her backpack and felt himself grinning. Her knuckles were turning white, and she seemed to have a newly discovered difficulty meeting his gaze. Maybe she had begun to feel the same energy building between them that he'd been fighting all evening.

Now, though, he was having a hard time remembering why he shouldn't just give in. If Corinne was his heartmate, then the issue of his magic no longer stood between them. She had seen through his enchantments, so no one could argue that his Fae nature had clouded her mind. If she was attracted to him, it was an honest attraction.

It was a strange twist of fate that humans should find something about the Fae so irresistible when their people had chosen to live so far apart, but there it was. Not even glamours could hide the fact that the Fae were magic, nor keep some humans from sensing it. Usually, when a human woman seemed intent on seducing Luc, he could write it off as a reaction to his glamour, as he had with Corinne's friend Ava. The other woman hadn't really wanted him; she'd been drunk on his power, which no matter how beautiful she might be by human standards took quite a bit of the shine off the encounter.

Corinne was the first human woman he'd ever felt this kind of attraction for. He usually gave the species a wide berth. He knew humans and Fae were physically compatible, but he'd grown accustomed to taking the women he wanted without the elaborate mating rituals humans observed, and he didn't picture a human woman appreciating the bold sexuality so common among his people. Besides, somewhere in the back of his mind, he'd always found it distasteful that with a human, there would be the possibility that it really wasn't him she lusted for; it was the magic he couldn't hide, not even behind the strongest glamour.

That magical attraction accounted for all the human stories of the seductive beauty of his race. Tam Lin had indeed been captivated by the beauty of the Queen of Faerie, but at least a little bit of that beauty had come from Her Majesty's particularly strong glamours. Those very tricks usually proved the undoing of any relationships between Fae and mortal. For some reason, humans tended to get all bent out of shape when they discovered that their perception of their lovers was based on a web of pretty lies.

But with Corinne, he wasn't lying. He couldn't. She would—and did—see right through him. The thought brought forth a surge of excitement.

"I don't mind," he told her, letting his smile curve into one that would have made a hunting Lupine proud. "I haven't gotten much chance to see your city, and it's a nice night."

Corinne stared at him while inside her lust battled with reason in a fight to the death. Ten minutes ago she'd been convinced she'd have to let herself out of Ava's apartment discreetly while the two of them jumped each other and screwed like rabid mink. Now that she thought about it, though, it did seem as if Ava had been the one giving off all the signals. Luc had done nothing to encourage the other woman, except be gorgeous and charming, and Corinne didn't think the man knew of any other way to be. For the first time in ages, a man had brushed off a seduction-minded Ava and turned to Corinne instead. She needed a few minutes to process that information.

Oh, it wasn't like Corinne didn't attract her fair share of men, and Ava wasn't the sort to go after a man she knew one of her friends was already making a play for. Corinne knew she had nothing to be ashamed of when it came to her appearance, either. When she decided to pull out all the stops, she could pull off *bombshell* like Sophia Loren in her prime. But Ava was on a whole other level. Men looked at her and saw not a woman, but a fantasy. Except for this man. He saw Ava and wished her a good night, but if the glint in his eyes was any indication, when he saw Corinne he wished for a different sort of night entirely.

So what was it that Corinne wished for?

Three hours ago it would have been to dump this entire mess on the head of the Council of Others and then not set eyes on another non-human being—except maybe Reggie—for at least a week. Now, though, she wasn't so sure. Her head still told her that the man—or rather, the Fae warrior—standing in front of her would be a lot more trouble than he was worth; her gut, though—and maybe a bit of real estate just south of there—told her that the only way to know for sure would be to try him out.

And boy, she bet he would be one hell of a ride.

While she hemmed and hawed, Luc simply nudged her elbow and began walking, heading up the block to the nearest avenue where the cabs cruised more frequently. "Let's go." He glanced over his shoulder and urged her to cross to the other side of the street. "You can make up your mind on the way."

Corinne wondered if she really could. In fact, she was still wondering when he raised one beefy arm—somehow coming up with two cabs—when he slid into the back of the taxi next to her, and when she gave the driver her address. In her own defense, she had a lot to wonder about. Not just the sex, which she'd already decided had the potential to be stupendous, but also the advisability of getting involved with a member of another species. And an out-of-towner at that. Once he found the Faerie Queen's nephew, Luc Macanaw would head right back to his homeland and right back out of her life. How would she feel about that? The man didn't exactly have *long-term potential* written all over him.

That sort of thing didn't usually bother Corinne. After all, she'd dated more than her fair share of men, and none of them had lasted so far. But she rarely decided to hop into bed with a man if she knew beforehand that he wouldn't be around for more than the time it took to deal with the buttons and zippers. She blamed her Catholic roots.

Being raised in the church just had a way of making a girl worry about looking like a total slut. Maybe it was the dress code.

And Corinne had to admit, something in the back of her mind looked at the idea of sex with a member of another species with a certain amount of alarm. She'd never slept with a man who wasn't human before. She supposed the fact that Luc didn't suffer from the furry form of PMS counted in his favor, but still, were humans and the Fae even, er, compatible?

Instinctively, her eyes dropped to his crotch and her cheeks heated. The evidence suggested they were.

Corinne sighed. Why were all the good ones married, gay, or another species?

Her gut weighed in on that one. It told her that Luc Macanaw could be one of the good ones. Mouthwatering face and body aside, in the few short hours that she'd known him, the man had displayed a sharp intelligence, polished social skills, and basic human decency. Or the Fae equivalent thereof. Frankly, she'd dated men who'd barely scored two out of three on that scale, so why did she hesitate?

She pondered that for a few minutes and could come up with only one explanation: sheer, unadulterated stupidity.

The man made her thighs tingle just to look at him! Time to yell *Bansai!* and have at it.

Clearing her throat, she angled to face him just as the taxi turned onto her street. "So, um, maybe you and I should spend some time laying out our game plan." She tried desperately to sound casual and just hoped she at least managed better than totally lame. "You could come up for coffee, and we could compare notes. My building is just up ahead."

Corinne gestured through the windshield then swore.

Luc cursed. "Before or after the police barrier?"

"After. Damn it."

"Hey, sorry, folks, but this is as far as I can go." The cabbie eased out of traffic and rolled up to the curb four blocks ahead of Corinne's building. "I dunno what the heck is going on up there, but it looks messy. Good luck getting through."

"Yeah, thanks."

Luc was handing through the fare before Corinne even managed to find her wallet inside her backpack. She slid out of the vehicle in front of him, almost jumping out of her skin when he helped her with a warm hand on her ass.

"I, uh, I guess you're going to get to walk me home after all," she said, shoving her hands into her pockets to keep them from returning the favor and grabbing his ass in the middle of the street. "Unless, you know, you'd rather just wait until tomorrow."

He grabbed her hand and started hauling her down the sidewalk at a speed that forced her almost to trot to keep up. "I'll be lucky if I can wait until we reach your bed," he growled.

"Oh. Then I guess you will be staying for coffee."

He shot her a glance that all but set her eyebrows on fire.

"I'll be staying for you."

Luc decided to take the strangled sound Corinne uttered at his blunt pronouncement as a good sign. Considering the sight that greeted him farther down the block, he could use all the good news he could get.

When the barricades went up, a crowd gathered. That was the way it worked in New York. People wanted to know what was happening. At the moment, the happenings had to do with at least forty protesters gathered in front of a beleaguered coffee shop and angry over the plight of laborers on plantations in Africa and South America. Judging by the broken glass and ceramic littering the pavement, the angry voices, and the news cameras strategically positioned on the scene, Luc could assume that nonviolent protest had gone the way of the dodo sometime in the last few hours. What irked him at the moment, though, was that all these people currently blocked his way between here and Corrine D'Alessandro's bed.

This had to change. Immediately.

Grasping her much smaller hand firmly in his, Luc set his jaw, firmed his shoulders, and prepared to bulldoze his way through the crowd of protestors, police, coffee shop workers, and on-lookers. If he had to knock people over, so be it. His heartmate had just not-so-subtly invited him to share her bed. He'd have knocked over Mab herself if she stood in his way.

Luc was so focused on dodging and weaving that he didn't even see the blow coming. Later he would curse himself, kick himself, and call himself ten kinds of fool, but he simply hadn't been pay-ing enough attention. He'd been thinking with his dick, and so he'd never noticed when a form shifted through the crush of bodies just behind him on his left and raised a short length of metal pipe in the direction of his head.

Thankfully, his instincts seemed to operate well enough even beneath the haze of lust that had clouded his other senses. He caught the swing of movement and turned just enough that the blow meant for his head landed on the meat of his shoulder instead.

Adrenaline kicked in before he even had time to think about what had happened. He shoved Corinne away, pinning her between him and the wall of the nearby building and keeping himself between her and the threat. His left hand shot out and grabbed for the man's arm, the one with the weapon in it, feeling skin and leather before the as-sailant twisted away and broke free. Even as he raised his right hand to the hilt of his sword, he knew it was too late. Whoever had come at him had already melted back into the crowd.

Luc scanned the faces nearby and saw nothing. Damn it.

"Hey!"

He heard Corinne shout even as the pain of the injury began to resonate, making his breath hiss in between his teeth. His attacker had been strong, very strong; and for the blow to have nearly staggered him, the choice of weapon must have been deliberate. Only a blow from cold iron could possibly pack that kind of wallop.

"Jesus Christ, that guy attacked you! Are you all right?"

"I'm fine," he said, lowering his hand from his sword and pressing it hard into the small of Corinne's back. "But we need to get out of here fast."

If he'd been rude before as he'd pushed his way through the milling crowd, now he was ruthless, using a combination of brute strength and magic to move every obstacle from their way. His pace forced Corinne to jog to keep up with him, but he couldn't worry about that now. The goal was to get her off the street and into the safety of her apartment before their mysterious attacker could double back and try his luck a second time.

"Luc, what the hell is going on?" she demanded as they broke free of the congestion and picked up the pace until she was running beside him the last two blocks to her building.

"Not now. Get your key out of your bag. Have it ready."

"It's in my pocket," she grumbled, but she reached for it anyway and drew it out as they turned for the entrance.

"Inside. Quick."

He shielded her back as she worked the lock on the main door, his eyes scanning for anything odd in the street around them. Everything looked quiet, but then things usually did just before trouble broke out. He heard the *snick* of the lock and hustled her inside even before the door was fully open. Hearing the thick glass close behind him made him feel only marginally better.

"Okay, upstairs. Which floor?"

"Fifth."

Luc bundled her into the elevator and took a last glance around the lobby and out the door onto the street. There wasn't a soul in sight. He breathed a sigh of relief and turned back to his heartmate just in time to see her jab the button for her floor with such force he could only assume she was imagining it to be his eye. Or another, equally sensitive portion of his anatomy.

"Okay, what the hell just happened?" she demanded, her voice hot and hard with a combination of confusion, fear, and adrenaline. "Who the hell just tried to bring a lead pipe down on your head in the middle of a crowded street? And why did you react to it by treating me like the damned president right after somebody yells that they have a gun? You're not the goddamned Secret Service."

"Actually, I am," he murmured. "I'm the Fae equivalent, anyway. What did you think the Queen's Guard were for?"

She looked ready to spit nails, all warm and flustered with adrenaline pinking her cheeks and speeding her breath. Actually, she looked like a woman who had been thoroughly aroused, and the sight went straight to Luc's groin. He needed to taste her.

He reached out, his eyes narrowing in surprise when she slapped his hands away with a sharp snap.

"Just what do you think you're doing?" she demanded. "You think you're going to get all touchy-feely after someone just tried to kill you? What is wrong with you?"

God, she really was gorgeous when she was angry. Wasn't that a human cliché? Luc had never thought he would say this, but in this case the humans knew what they were talking about. Her eyes snapped with temper and her skin flushed with heat. He needed to show her how arousal could be converted from anger to sex in the space of a heartbeat. Maybe less.

"I'm not dead," he purred, stepping forward to crowd her against the elevator wall, "and neither are you. We're not even hurt, but that doesn't mean our hearts aren't pounding and our bodies aren't humming. That's the adrenaline. It makes a body feel alive."

He lifted a hand, stroked fine dark strands of hair away from her cheek, trailed the backs of his fingers across her smooth, warm skin. He felt her tremble and wanted to roar in triumph.

"Don't you feel alive, Corinne? Don't you feel . . ." He leaned in, breath fanning the soft curve just behind her ear. ". . . excited?"

He'd never be sure if he'd fallen on her like a starving man, or if she'd yanked him down like a lightpost flyer. When it came right down to it, he'd never feel moved to care. The first touch of her lips felt like home and tasted like brandied cream.

Luc growled his pleasure against her mouth and wrapped his arms around her, dragging her body hard against his. She felt small and delicate compared with him, so tiny he could almost wrap his arms around her twice, but she didn't kiss like a retiring flower; she devoured him. Her mouth bloomed under his, her body stretching and heating, her hands clinging to his shoulders as if she couldn't imagine a reason to let him go. Lady help him, he didn't want her to.

Her lips parted eagerly for his tongue and he plunged deep, seeking the unpolluted taste of her, the flavor that lingered in the soft, inviting recesses of her mouth. He could sense in her the same lust that threatened to send him over the edge, which wasn't helping his struggle for control.

Then the elevator dinged and the doors slid open and he had to drag himself back to reality to keep from throwing her down and taking her there in the hall of her apartment building. He may never have been involved with a human woman before, but he'd heard they tended to frown on public sex. Compared with the Fae, humans were just prudes.

"Apartment," he said, his voice raw and hoarse and tight with need. "Key. Hurry."

"Left. Second door on the right."

He picked her up and ate up the distance with long, loping strides. It would be faster this way, when he didn't have to wait for her shorter legs to keep up with his. She didn't bother to protest. She just buried her face in his shoulder, small white teeth digging in to the tight, flexing muscle, even as her fingers fumbled for the key to her door.

"Hurry," he repeated, following her directions and pressing her up against the smooth white surface of her door. She scraped the key against the lock, swearing when her shaking fingers missed the keyhole twice. Luc rubbed his hips against her in encouragement.

She dropped the keychain.

"Shit!"

"Let me." He had the key in the lock and the door swinging wide before she could so much as nod. He herded her through, kicked the panel shut behind him, and saw to his great relief that there was enough light in the sparsely decorated room that he could make out the sofa immediately. Picking her up, he tossed her onto the soft cushions and followed closer than her own shadow.

The taste of her lingered on his tongue, and he'd have sold his soul for more of it. She felt like paradise, the feel of her curves under his hands, the smell of her, warm and musky and so essentially female that he literally felt dizzy. Thank the Lady he'd finally gotten them horizontal. Taking advantage of his own good sense, he framed her face in his hands and dove back into her brandy-flavored kiss.

"Mm."

Her throaty moans drove him crazy. This human he'd been afraid of shocking apparently didn't know she was supposed to be significantly less aggressive than a Fae woman. Her hands wove themselves though his hair, nails raking his scalp and sending tremors shivering down his spine. They kneaded his shoulder like kitten paws then dove between their bodies. She shifted position, wrapping one slim leg around his hip, opening herself and letting his body sink deeper against her, but she never interrupted their kiss.

Their mouths fed on each other as she maneuvered her hands with surprising dexterity in such tight quarters to attack the buttons of his now too-tight jeans.

Luc barely managed to stop himself from releasing them with magic. Instead of whisking them both naked with a flick of his fingers, he savored the maddening slide of her fingers over his hips and thighs, the brush of knuckles against his straining erection, as she struggled with metal and denim.

When she finally got the last of the buttons open, she moaned her relief against his mouth and slid her hands inside to close reverently around him. Slim, feminine fingers curled and flexed, exploring silky skin and lingering over urgent hardness. Lady knew, there was no way on *Ithir* he could possibly get any harder, short of turning completely to stone. And even then, it would be a close call.

Her other hand burrowed lower to cup him in a tender palm. The satisfied purr she gave when she did that almost finished him in her hands, and he cursed his own impatience. He felt like a boy again, too eager to pleasure the woman who promised him a taste of heaven. He'd be damned if he'd disgrace himself.

He tore his mouth from hers just long enough to strip his shirt over his head and toss it away. Before he had time to grasp the hem of hers, she dove headfirst for his bare chest and laid her warm, clever tongue against the hollow of his throat. He cursed. Between her stroking hands and her darting tongue, he didn't stand a chance. If he didn't stop her right now, he'd never be able to live with himself. And Corinne certainly wouldn't be asking for a repeat performance. Easing her hands from his body, he decided it was his turn now.

In one dizzy rush of motion, he stripped her T-shirt over her head and flung it away into the darkness of the room. Before she could do more than blink up at him, he had her pants, shoes, and socks off and was kicking out of his jeans, leaving them to join the pile of abandoned clothes on the floor. Naked, he forced her legs apart and settled himself in the saddle of her hips. No place in this world or his own had ever felt more like home.

Bracing the weight of his torso on one hand, he curved the other around her breast, flicked his thumb over her erect little nipple, and grinned down at her.

"Hey," she protested, even as she parted her thighs wider and wrapped her smooth, golden legs around his hips. "You're not fighting fair. I was enjoying myself."

Luc ducked his head until he could scrape his teeth over the delicate tendon along her shoulder. "I'm not fighting at all." He inhaled deeply to capture her scent. It was a heady mix of honeysuckle, clove, and warm, willing woman. "And I'd much rather we enjoy ourselves together. What do you say?"

He rocked his hips against hers, savoring the music of her ragged gasp. Goddess, he couldn't wait to be inside her.

Teeth clenched, he rose up above her, watching the arch of her throat as she threw her head back, the fluttering of her eyelashes when he gently kneaded her full breast. He stared down at her, at the dark, expressive eyes currently narrowed in arousal, at the warm, olive skin flushed with passion. He could stare at her forever, he realized, and never see enough. She held the whole universe within her. His whole universe.

"I say I'm way ahead of you," she murmured, and her mouth curved in a smile so slow and warm and sexy he felt his heart stutter before it raced forward with excitement.

"Then let me catch up." He grinned and slid into that smile like a runner stealing third.

She shifted beneath him, not content to let Luc set the pace. Her hands stroked over the taut, flexing muscles of his back, feeling they way he moved and shifted above her. The clasp of her thighs urged him toward her, and the sweet, sharp hunger of her kiss removed the last film of anticipation. It was time to experience.

His hands shifted, sliding beneath her hips to lift her to him, and she met him, hands clinging, back arching, calling him home with a heated siren song of pleasure. He dove into her like a pool of clear, crystalline water, letting the sensation of joining envelop him in silent perfection. The only sound was the too-rapid beat of their hearts as even the breath seemed to freeze in their chests for that one amazing moment of recognition.

They had found each other. The search was over. All was right with the world.

Time stood still for a second, no longer. The urgency of their passion was too strong to allow for any more. With a groan, Luc snapped and gave in to the driving need to move, to touch, to feel.

His hands stroked and savored, his body moving in a primitive rhythm that seemed directed by something within himself he'd never known existed.

Corrine cried out, her head dropping back to the cushions even as her hands clutched at his shoulders. She tugged as if to pull him nearer, and Luc obeyed, pressing their sweat-slick bodies together from neck to groin, feeling the way she fit him as if someone had taken a mold and designed her just for him. He'd never felt anything as amazing as this woman, as the way she made him feel, just by being. He clutched her to him as if he could crawl inside her skin, get so close to her that not even the air could separate them.

The feel of her body cushioning his drove him crazy, almost as crazy as the pleading whimpers that issued from her parted lips with each ragged breath. He crushed her mouth under his, swallowing those whimpers, catching them on her tongue, and returning them in the form of his own deep, rumbling groans.

For hours they strained together—or what seemed like hours to his fevered brain—struggling with the instinctive need to become one, but in the end they gave in to the inevitable. Pleasure overtook them and she gave a choked cry, her body convulsing, leaving Luc to follow her into ecstasy. With the feel of her shuddering and sobbing beneath him, it didn't take long. Three hard, endless thrusts later, he exploded, emptying his entire being into her, until all he could do was sink heavily atop her and wonder whether this amazing woman was really human after all.

Seven

Corinne lay beneath him, heart pounding, lungs aching, muscles burning, and struggled to remember the last time she had been this wrung out by sex. She couldn't. She'd never experienced anything like it. It had been like being hit by a tidal wave, the adrenaline of the attack suddenly morphing into a need so sharp it had been like a knife in her flesh. The urgency and desire had felt almost unnatural, like a spell that compelled her to get as close to him as possible before she took her next breath.

Judging by her present position, Corinne thought she'd managed that well enough.

Wary, she checked for any lingering signs of that driving need, but it seemed to be gone. Oh, she still wanted him, but this time she felt she could wait another few minutes if she had to. Though she'd like it if she didn't have to.

He covered her like a duvet and generated more heat than an electric blanket without the pesky need to plug him in. Just call her an environmental crusader, cutting down on power consumption one bout of hot, sticky sex at a time.

Luc stirred above her, nuzzling the curve of her shoulder, stroking his hands down her sides to cup her ass for an affectionate squeeze. Humming in pleasure, she shifted beneath him, stretching abused muscles and not even wincing at the resulting aches.

"Are you okay?" His deep voice sounded even deeper than usual, more like a rumble of distant thunder. She felt it as much as heard it.

"Mm, I thought I was pretty damned fabulous, didn't you?"

He chuckled, his shoulders shaking beneath her fingers. "Oh, absolutely. But I was actually wondering if I hurt you."

If her eyes had been open, she'd have rolled them. "Oh, please. Is that in a manual all men read or something, so you all feel compelled to ask it afterward?" She turned her head until she could reach his shoulder and taste the salty tang of his skin. "Trust me, I'm not easy to hurt, and if you did manage it, I can guarantee I wouldn't have sounded quite so happy a few minutes ago. Pain is definitely not my kink."

He grunted in satisfaction and pulled her closer, bodies still joined, heart rates still somewhere north of normal. It felt good, she decided, to lie here with him, all warm and sated and cozy. She felt comfortable with him, she realized, despite how briefly they'd known each other. She winced, realizing she'd broken a personal record by getting naked with Luc a mere four and a half hours after first meeting him. Still, there was no awkwardness in being stretched out beneath him and around him on her cushy living room sofa. It felt . . . nice.

Though now that she thought about it, being able to breathe would feel pretty good, too.

She nudged his shoulder. "Luc?"

He grunted but didn't move. Typical male.

"Luc, I hate to ruin the mood here, but you're getting kind of heavy, and I'm starting to think those spots I'm seeing might be a sign of oxygen deprivation rather than just good sex."

"Great sex," he corrected, but he was already wrapping his arms around her and flipping so that he lay on his back on the sofa and she draped over him instead. "But yeah, since I probably outweigh you by a good hundred pounds."

Corinne definitely approved of the new arrangement. He made an excellent mattress. Extra-firm for comfortable support. Now she had room to stretch, which she did with great satisfaction, the friction of her skin gliding over his bringing a satisfied smile to her face. Satisfied, hell. She probably looked like the Cheshire cat. Only bustier. And less furry.

Bringing her knees up alongside his hips, she pushed herself to a sitting position with every intention of swinging her leg over his hip and climbing off the well-used sofa. She definitely needed a shower and, come to think of it, something to eat. As her stomach had begun to point out to her, she'd

just burned off one hell of a lot of calories and it
had been hours since dinner.

The problem with her plan lay in the execution.
Sitting up astride Luc's hips realigned their bodies
and solidified the intimate connection they had yet
to break. She shivered, her breath sighing out as a
residual burst of pleasure set her nerves back on
alert. She planted her hands on his chest and lifted
her hips to separate from him, only to find his electric eyes locked on her face, as focused as if neither
of them had climaxed like an atom bomb just minutes ago.

He watched her through narrow slivers of green
so intense they seemed almost to glow. The color
looked even darker and more vibrant than before.
In fact, everything about him seemed more intense
than it had an hour ago. His eyes looked more
exotically slanted; the slash of his brows, darker
and sharper. His cheekbones seemed more prominent, and the line of his jaw looked like it could
have been chiseled from granite. He looked like
the man she remembered, just . . . more. Sharper,
clearer, more defined, and more unbearably attractive.

His hands closed around her hips, fingers biting
into her flesh as he encouraged her to sink more
heavily onto him. Apparently her plans for that
shower would have to wait. He guided her into a
steady rhythm of long strokes seemingly designed to
make the top of her head fly off and her nervous
system short-circuit like an overloaded breaker

switch. She moaned when he released her and sent his hands stroking up her torso to cup and cuddle her breasts in his large palms.

Her hands clenched in the unyielding muscle of his chest, and she locked her elbows to keep her arms straight and give her even more leverage to ride him. He matched her pace seamlessly, his body flowing into hers, muscles bunching and shifting beneath her.

"Bend down." He gave the order in a voice so harsh with gravel it took her a moment to realize it was more than a wordless groan. "I need to taste you."

She bent, bringing herself within reach, until his mouth closed hot and strong around her nipple, and she whimpered in pleasure. He drew on her with hard suckling motions, as if he could draw her heart out through her breast. The little bud contracted, beading tight against his tongue. The feel of his mouth on her sent shock waves racing through her to the spot where their bodies joined. Overwhelmed, she wrapped her arms around his head to cradle him closer.

Her body and heart ached with the beauty of the moment. Corinne had had good sex before—she'd even had great sex a time or two—but she'd never had this, whatever this was. *Sex* seemed like such an inadequate word. This went beyond a mechanics of tab A and slot A. This felt more like soul A and soul B matched on some sort of elemental plane of need and fulfillment. What one sought, the other gave; what one offered, the other welcomed. Body matched body, breath matched breath, heart matched heart. It made her head swim and her senses ache and her soul rejoice.

And it made her wonder how she would continue to breathe when it finally ended.

That happened all too soon. As much as her soul wanted the joining to go on forever, her body reached its limits with a shudder and a sigh. She came apart on a long, quivering moan, her body clenched tight around him, pulling him after her into the shattering pleasure. Wanting to see his face in that perfect moment, she forced her eyes to open and watched as his jaw clenched and his breath caught and his eyes went dark and blind while he poured himself into her.

That's when she noticed the glow.

At first she tried to blink it away, but the glow remained, a bright, golden aura that radiated from him like a halo. It made her eyes widen and her jaw drop as a voice inside her head whispered something she decided not to strain to hear, something true and profound and way too much for her to deal with just yet.

"Um, Luc," she whispered and pointed to the glow that emanated from his warm skin, "is that, uh, normal?"

He froze and eyed her warily. "Is what normal?"

She pointed again. "That."

He shrugged. "It's a Fae thing."

"A Fae thing," she repeated, voice flat. "So that

happens every time. Whenever you have sex, you just . . . glow."

The man looked a lot less comfortable than she'd expect of someone who should have been boneless and exhausted after a couple of truly exceptional orgasms.

"Luc?"

"Whenever the sex is like this? Yes."

Corinne paused to consider that. Okay, really she paused to savor the knowledge that she'd managed to rock the world of someone who could make the most ardent man hater on earth rethink her devotion to the cause. She decided pretty quickly that there were worse feelings to be burdened with.

"Okay," she allowed finally. "Something to get used to, I guess. And look, it's already fading."

He grinned, looking smug and sly and too damned sexy for his own good. Or hers, for that matter. "Want to charge me up again?" he purred.

Corinne laughed. "Please. Unless you're the most mature-looking eighteen-year-old I've ever seen, you're going to need a few minutes for your body to catch up to your intentions, Romeo. Nobody's got that much energy."

Luc wrapped his arms around her back and pressed her to him as he sat up and swung his feet to the floor. "I'm afraid you don't know very much yet about the romantic inclinations of men from Faerie, sweet Corinne, but don't fret; I'll be more than happy to see to the gaps in your education."

He slipped one arm under her bottom and stood, lifting her with him as easily as if she'd been made of feathers. Instinctively, she wrapped her legs around his waist, hooking her ankles together behind his back and holding on tight. Luc gave a pleased little grunt and leaned in to kiss her, exploring her warmth with way more enthusiasm than any man should have been able to muster by that point in the evening. Corinne couldn't even be sure her own enthusiasm was up to the task.

She pulled away to suck in a deep breath, prepared to break it to him gently that friction led to heat led to chafing led to rest periods involving long soaks in deep bathtubs, but before she could speak, he began to trail slow, heated kisses down her throat the delicate skin over her collarbone. He paused there to nibble and Corinne forgot entirely what she'd been about to say.

"Which way is the bed?"

Her eyes crossed when his right hand shifted to squeeze her ass with affectionate intent. Giving up, she let her lids drop. "Left," she gasped.

He took the doorway to the left, walked down a short hall, and located the partly open door to her bedroom. Shouldering his way inside, he carried her to the side of the full-size mattress and dropped her. She bounced on the springy coils.

"You need a bigger bed." The complaint didn't stop him from following down to the surface, but she could see his point. Even conserving space by stretching out directly on top of her, his feet likely hung over the end of the mattress. "This is too small for the two of us."

She wrapped her arms around him and shivered when he buried his face in the warm hollow behind her ear. A man could make her rob banks by scraping his teeth over that delicate skin, she realized. Just like he did right then.

A disconcertingly girly little squeak escaped her lips. "So either learn to be inventive, or find someone else to crawl into bed with."

"I think not." His voice issued in a raspy murmur then traveled along her spine like caressing fingers. Looming over her in the dark, he pushed himself back to his knees so that she could see the way his skin began to heat and radiate that strange, incandescent light.

Maybe the man had something to prove to her after all. Her poor, aching body clenched in protest.

"Uh, Luc," she began, bracing her hands against his chest as if that feeble gesture could hold off a man of his size intent on conquest, "I'm not sure this is a good idea. Or even physically possible. I'm, um, a little sore at the moment."

Luc grinned, white teeth flashing in the darkness. She saw his eyes glint with deviltry just before he positioned himself between her legs and hooked her knees over his shoulders. "No problem. I think I'll just improvise."

Corinne woke on her stomach to the feel of clever teeth nibbling at her spine and silky dark hair tickling her skin. She frowned. "That was a damned sneaky way to solicit an invitation to stay the night."

Her voice sounded raspy with sleep, what little of it she'd gotten, and her muscles felt soft and pleasantly achy.

"Mm, maybe," he said from somewhere around the bottoms of her shoulder blades, "but it was effective."

She snorted. "Yeah, and you saved on your hotel bill."

She could feel his mouth curve against her skin. "Last time I checked, Graham didn't plan to charge me for the room. But you never know. He's damned capitalistic for a werewolf."

Surprise had her craning her head to look at him. "You're staying at Vircolac?"

"Uh-huh." His tongue traced a pattern between two vertebrae and his hands slid up and around to close over her breasts. "I usually do when I visit. It's convenient. And the chef there is talented."

She rolled her eyes and turned her head to stare across the room at the closet door. "I can't believe Missy didn't warn me about you," she muttered.

"Graham's mate? I haven't met her yet." He slid back up the bed and curved his body around hers, like spoons in a drawer. His hands squeezed her breasts affectionately, and his lips brushed lightly over the top of her head. "But I heard a lot about her. He's smitten."

"He'd better be, after everything she went

through for him." She flipped onto her back and leveled a meaningful glance at Luc. "Fair warning, the minute you tell me about some weird Fae sexual tradition involving being hunted down like a stray dog, or mating in front of a live studio audience or something, I'm outta here."

He raised an eyebrow. "So then I imagine you don't want to hear about the four purified virgins, the consecrated gourds, and the chocolate pudding, huh?" She felt her eyes widen for a second before he gave up on the attempt and laughed. "Don't worry. No mate hunts for the Fae. Although I do personally happen to have a fondness for chocolate pudding . . ."

She punched him. "And I have a fondness for sharp objects, so watch it, beagle."

He grinned unrepentantly. "I couldn't resist. You have some of the most ridiculous notions about the Fae. And you're so cute to tease."

"Remember how cute I am when I'm amputating body parts." She mumbled the threat more out of a sense of obligation than any real intentions, and he must have understood, because he looked remarkably unafraid. She would have to work on her delivery.

A glance at the bedside clock told her she'd woken half an hour later than usual, which mattered not a lot. Technically, she had set this day aside for interviews, so she didn't need to go to the office at all. That was a good thing, too, considering her newly acquired sidekick. With the witnesses, she could pass him off as a photographer or something, but if she tried that with anyone from her office, the jig would be up before she even got the words out.

Hiding an enormous yawn behind her hand, she pried Luc's arm from around her waist and pushed herself out of the bed. She stood for a minute beside it, making sure everything worked—and feeling vaguely surprised that it did—before she headed toward the bathroom. "I'm going to go take a shower," she called over her shoulder. "If you're still here when I get out, I suggest you at least have breakfast ready. It'll go easier on you that way."

She heard him laughing through the closed bathroom door and contemplated opening it to tell him she hadn't been joking. Oh, well. He'd figure it out.

A hot, hot shower managed to steam away most of her morning brain fog and a good bit of her soreness as well. Somehow with the water beating down over her head, relaxing her muscles and pinkening her skin, she found it a lot easier to outline the path forward and see the benefits of joining Luc in the hunt for this Seoc character. She also found it easier to acknowledge that after so many months of going on about her life as if she didn't know that the things in the stories her grandmother used to read her before bed at night actually existed, she'd just now managed to get herself all tangled up with what amounted to a crisis for the Others. She might even just manage to acknowledge that she maybe cared about what happened to them.

If someone had asked her about it a year ago, or even a month ago, she would have replied without hesitation by saying that if vampires and werewolves existed, and if *Faerie* was more than just a derogatory word for a homosexual male, she didn't want to know about it. Life had been simpler back before she knew, simpler and a whole lot more appealing.

Working a handful of herbal shampoo into a lather, she contemplated what it would mean to the Others if she and Luc failed at their missions—if Luc didn't find Seoc before the human public started asking the right questions about his identity, and if she didn't manage to turn the story into more spoof than scoop to control the potential damage.

First off, the Others as a people could be in very real danger. She supposed there was a scenario where the human public greeted the revelation with awe and wonder and learned to embrace them as a valuable part of society at large, but she had a feeling that didn't rank as the most likely scenario. Missy and Reggie had told her that a growing faction of the Others felt the time was coming when Unveiling themselves would be inevitable, and the Council—meaning Rafe—had quietly begun to take steps to prepare. In other words, he was setting up a PR engine that would spin the biggest news story in human history in the way that would generate the smallest chance of worldwide panic and outright war among the species. Which, Corinne thought, was likely a smart move. But the most likely outcome of this story breaking right now was mass hysteria, the kind that resulted in lynch mobs and vigilantism and her closest friends being at risk of serious injury or death. Frankly, Corinne was willing to do a lot more to keep Reggie and Missy and their families safe than file one bogus news story.

Second, from what Luc had told her, she figured that the separate existence of the people of Faerie would come to an abrupt and unwelcome end. He'd been right about that. If humanity in general suddenly discovered that an alternate reality existed where magic made the world go round and the natural resources remained pristine and unexploited, there would be a stampede for the border so fast, people would get trampled in the confusion. Then they'd go right ahead and trample over Faerie. Which could very well lead to a second front of warfare. Corinne couldn't imagine that the Fae would give up sovereignty over their domain without a fight, and if Luc was any example of a soldier among their people, it would turn out to be an ugly and bloody struggle. She couldn't live with herself if she didn't do everything in her power to prevent that.

And finally, Corinne thought about the picture she'd formed of this Queen Mab from the little bits and pieces Luc had let slip yesterday. *Scary* seemed like a good word to sum up her impression of the Fae monarch. If the Queen had sent Luc here to complete a task, and Luc failed . . . well, Corinne had no idea what Mab would do, but she felt pretty sure that it would put one hell of a damper on the budding relationship between Corinne and the captain of the Queen's Guard.

Corinne squeezed the last of the rinse water out of her hair and reached up to turn off the shower. Somehow that last part scared her almost as much as the possibility of a global and an interdimensional war put together. Why in God's name should it mean so much to her to hold on to a man she'd known less than one day? A man who had so far offered her nothing but sex—truly, stunningly mind-blowing sex, but still—and who had said not one word about whether he planned to so much as leave a forwarding address with her when he finished his job and went on his merry way back to his own world? A man who wasn't even of the same species!

Wrapping a towel around herself, she admitted that the species thing bothered her a lot less than she had anticipated. When Reggie and Missy had gotten involved with their respective husbands, Ava, Danice, and Corinne had privately sworn that none of them would ever hook up with a non-human man. But then Danice had met Mac Callahan and disappeared for a few days only to come back glowing with love. And aside from his pointy ears—and the glowing and the magic and the ability to make her lose her mind with sex—Luc seemed like a nice, normal guy. The sort of guy she

had always hoped she'd meet one day. He was
sane—or at least as sane as she was—employed,
handsome, and sexy. If he could do something
about the pointy ears and the glowing, she could
picture him being the man she brought home to
meet her family—

And, whoa, she was getting way ahead of herself
here.

First things first. The priority was to help Luc find
Seoc. After that, she could worry about either
picking out the china, or hiring a hit man to off
Luc and hide the body.

Pushing the worries aside for the moment,
Corinne finished toweling herself dry, used a blow
dryer to bring her hair from sodden to comfortably damp, and padded cautiously back into the
bedroom to dress. Luc was nowhere to be seen, so
either he'd gotten a hot lead on Seoc while Corinne
was in the shower, or he was at least pretending
to take care of breakfast. Somehow, she saw him
as more the roast-a-hunk-of-flesh-over-an-open-fire
type than the scrambled-eggs-and-fresh-squeezed-
juice type, but since she couldn't hear the fire alarm,
she decided to go with cautious optimism.

Panties, bra, red tank top, and khaki cargo pants
passed for her ensemble of the day, and she carried
a pair of white tennis socks and white canvas
sneakers with her into the kitchen. She braced herself for Luc's potential absence, then had to brace
herself again not to let him see how pleased she
was to find him piling toast onto a plate and carry-

ing it to her tiny kitchen table. He looked up at the sound of her footsteps.

"Honey?"

Corinne cocked an eyebrow. "Yes, snookums?"

He grinned. "I meant, do you have any honey?"

"I dunno. Check the cabinets."

He started opening doors while she sat down at the table and pulled on her socks and shoes. By the time she finished tying the laces, he had the honey on the table along with jam, butter, and a plate of segmented apples, chunked bananas, and the neatly sliced corpse of the kiwi she'd bought on a whim and hadn't figured out what to do with.

"Thanks." She popped a piece of banana into her mouth, swallowing just as a thought occurred to her. "Um, are you a vegetarian?"

Luc looked up from spreading thick layers of butter and honey onto his toast. "No, why?"

She nodded at the meatless breakfast, and he smiled.

"No, I'm just a lousy cook. I never saw a stove until the first time I came to *Ithir*. We don't have them in Faerie."

Corinne swallowed a bit of toast. "How do you cook?"

"We don't. We use magic."

"Oh. Well, I suppose that's gotta be convenient."

"Very." Her kitchen was so compact that he didn't even have to get up to fetch the thermal carafe from her counter. He just twisted around in his chair and snagged it before turning to offer it to her. "Want some?"

Her mouth was full of jammy toast, so she just nodded and held her mug out for him. He poured it full before topping off his own and filling his plate with more toast and fruit.

Because she was watching him, Corinne didn't notice anything wrong with her coffee until she took a big sip. Then she sputtered. "What the hell . . . ?"

Luc looked up. "What's wrong? If you don't like Earl Grey, why was there a boxful in your cabinet?"

She choked, reached reflexively for her coffee mug, and jerked back as if she'd been stung. "Tea?" she coughed. "You made me tea?"

"Is that wrong?"

"It is if you want to live to see tomorrow." Holding her mug at arm's length to be sure the foul, watery brew in it wouldn't do her any further injury, she carried it to the sink and dumped it down the drain before pulling her Krups automatic drip to the front of the counter and putting on a pot of coffee. "How the hell am I supposed to get through the day with nothing but leafy water to fortify me?"

Luc sat back in his chair, cradling his cup and watching her with an expression of baffled amusement. "I didn't realize you needed fortification."

"I do if I'm going to spend my day interviewing people about the elf-who-got-away."

"Fae."

"Whatever."

Before the coffee finished brewing, she pulled out the pot and poured herself a cup. She'd taken her first sip before she even sat back at the table.

"Did the info about the models change your game plan? Or do we still plan to hit the sex shop owner at ten today?"

Corinne popped a piece of kiwi, decided it was just fine plain now that he'd removed the fuzzy rind, and chewed thoughtfully. "Well, I think we should run down the list and compare thoughts, but my gut tells me that Walter Hibbish is our best bet."

"The rabbi? So we are changing our plans."

"No, Hibbish is the sex shop owner."

"What's the rabbi's name? Paddy O'Brien?"

"Cute. It's Levi Aaronson." She gulped down another mouthful of coffee, then went to the living room to retrieve her notebook from her backpack. The sight of their clothes scattered across the floor gave her a warm, rosy feeling that had nothing to do with embarrassment. Why be embarrassed about such a delightful evening? She did frown, though, as she sat back down at the table and examined his fully clothed form. Clothes different from the ones he'd been wearing yesterday. "Do you always carry spare jeans around in your pocket?"

He grinned. "You mean the clothes? I conjured new ones. I like a fresh T-shirt in the morning."

"Conjured? You mean they're magic?" She

reached across the table and fingered the heather-gray cotton. "Are they like the emperor's new clothes? You're really naked, and only you and I are the ones who know?"

"Sweetheart, we're all naked underneath."

She laughed and drew back. "That must be a pretty handy skill."

"It saves time."

"Right." She flipped open her notebook and sipped her coffee. "Okay, so altogether we have six names. The models Ava gave to us are Leena Thomas, Marlie Hasek, and April Brodeur. Plus Hibbish, Aaronson, and the bartender, Mark Ingram. I called and asked Hibbish if I could stop by this morning at ten, so it makes sense to keep that appointment, but it probably wouldn't be a bad idea to give a call to the others on the list to see if we can set anything else up. I'm assuming that the sooner we talk to all of them, the better. Right?"

"Absolutely. Do you want to make the calls, or should I?" He glanced at the digital clock on her microwave and waggled his eyebrows at her. "We have an hour and a half until we have to be at the sex shop."

"Stop trying to make it sound dirty. We're going strictly on business."

"I said nothing different."

She handed him her cell phone and pulled the kitchen landline onto the table beside her. "We'll split them up. It'll take us half an hour or so to get to the shop. This way's faster."

"Someday I'll have to teach you that fast is overrated." Another waggle.

She rolled her eyes. "And you really think we're going to get anything done if you spend all day thinking up sexual innuendos?"

He shrugged. "Think of it as our own personal version of good cop, bad cop."

Corinne sighed into her coffee to hide the fact that bantering with him had quickly become one of her favorite pastimes. "Yeah, if we can't win them over with charm, we'll baffle them with non sequiturs."

Eight

The blazing pink neon should have been their first clue. Of badness.

Walter Hibbish's sex shop, The Pink Pillow, turned out to be one of those places people gave directions to using the phrase, *You can't miss it.* And Corinne couldn't. No matter how much she would have liked the opportunity to protect her poor, unsuspecting retinas. She spotted the store-front from a block and a half away.

She strolled through the East Village beside Luc, stubbornly taking her time, both because they had the time to kill—having left early, as she'd been trained to do by her obsessively punctual mother— and because a part of her just wanted to savor the feeling of walking beside a man who actually in-spired fantasies about having him as a permanent part of her life.

The thought first ambushed her in the lobby of her apartment. She'd stopped at her mailbox on their way out, and the jerk in 507, who had the box next to her, had elbowed her trying to wrestle a padded envelope out of his box and hadn't even apologized. Luc had tapped him on the shoulder, informed him of the oversight, and waited until 507 got a good look at him, went pale, and hastily apologized. That's when Corinne caught herself thinking that she'd forgotten how nice it was to have someone around who cared enough to defend her from the small realities of everyday life.

When she'd realized what she was thinking, she'd gone a little pale herself, being a largely independent sort, though she'd shaken it off as an aberration and moved on. But then when they were walking down the street—with Luc deliberately positioning himself beside the street, to keep her away from the curb—she had read through her mail, and he had asked her what about the junk mail that had filled her box was making her laugh. Corinne had found herself reading parts of a particularly ridiculous flyer to him out loud. They had laughed together, and she'd thought how much she enjoyed talking to someone who seemed to understand her slightly warped sense of humor.

Being with Luc just felt . . . good. Never mind that he had popped into her life without a by-your-leave, had turned her world upside down, had given her the most amazing orgasms of her life, and had recruited her for some sort of top-secret Fae mission. The man just seemed to fit, at her side, in her apartment—even if he did hang off the end of her bed—and into her thoughts. She couldn't remember ever feeling so comfortable with a man before. Certainly not with one who stood on the other end of a vibrating current of sexual tension that seemed to arc between them constantly. Even with the electricity of that burning up the atmosphere, she felt relaxed with Luc. He made her feel more completely herself.

And if she thought about that too hard for too long, she was going to tie herself up in the kind of knots Boy Scouts earned merit badges for mastering.

She thought she was doing fairly well living in the moment as they strolled down the street to the monstrously colored shop in the middle of the block. Then she yanked open the glass door and stepped into the pink hell of her foulest nightmares.

Apparently someone had taken the shop's name a little too seriously. The walls glowed with a high-gloss paint the same sickeningly intense shade as Pepto-Bismol. They seemed to radiate an unearthly light that even the dark, cheery red trim around the windows and doors and along the floor and ceiling couldn't moderate. Everywhere she looked, she saw evil, and she wasn't talking about the sex toys; she meant the decor. Pink marabou and dyed faux fur clashed hedonistically with silk, satin, velvet, and brocade in all the horrifying shades of pink, rose, red, scarlet, mauve, and the occasional purple a body could imagine, and Corinne had a damned fine imagination.

Unfortunately, another five minutes in this place, and she'd need that imagination, because she could feel her retinas being seared off where she stood.

She heard Luc's pained inhalation beside her and hoped his own sense of taste was as offended as hers. If he suggested bringing a single drop of this virulent mess into her apartment, she was going to have to kick him. In the nuts.

It took a second to even remember what they were doing here. The decor was that big an assault.

Since they had decided that Corinne—as the one with a legitimate reason to be poking around and asking questions—should be the one to poke around and ask questions, she took a deep breath and mustered up the resolve to walk deeper into the abyss of bad taste. Swallowing back a surge of nausea, she blinked her watering eyes and fixed her gaze firmly on the maroon carpet, not looking left, right, or up as she made her way across the floor to the counter in the corner of the shop. Luckily, her field of vision remained broad enough that she could see the counter getting closer to her knees before she walked into it, and stopped. Bracing herself for the sensory onslaught, she looked up to meet the entirely disinterested gaze of the clerk behind the register, a young woman with black-tipped blue hair, purple lipstick, and enough shiny silver facial piercings to give an airport metal detector a heart attack.

Sighing, Corinne fished a business card out of her pocket and slid it over the counter. "We're here to see the owner."

Shiny and Bored barely looked up from her puffy pink emery board. "Yeah? Who're you?"

Corinne glanced down at her card and back up at Shiny. She waited a heartbeat. "We're with the *Chronicle*. He knew we'd be coming by."

So it was a little fib. She had called and left a message. Walter Hibbish should know, if he'd checked his machine.

"That so." The clerk snapped her gum and went back to filing.

Corinne resisted the urge to take out several days of frustration on Miss Unconventional and Uncooperative. Instead, she leaned over the counter and bared her teeth. It was supposed to look like a smile. Sort of. "Why don't you go tell him we're here. Don't worry. We'll wait."

This time, Shiny actually lifted her head and sized them up. Well, her glance slid right over Corinne and chose to invest its energy into sizing Luc up. To mentally try him on for size, judging by the way Shiny's eyes widened and glazed over just a bit once she'd taken in his full glory. If the amount of time she lingered there was any indication, she seemed to be conjuring particularly vivid mental pictures of his crotch.

Corinne was about to get Shiny's attention by yanking hard on the silver ring in her eyebrow when Luc distracted her. He leaned over the counter, flashed Shiny a charming and patently insincere smile, and added his weight to Corinne's.

"Please," he purred. "We'd appreciate it."

Corinne wondered how much the flirtatious Fae would appreciate a trip to the emergency room.

Her mouth curving in what might have passed for a smile—had she been about three days past dead—Shiny nodded, slid off her stool, and gave Luc a smoldering look. "Wait while I tell him you're here."

She disappeared through the door behind the counter without another word but with one last, lingering glance at the fly of Luc's jeans. She just missed hearing the new nickname Corinne invented especially for her, but that was likely a good thing.

Grumbling under her breath, Corinne gave the door a sour glare and slung around the backpack she used in place of a purse. She knew Luc wasn't to blame for the walking corpse's blatant ogling, but rationality didn't seem to have a lot to do with the uncomfortable level of jealousy that had fallen onto Corinne's head like a cartoon anvil. God, she couldn't even remember the last time she'd been so wrapped up in a guy that she'd managed to get irrationally jealous over him. When had that been? High school?

To distract herself and hopefully shock herself back down to earth, she pulled out her notebook and decided to do her job for a few minutes. Might as well make use of the time it took Shiny to deliver her message to scope out the store. If she was going to write an article that would pacify Hank without compromising the security of the Others' secrets, Corinne would need to pack in as much color as possible. She doubted there was a place on earth more colorful than this one. Frankly, if such a site existed, she prayed she'd never have to go there.

Rummaging for a pen and wishing she could put her sunglasses back on without feeling somehow rude, she looked around the shop, this time tuning out the horrendous decor and the presence of the Fae warrior beside her. She didn't need to notice the decorating scheme again to know it would play a prominent role in her description of the place. Some things a girl could never forget.

In a city full of sex shops, they tended to boil down to three categories. On one end of the spectrum, you had the kind of place that flourished in Times Square during its heyday, before Giuliani and Disney got hold of the neighborhood and cleaned it up nice for the tourists. Those were the sleaze museums, the places where anyone in their right mind wore rubber gloves, a biohazard suit, an impenetrable disguise, and still thought twice about touching anything. They catered to the lowest sort of hustlers and vagrants, along with anyone with a quarter and a strong stomach who wanted a couple of minutes alone in a dirty viewing booth. Come to think of it, no one in their right mind would step foot in one of those to begin with, biohazard suit or not.

At the opposite end of the scale, you had the upscale shops, the ones that made the papers for reasons besides their indecency arrests. They had well-lit, tastefully decorated retail spaces, with polite, well-educated, and well-informed staff who took care to be both helpful and non-intimidating. They carried quality products and catered to couples looking to add spice to their relationships, or to women who were too intimidated or embarrassed to venture into a less welcoming environment.

Then you had places like The Pink Pillow. Somewhere between trash and good taste, it sold a huge selection of goods at reasonable prices in a neighborhood you wouldn't be afraid to walk through under normal circumstances. The staff were iffy—clearly—but they probably didn't have any serious criminal history and they could ring up a sale easily enough, even if they couldn't discuss the chemical components of lube like a Nobel scholar. These shops retained just enough of the sleaze factor to give the average conservative a thrill, but not enough to scare him or her away. In fact, if she hadn't been so off balance, Corinne might have had some fun browsing. While she appreciated the Toys-in-Babeland-type places of the world, her pocketbook appreciated the Pink Pillows.

In reality, aside from all the . . . pink . . . there really wasn't anything wrong with the shop, or its merchandise. Looking around, Corinne spotted half a dozen brands she recognized, from the maker of flavored massage oils on a small multi-tiered shelving unit, to the silicone dildo manufacturer occupying a prominent place against the wall. She wondered briefly if that much familiarity with the world of sex toys said something about her character, but shrugged it off. Everybody had to have a hobby.

"Are you going to ignore me for the rest of the day?" Luc spoke from right behind her, apparently bent on following her through her tour.

Corinne jumped. "I'm not ignoring you."

"Because it's not my fault that woman was staring at me."

She forced a laugh. "I'm really not upset about someone leering at you. Sheesh, do I look like I have time to even notice every time a woman gives you the eye? I have a day job, remember."

Luc raised a brow, but he let it go, for which Corinne felt grateful. How was she supposed to explain to him that she wasn't upset by the ogling, only by her own reaction to it? She wasn't sure it made sense even in *her* head.

She scribbled down notes as she walked through the shop, which turned out to be a good deal bigger than the average Manhattan storefront, or at least the average storefront in the East Village. There seemed to be plenty of room for attractive displays and for the half a dozen other customers to avoid one another as they browsed. In fact, if it weren't for the god-awful pink everywhere, Corinne might have made it a point to come back, but she couldn't think of a good reason to risk permanent vision impairment when she already had Blowfish bookmarked on her web browser.

She raised an amused eyebrow at the life-size blow-up boyfriend who stood propped up next to a colorful display of condoms, but her attention really caught on the far side of the shop and the table stacked high with edible goodies. She had a deep weakness for the combination of sex and chocolate. But oddly enough, she'd never experimented with chocolate pudding. With or without the ceremonial gourds.

The body paint got a cursory glance—she preferred to go with real chocolate syrup, since it tasted so much better—but she lingered for a moment on the raspberry bindi set. Then her eyes widened and her hand shot out to snag a long, thin box with an intriguing cover illustration.

"Ooh," she murmured to herself as her mouth slid into a grin, "chocolate tattoos!"

She dropped her notebook on the table and flipped the box over to scan the information on the back, trying to block out the mental picture of stenciling her name in chocolate on some choice body parts of the Fae warrior who still trailed after her with his hands in his pockets and a scowl on his face. Maybe she could add the word MINE across his ass in those gothic-looking chocolate capital letters.

"You know, at some point we're going to talk about what's going on here."

Corinne looked up from the chocolate. "You mean aside from crimes against the sighted community?"

"Not what's going on in this store. What's going on between us."

She shook her head and hoped she hadn't just gone visibly pale. "I told you, I'm not upset about the ogling, and I wasn't ignoring you."

"But you are upset about something."

"No, I'm just working."

"Corinne, you need to feel comfortable sharing things with me. We're in this together."

She played it deliberately stupid. "Believe me, if I see or smell or think of anything that will help us find Seoc, I will absolutely let you know. Now relax."

He didn't budge. "You know that's not what I'm talking about. You keep trying to act as if there's nothing between us, as if you don't have the right to be jealous if a woman makes a pass at me. We need to talk about us."

"I wouldn't have called a few leers and the sad lack of a poker face a 'pass' necessarily—"

"Corinne." He snapped out her name, sharply enough to force her to look up at him.

She abandoned stupid and tried for dismissive. "Look, I really don't think that's going to be necessary."

"You don't? Hm, then I imagine you might find it a little awkward when the first baby comes along."

The box of tattoos clattered to the floor with the impact of a Howitzer shell.

"When *THE WHAT* does *WHAT*?"

Luc couldn't quite decide if he found the expression on his heartmate's face more insulting or amusing. She looked as if someone had just explained to her that her regular coffee had secretly been replaced with dehydrated, powdered babies' fingers.

"When the baby comes," he repeated—whether to punish her or to force the issue of their relationship out into the open, he wasn't sure. "Darling, don't tell me you don't want children."

She stared at him for a minute, narrowed eyes assessing his intent before she unclenched her fists and drew in a hissing breath. "You're a bastard, you know that?"

"I think that all depends on point of view, really. In your eyes I'm a bastard for talking about the future," he explained calmly. "In my eyes, I'm simply refusing to let you avoid the subject of our relationship like the proverbial grasshopper to my ant."

"If you were an ant, I'd so step on you right now."

"Temper, temper."

"Okay, you really want to do this here?" She planted her fists on her hips, a pose he supposed he preferred to having those fists swung at his face, and glared up at him. "You really want to talk about our relationship—which so far consists of nothing more than about three hours of admittedly fine sex, by the way—here. In a god-awful-tacky sex shop, in front of a handful of strangers, with the kindly gaze of—" She read a nearby label. "—Inflatable Amy, Your Go-to Good-Time Girl! looking on? Frankly, I think the romance factor may be a little shaky."

He grabbed her around the waist and boosted her up to sit on a display table, bringing her face at least a few inches closer to his. He imagined his expression when he leaned in might have intimidated a lesser woman. "You might be telling yourself that the only thing between us is sex, Corinne, but I know you don't believe it. You're not stupid, and you're not blind, and to dismiss what's happening would require you to be both."

"I don't *know* what's happening between us," she ground out, her eyes meeting his in a way that spoke of both defiance and discomfort. He could read the confusion in the brown depths. "Twenty-four hours ago, I didn't even know you existed. Now, in the space of less than a day, I've had to deal with the worst story assignment in the last millennium, a meeting with the Council of Others, the discovery that the Queen of Faerie's idiot nephew is currently gallivanting through Manhattan and threatening the safety of some people I love like family, and the fact that I've just met a man who makes my knees quiver every time he gets within three feet of me. I've got a lot on my plate, so cut me a little slack, okay?"

"No."

Her eyebrows shot toward her hairline. "No?"

"No," he said. "I'm not cutting you a damned thing. You're not the only one in this situation, and you're sure as hell not the only one in this relationship. You seem to keep forgetting that I've known you for exactly as long as you've known me. Do you think this hasn't caught me by surprise? Sometimes that's just the way these things work. Sometimes you stumble over the things you need most while you're busy looking for the ones you don't even want."

"You don't want to find the Queen's idiot nephew?"

"If it were up to me, the little menace would have suffered a fatal accident shortly after birth. The point is, it's not up to me. And neither is this thing between us. We're both just going to have to get over it and deal."

"Because you're not leaving until this is finished." She sounded tired and worn out. "Right. I get it. So let's get the hell on with it."

Damn it, she just wouldn't understand until he laid it all on the line, would she?

"No," he said, catching her chin in his hand, and holding her gaze with his. "You have to get used to it because I'm staying whether this gets finished or not. I'm just staying. Because you and I are together from now on."

He watched as his words registered with her and enjoyed the parade of expressions across her face. Excitement, lust, shock, confusion, and terror all made an appearance as she studied him. His brain told him he should gloss over it—pretend that it hadn't happened or that he'd been joking. When his heart and other assorted parts encouraged him to just rephrase it from *You and I are together* to *You're mine and I'm going to spend the rest of our lives keeping you so busy you won't have time to argue with me,* he thought his words made a good compromise. Because his other parts offered a really good argument in favor of option number two.

She pursed her lips, and he banished the thought of what he'd like her to purse them around. "You certainly work fast," she said, slowly, almost visibly fighting the desire to panic.

He shrugged. "What can I say? I'm decisive."

"And you've decided this?"

I've decided lots of things, including that the best way to keep you from fighting with me is to keep you so distracted that you can't remember what you wanted to fight about in the first place.

"Fate has decided it. I'm just along for the ride." Tact, he reminded himself. Tact. "I'm as shocked by it as you are."

She barked out a laugh that didn't sound at all amused. "Somehow, I doubt that."

"You should have a little more faith. Look at this from my point of view—I came to *Ithir* to find an annoying royal brat with the common sense of garden moss, and instead I found you. I think *gobsmacked* is an appropriate estimation of my current frame of mind." He saw her hesitate and tried an engaging smile. The captain of the Queen's Guard rarely bothered with engaging smiles, but maybe she wouldn't notice if his looked rusty.

"Yeah, that's a bit more British than I'd have gone on my own, but I think it works." She shifted her weight to brace her hands on the edge of the table and lean forward a little. He took it as an invitation to wrap his arms around her and cradle her to his chest. Mostly just because she felt so right there.

"How is it that you can be so calm about this?" she wondered, her voice partially muffled against his shoulder. "You might claim to be gobsmacked, but you don't act like it. You act like you're taking it all in stride, which just makes me feel like an even bigger idiot. I feel like I'm on some sort of roller coaster, only someone blindfolded me so I can't even tell when I should be getting ready to scream."

He squeezed around her and tried to tease. "Why should you scream? Is the idea of having me in your life really that terrifying?"

She sighed and answered the question seriously. "No. But yes. I'm not terrified of you. You're just . . ." She hesitated. "You're not what I was expecting in a lover."

"You mean I'm not human." He didn't mean it as a condemnation, just as a truth. He knew Corinne had to be wary of the Others, including him, and he couldn't really blame her for it. She'd been brought up to believe that creatures like him were only to be found in storybooks and scary movies. Even after she'd found out the truth, that legacy represented a lot of mistaken beliefs to overcome.

"That sounds so . . ."

"Maybe, but that doesn't invalidate your right to feel that way." He sighed and took her by the shoulders, cupping the curves in his hands and urging her back far enough that he could look into her face. "Look, I'll make you a deal. We'll take this one step at a time, okay? Right now, we'll concentrate on finding Seoc, and I'll try not to do anything to scare the pants off you. But in exchange, you've got to start trying to get a grip on what we have between us, because I can promise you it isn't going to go away. And neither am I. Deal?"

She hesitated, her wide brown eyes searching his face for something. She must have found it, or found something she wanted, because she pursed her lips and nodded slowly. "All right. It's a deal."

"Thank the Goddess," he sighed, flashing her a grin and squeezing her shoulders before he lifted her from the table and set her back on her feet. "Now, should we get back to business?"

Before Corinne could respond, Shiny reappeared from the back of the store, followed closely by a bald head that peered around the heavy curtain and fixed on Corinne.

"You're the reporter?"

Nine

The bald head barely waited for her to nod. In fact, he might not have. "Come on in back. I'm right in the middle of something."

The head disappeared and Corinne blinked. "Who was that?"

Shiny shrugged. "The owner. You better hurry up. He won't wait around for you."

Corinne couldn't decide whether to feel upset by the interruption, or intensely relieved. Luc might have been ready to steer the conversation back to business, but she still had a few questions she was dying to ask. Like, *What the hell are you talking about?* Still, it quickly became apparent that Shiny was right and Hibbish didn't intend to wait around for them.

Gesturing for Luc to follow her, Corinne pushed through the heavy drape and hurried through a short entry then around the corner of a shelving unit. She saw piles of stock, apparently separated by categories, and in some cases by color and/or size. The choices stocked by The Pink Pillow were quite, uh, impressive. Not to mention distracting.

One particular battery-operated accessory had her tilting her head this way and that in confusion until she nearly forgot about the rest of her surroundings. She just followed the path through the shelves until she rounded a corner and something entirely non-mechanical caught her attention. It took about three seconds for what she was seeing to register with her unsuspecting brain, and she froze in place with the abruptness of a gunshot.

Good Lord! What had she just walked into?

She heard a chuckle behind her and a gust of warm breath against her ear. "When he said he was in the middle of something, I didn't think he meant anything quite so . . . literal."

"Um, me either."

Corinne swallowed and felt Luc's hands settle on her shoulders. He had stepped into the back room right on her heels, and since he was so much taller, he had an unobstructed view of the sight that greeted them. She could only wonder what it looked like from his angle.

She did try to look away. It seemed like the polite thing to do. She wondered briefly if she should have stared at the hideous pink walls outside for a little longer so she could have been struck blind by the garish colors. That way she would have been unable to see the horrific sight now before her.

Sheesh, she thought, *can this day get any weirder?*

In the back room of the shop, the man she assumed was Walter Hibbish stood hip-deep in a pile of mostly naked bodies with a camera pointed straight at some of the most naked bits. Okay, the most unclothed bits. *Naked* might be a bit misleading, since they all seemed to be covered with something that looked like pastel-colored whipped cream.

"Sorry I can't take a break to talk to you," the shop owner said in between snaps of his shutter, "but this stuff is gonna be on the shelves next week and I need to get these shots done and printed up for the display. A little to the left, Hildie. Good. Is that okay?"

Corinne blinked and grabbed for her composure. "Well, I would have said to try it with that top leg a bit more bent, but yeah, it looks fine to me."

Luc snorted behind her.

"Oh, I meant—hey, wait. I think you may be right. Deb, try bending your top leg just a little farther toward Maura. Great." The camera snicked again. "Hey, good call, Ms. . . . ?"

"D'Alessandro." Corinne stepped forward, figuring that if she pretended she wasn't in a room with a pile of naked women, a man she wanted to jump on and spend a few hours licking, and a weird middle-aged man with a camera, then she should be able to conduct this interview just fine. "Corinne. From the *Chronicle*. Sorry, but I thought you were expecting me."

"No. Should I be? We already run a regular spot in your paper. More tongue, Lil. Fabulous!" He glanced over his shoulder at her and spotted Luc standing in the background. "Who's he?"

Luc beat her to the punch. "Luc Macanaw. I'm an associate of Ms. D'Alessandro's. Thanks for agreeing to meet with us."

Corinne had intended to introduce him as her photographer, but seeing the profession—or at least very serious hobby—of the man they were about to interview, she figured *associate* would be safer. It was nice to work with someone who could think on his feet.

She was about to forge ahead with the questions, but something distracted her. Specifically, five pairs of feminine eyes distracted her when they turned at the sound of Luc's deep voice and took on the bright gleam of interest. She fought back an urge to curl her fingers into claws or to slap a sign on Luc's back reading, MINE! And just in case they missed seeing that one, she'd put another, permanent one someplace lower. But now that she'd had time to think, she decided the second tattoo wouldn't be on his ass, and it wouldn't be made of chocolate, and—

Damn it, she needed to get a hold of herself. This jealousy thing was going to get real old real fast, especially if Luc continued to do absolutely nothing to warrant it.

Hibbish seemed to notice the looks, too, but he had a slightly different reaction. "That's it!" he shouted, camera snapping frantically. "That's exactly the look I need. Hold it. Hold it. Perfect! Wonderful!"

Corinne's teeth clenched so hard she feared lockjaw, but Luc didn't seem to have any such trouble. In fact, he flashed the heap of women a playful grin and reached for a tall, black can from the assortment on a nearby table.

"Kissy Kreme?" he asked, his eyebrows rising.

"Yeah. Great find. Come on, Jennie, smile for me." Hibbish paused to adjust a flash umbrella, then resumed shooting. "It's brand new, but I know it's gonna be big. It's fun, colorful, all natural. Customers are gonna eat it up."

"I think that's the point," Luc said, his voice low and clearly intended just for Corinne. That damned murmur of his was lethal. She watched, feigning disinterest while he flipped the can over and began reading from the blurb on the back. "'Sweet, creamy and sensual—just like the perfect lover should be.'"

He looked up at her with an intent expression that she'd have to be dead not to be affected by, but she covered her melty-ness with a snort, since the last thing he needed was another advantage over her. At least, she hoped she'd done sufficient melt-coverage, but his eyes just sparkled at her as he continued to read.

"'Kissy Kreme brings a new dimension to your love play in five unique flavors that blend wholesome ingredients with wicked intentions. Cover your lover's tastiest bits with the sweet flavor of raspberry, mint, chocolate, orange, or strawberry cream and delight your senses to the fullest. Because kisses taste better when they're creamy. Bon appétit!' Hmm, sounds yummy," he said, looking back up at her with speculation and intentions that went well beyond wicked. "Don't you think, Corinne?"

"Come on, girls, act like you're having fun, will ya? It's great stuff," Hibbish said to them over his shoulder. "Go ahead. Give it a try."

Luc's mouth twisted into a subtle curve, the one that seemed to eat away at the ability of Corinne's knees to actually do the job of supporting her weight. "Thanks. Don't mind if I do."

The man's mouth ought to be outlawed, Corinne decided as she watched him check labels until he found the one he wanted. Lifting it from the table, he extended his free hand to her and made her stomach do a wobbly cartwheel.

"What do you say? Care to try?"

When she found herself all but blushing like a virgin, Corinne drew the line. She hadn't let a man intimidate her with sex appeal since Tony Melitti in the ninth grade. Squaring her shoulders, she cocked one eyebrow, put one hand on her hip, and let the other brush teasingly across Luc's upturned palm. "Absolutely," she purred in her best Jessica Rabbit. "But you go first. So I can watch."

"Thanks. I think I will." Predatory hunger radiated from his big, beautiful body as he caught her hand in his and sidled right up next to her until she could feel every inch of his body pressing up against her.

Sweet Mary Magdalene, the man felt like heaven.

All heavy, roped muscle and exotic scent, he gave off heat like a blast furnace, but Corinne already knew he was a hell of a lot nicer to curl up to during a cold snap. She watched his crystal-green eyes go all lazy and seductive and fought back the urge to wrap her arms around his neck and scale him like a prison wall. Just the thought of wrapping her legs around his waist and feeling his arms reach around to hold her steady made her pant. She could almost feel those enormous hands of his kneading her muscles again, easing the burning ache his nearness caused. She remembered the width of his shoulders blocking out the light, the weight of him pinning her to the cushions of her sofa, the scrape of callused skin against hers . . .

The hiss of the spray can yanked her back to reality just before her fantasy life caused her to embarrass herself. If thinking about him drove her to the edge like this, she'd hate to imagine what might happen the next time she got her hands on him.

He already had his on her. Eyes gleaming, he held her gaze captive while his fingers pulled the neckline of her tank top and the strap of her bra to one side, exposing the golden slope of her shoulder. The can hissed again as he pointed the nozzle at her bare skin and painted a line of thick, pale blue whipped cream from the side of her neck to the edge of her shirt. Then his head lowered and she felt his breath in hot contrast with the refrigerator cool of the cream.

"Chocolate pudding aside," he whispered as her breath froze solid in her chest, "you can never go wrong with the taste of fresh raspberries . . ."

His head dipped, and his lips parted, and her world spiraled out of control at the feel of his tongue sliding hot and moist over her cream-covered skin.

Her head fell backward as if her spine had melted, and that's pretty much how it felt to Corinne—like she'd become nothing but a great, big, boneless pile of goo. Well, if goo could feel so desperately needy. She pressed her chest against his, the pressure offering a slight easing of the ache in her breasts. His tongue licked and stroked muscles and nerves and tendons as he ate the cream from her skin. His lips pressed and teeth scraped, and it felt like he touched each separate nerve ending and coaxed it to quivering alert. Her knees quivered like jelly and her stomach had filled with hyperactive butterflies, while her head swam a leisurely backstroke, content to let Luc feast on her flesh as long as he wanted. If she was lucky, it would be a long, long time.

The click of the camera shutter barely penetrated her consciousness, but the loss of his kisses did. He pulled away and straightened to his full height. She whimpered and reached up to pull him back toward her, dying for more of his magic touch.

"Oh, my God, you two are amazing!" Hibbish let his camera fall to his chest, dangling from the woven strap while he palmed his bare head in his hands and tapped out an obscure rhythm in what

Corinne guessed was a gesture of mental overload. "I've never seen anything like it! Tell me what you charge. I'll pay anything! Anything you want, just so long as you sign a photo release so I can use that shot on the Kissy Kreme display. Name your price."

Corinne barely registered the shop owner's babbling as English, her senses still reeling. It took a second to transition from the impulse to climb Luc's body like a rope wall, to acting like a mature professional with a job to do and information to elicit. With her eyes still locked on Luc's face, she saw his expression sharpen. He turned to the shop-owner-*cum*-photographer.

"Anything?" he repeated.

Hibbish nodded. "Absolutely. That picture I took of you two is gonna sell a whole truckload of Kissy Kreme. For God's sake, you can have my firstborn child. Just give me ten minutes to call my wife and let her know."

Luc squeezed Corinne's hand, as if encouraging her to keep silent. As if she had yet recovered the power of speech. Ha. The man clearly didn't understand the potency of his own kisses. "We appreciate this, Mr. Hibbish. Can you start by . . . ?"

"Whoa, wait a second there." The man held his hands out in front of him and backed up half a step. His friendly expression closed down like a Popsicle stand in October, and he shook his head. "If you're here lookin' for Walt, I'm afraid I can't help you."

That managed to yank Corinne out of her lust-induced fog. She frowned. "What? I thought *you* were Walter Hibbish. I looked it up. The Pink Pillow is owned by Walter M. Hibbish."

"And Harvey Weitzel. They're partners. We're partners. I'm Harvey," Weitzel explained. "But I haven't seen Walt in nearly a week."

"Have you reported him missing?" Damn, that news threw Corinne for a loop, but her instincts were kicking in now. Maybe this assignment had caused her to stumble on to real story. "Do you know where he was last seen?"

"Yeah, I reported it, since he hasn't returned any of my calls, but I'll tell you the same thing I told the police." Weitzel turned away to begin breaking down his equipment from the shoot. The models reached for their robes, still watching Luc out of the corners of their eyes. "I don't know nothing about where he might be. Walt and I never lived in each other's pockets, and when one of us wanted to take a little break, we never felt the need to explain it. He could be anywhere. Chances are he'll turn up in a week or two. You can try back then."

"I won't need to try back then. I'm working on a story, and I need to talk to him now."

"Then I hope you got a nose like a bloodhound, 'cause I can't think of any other way for you to find him." Weitzel gave a regretful shake of his head and zipped his lens into a protective case. "Sorry I can't tell you more. But if you wanna do an article on the store instead of just on Walt, I'd be happy to have a sit-down. The publicity would be great."

Corinne blew out a frustrated breath and shoved her notebook back into her bag. "Sorry, but I have to run that by my editor first."

Weitzel looked disappointed for a minute, then shrugged it off and offered her a smile. "Oh, well. That's how it goes, I guess." He picked up a can of Kissy Kreme and handed it to Luc. "Here. Take a freebie. Just for coming. Tell your friends about it, too. We'll be all stocked up by Wednesday."

By Wednesday, Corinne sincerely hoped she could forget The Pink Pillow had ever existed, but she just nodded and left the thank-yous to Luc. He seemed to be good at them.

"Look, I'm sorry you went through all this trouble for nothing," the shopkeeper said. "Unless you change your minds about the photos it's like you wasted a trip. Why don't I walk you out and tell my girl out front to give you a special discount. Anything you want, twenty percent off."

"Thanks, Harvey, that's very generous of you," Luc said, taking Corinne by the elbow and guiding her forward. "We appreciate all your help."

Weitzel shrugged as he set aside a soft-sided camera case and led the way toward the doorway they had entered through. "No problem. I wish you luck on your story. Sorry I couldn't give you more information."

"Yeah, me too," Corinne muttered under her breath, stepping back into the shop with Luc right behind her. They exchanged pleasantries with Weitzel, but when the curtain fell closed behind them, she crossed her arms over her chest and immediately dropped them back to her sides. She gave a frustrated sigh. "Fabulous. Just what we needed. Now we've got a great big blank from what was supposed to be our likeliest source. What now?"

"Well, we could always pick out a few things to . . . console us until we decide what to do next."

Luc's suggestion startled a laugh out of her. "I suppose that's one way to make lemonade, but before we, ah, stop for refreshments, what do you say we put in a bit more than an hour of hard work for the day and see what else we can find out about Walter Hibbish?" Her eyes slid back to the display of chocolate tattoos she'd noticed earlier, and her smile turned wicked. "Then if you're a very good boy, maybe we can take a break later on."

She snagged a box and sashayed over to the cash register. "After all, we'll need to keep our strength up."

Luc's mind was filled with two primary thoughts as he bustled Corinne away from the shop and down the street. On the one hand, they needed to figure out what it meant that one of the last mortals to make contact with Seoc had disappeared without a trace; on the other, he needed to understand why the taste of Corinne D'Alessandro went to his head faster than Faerie wine.

He knew she was his heartmate. Even if he'd wanted to deny it, that part had become abundantly clear when she'd seen through his glamour last night. Still, just being his perfect match didn't explain why the one little taste of her in the back of the sex shop had nearly snapped his control. He hadn't touched anything more intimate than her shoulder. Heartmates were said to possess a strong, elemental attraction to each other, but could this really be what the stories were talking about?

For a man who'd learned the finer points of sex from nymphs and dryads, a man known as one of the most desirable warriors in Faerie, Luc couldn't fathom why one human woman should be able to seduce him simply by breathing. For Goddess's sake, he'd spent the entirety of last night having her as many times as he could manage. He should be sated, but he'd wanted her again the minute he'd woken, and the desire had only increased with each passing second. How in *Ithir* was he supposed to function like this? If this was how all heartmates felt for each other, it amazed him that he'd ever seen any of them outside their bedchambers.

"Luc?"

The sound of her voice surprised him. He'd been so caught up in thinking about her, he'd almost forgotten about her. She stared up at him with those wide, earth-colored eyes, and he felt his blood head back south. "Sorry, what?"

"I knew you weren't listening. I asked what you

think it means that Hibbish has gone missing. I saw the look on your face when Weitzel first mentioned it. You have some sort of theory."

He weighed his words for a moment before he answered. "Not so much a theory as a whole lot of questions that I'd really like answers to."

She frowned. "What do you mean?"

"I think it's a pretty odd time for Hibbish to go missing, don't you?"

"I think *odd* is pretty much at the root of this whole situation, but then I'm still trying to accustom myself to the idea of there being a Queen of Faerie, or a place called Faerie itself, so I don't think I'm one to judge. I'm more interested in what you think is odd."

He sighed. "I think it's odd that Hibbish has disappeared so soon after sighting Seoc."

"Explain."

It must have been nearing lunchtime, because the sidewalk had begun to fill up with pedestrians, and Luc had to pull Corinne out of the way of a small gaggle of young people who seemed oblivious to the fact that they were expected to share the world with anyone else. He grimaced. "Come on. We can't stand here and chat all day. I saw a coffee shop down on the corner. Let's grab a table and swap theories. And maybe some more of that foul brew you love will put you in a better mood."

"My mood is just fine, but I never say no to a cup of foul brew." She let him guide her down the block and inside to the table a harried waiter indicated.

"Fine, is it? I suppose that's why we had to have that little relationship talk in the middle of that atmospheric shop."

She had the grace to look abashed. "Okay, so my mood is greatly improved."

"And think how much further it will improve after a cup of coffee." Personally, he didn't see what humans liked so much about the dark, bitter liquid, but if it made Corinne happy, he'd be delighted to provide it.

He thought he heard her murmur something about torture, revenge, and Altoids as he helped her into her seat, but when he took his own and glanced across at her, she just smiled sweetly. The expression gave him the willies. Talk about unnatural. He gave her order to their waiter, along with a request for a pot of Darjeeling with lemon and turned back to their conversation.

"So what's your theory about the weirdness?" she asked as soon as they were alone again.

He paused, taking a moment to weigh his answer. It wasn't so much a matter of deciding how much of the truth to tell her as deciding how to tell her so she would understand without getting freaked out. "Have you ever heard of a Changeling?"

Her eyes widened. "Oddly enough, I have. A few months ago, I would have assumed that when you asked about a changeling—small *c*—you were

referring to the folktales about how fairies—small
f and one *e*—used to exchange their sickly or mal-
formed offspring for healthy human babies, whom
they then raised as their own children back in
fairyland. But last summer, another friend of mine
actually met a guy who calls himself a Changeling,
so I'm going to assume you're talking about the
kind with the capital *C*."

"Definitely a capital *C*. The other sort haven't
happened in a long, long time. Not since the very
beginning of our time out of *Ithir*. These days, the
term always refers to the offspring of mixed
parents—one Fae parent, and one human."

"Really? Danice just said it meant half human
and half Other. She never mentioned the Fae, even
when she married the guy. The jerk."

"Last night, when I first explained what I was
doing here, I mentioned that the only way to travel
between here and Faerie, and vice versa, is to use a
magical doorway. Remember?"

She nodded.

"Good. The thing is, that wasn't always true. It
used to be that the Fae could build a kind of portal, using magic, and do it anytime and anywhere
they wanted. But having that power led to abuses,
like stealing human children. So a long time ago,
that power was stripped away; from then on, the
only paths between the worlds were the doorways.
That's one of the reasons why taking human babies back to Faerie stopped, because in order to
make the trip, the Fae would have to not only find

the right baby and make the switch, but also find the nearest door between the worlds and get the baby through before getting caught. It just got too tough. And since the Queen could hardly afford to seem like she approved of the whole practice, she didn't exactly make those doors easy to find."

He closed his mouth as their server approached and waited until he was done before leaning forward to continue his tale. "But some Fae continued to find them. Worse than that, some humans found them, too, and a few came into Faerie looking for the lost children. Once, a human man managed to convince some of his neighbors that the Fae were responsible for the death of their crops and their cattle, and they formed a small army to attack us. That was an extreme example, but it made an impression on the Queen. Eventually, she decided to close almost all the doors between the worlds so she could control the passage of anyone into and out of Faerie."

"Sort of like the Berlin Wall of alternate realities, then."

Luc gave an amused snort. "Well, I suppose there are worse analogies. Anyway, all but five of the doors in *Ithir* were permanently sealed, and the five that were left were all charmed so that while they exist at different corners of the world in *Ithir*, in Faerie they all open into the Queen's palace."

"And she's a one-woman border patrol?"

"She makes the decisions about who passes, yes. Very, very rarely someone discovers a new door that has opened on its own, but those are shut as soon as they are discovered. I heard that the one leading to the Winter Court was closed just recently after some sort of incident there."

Corinne frowned. "Then how did Seoc get here to begin with? For that matter, how could you have gotten here in the past like you said you have?"

"I had permission," he said. "And we think Seoc snuck through one of the palace doors when a room was left unguarded."

Her eyebrows climbed toward her hairline. "I bet that as the head of the Queen's Guard, that really chaps your ass, doesn't it?"

He frowned. "It doesn't make me happy. While I had a man stationed in the room the night Seoc went through, he was distracted from his duty, and it is ultimately my responsibility to make sure that kind of thing doesn't happen."

"I wasn't saying it's your fault. I just want to have my facts straight."

"Well, the fact is it doesn't matter how Seoc got here, because he's here now and so are the five doors back to Faerie. But those are the only doors on *Ithir*. A door can lead to any number of alternate dimensions; Faerie is only one of them. The only way for Seoc to tell where a door goes is to have been told in advance, or to try it and see what happens."

"And he's the reason why we're having this conversation." She frowned. "Wasn't the point of this conversation originally to discuss why Walter Hibbish disappeared?"

He had to give her points for persistence. "I'm getting to that."

"Get faster."

"Fine. I think Hibbish disappeared because Seoc was experimenting with the doors and needed someone to test them on."

Her eyes widened. "You think Seoc killed Hibbish?"

"No, I think he sent him through a door."

Ten

Corinne did her best to wrap her mind around the information Luc was giving her, but she just didn't think her brain was that flexible. Maybe she should look into mental yoga.

She shook her head. "But you just said that the Faerie Queen closed all the doors between *Ith*—um, between here and Faerie. So how did Seoc send Hibbish through one?"

"He didn't. At least, he didn't send Hibbish through to Faerie. I think he sent him into limbo."

Her jaw dropped so hard, she almost heard a crash. "He sent that guy into eternal nothingness?"

Luc's mouth curved in a brief grin. "Not exactly. Limbo isn't any one specific place. It's what we call the place between any two worlds. It doesn't technically exist, so a being who can do magic can shape it to be anything he or she wants."

Corinne grimaced. "You sound like a theoretical physicist."

She knew whereof she spoke. She'd dated a theoretical physicist for a while in college. She still got occasional flashback headaches.

"Okay, so Hibbish is . . . somewhere that's not here and not Faerie. But why was Seoc experimenting with the doors? Are you telling me he came to—er, he came here without already knowing what door he'd need to get back? No one could be that stupid."

"You haven't met Seoc."

"Huh?"

"He's exactly that stupid. Now I think he's looking for the doorway back."

"You're kidding me."

He shook his head. "I wish. One of the five remaining Faerie doors is here in Manhattan." He topped off his tea and added a fresh slice of lemon. "Mab opened a new door for me when she gave me permission to come here, but she's the only being I know capable of still using that kind of magic. Seoc needs to know where the permanent door is, and I think he's trying to find it."

"But what's so bad about that? If all of you want him to go back to Faerie, and he's trying to find his way back there, why not just let him? Or better yet, help him find it and get him home even quicker."

"Because I don't think he's looking for it so he can use it to go home. I think he's looking for it so he can prop it permanently open."

He said it so gravely and with such a forbidding frown on his face that Corinne could only speculate. "And that would be a bad thing."

He nodded. "That would be the thing I told you about last night. That would allow anyone and anything that wanted to travel between our worlds to do it. That would upset the balance between them. That would do all those bad things I told you about last night."

Corinne blew out a breath. "Right. So then it's important for us to stop him."

"You could say that. But first, we have to find him."

"True." She drained her coffee mug and frowned. "Well, I was going to focus this afternoon on finding Hibbish. He gave the most complete statement about seeing Seoc, so it made sense that he'd be able to give us the most details, but his sighting wasn't the most recent."

"Whose was?"

Corinne pulled out the notebook to double-check. "Rabbi Aaronson. He reportedly spotted Seoc near his synagogue in Morningside Heights."

"That's farther uptown, isn't it?"

She nodded. "North of Central Park. And that was just three days ago." She reached for her cell phone. "He was one of the calls I made this morning. I left my number on his office machine. Let me see if he called back."

He watched while Corinne dialed her voice mail, seeing her impatience grow as she navigated through the prompts to listen to her new messages. When he saw her go pale, he knew something was very wrong.

"What?" He reached across the table to cover her hand with his. Her fingers had gone icy cold.

Corinne shook her head and put the cell on speaker before laying the phone down between them.

"This message is for a Corinne D'Alessandro." The woman's voice sounded think and shaky, as if she were very old or very upset. "Ms. D'Alessandro, this is Rebeccah Silver from the Temple Beth Elohim and the office of Rabbi Levi Aaronson. We received your request for an interview, but I'm afraid that Dr. Aaronson has . . . Dr. Aaronson was killed last night in a mugging near his home. I hope—" She broke off, drew a raspy breath. "I hope you'll understand if I refer you to the media relations office at the Jewish Theological Seminary with further questions."

Corinne pressed the button to end the call. For several minutes, they both remained silent, considering the implications. For her part, Corinne wasn't quite sure what to make of the news. This was New York. Muggings happened, and sometimes, people died; still, this was at least the third coincidental event to make her list since she'd first heard about sightings of an elf on the streets of Manhattan. So far, nothing had linked directly to the subject of the sightings, but the questions were beginning to pile up.

She spoke first. "You don't think that Seoc would have—"

"No." Luc spoke firmly. "I can't picture it. You don't know Seoc, but he's . . . he's just a boy. He's spoiled and immature and willful, and I don't think he's stopped one time in his ridiculous life to consider the consequences of his actions, but he's not a killer. I don't know if he'd be able to manage a kill if he tried."

Corinne drew back. This was news to her. "When you say boy, you don't mean he's a child, do you?"

"No, of course not. He's legally an adult, though not by much, according to Fae standards. He's only just over three hundred. But he's not a child; just an idiot."

Corinne choked on her coffee. "Three hundred? As in *three hundred years old?*"

"About that. Three hundred and seven or eight, I think."

"And you call that a child? What are you? Four thousand? Give or take?"

"Don't be ridiculous." He shot her an impatient stare. "I'm only nine hundred and twenty-seven."

"Oh, well, I guess you're lucky Dmitri doesn't make you sit at the kids' table for Thanksgiving dinner!" Corinne set her mug down with shaking hands. If only it were filled with vodka instead of Kenya select. "Nine hundred twenty-seven. Holy Jesus."

Some of her distress must finally have filtered through to Luc. His expression softened and he reached for her hands, cupping his fingers around hers. "Try not to panic," he said. "Time is different in Faerie, and the Fae age differently from humans. Technically I've lived somewhere in the neighborhood of that many human years, but to my people I'm in my prime, nothing more. Think of me being around, oh, thirty-five or thirty-six."

Her fingers continued to tremble. "Is that what it comes out to in the New Math?"

He chuckled.

Corinne struggled to breathe slowly and deeply. She could handle this; really she could. So what if the newest man in her life was older than the country she lived in? Was that really such a big deal? After all, Reggie was one of her best friends, and Reggie's husband was even older. He'd topped a thousand before the two of them even met, which meant Luc was practically wet behind the ears in comparison.

Yup, wet behind his cute, pointy ears.

"Oh, God."

Luc squeezed her fingers. "Do you need to put your head between your legs?"

"I'm not going to pass out." Probably. "I just . . . I need a minute to cope, that's all. Just give me a minute."

He fell obediently silent.

Okay, Corinne told herself, taking another deep breath. *Think about this calmly. Rationally.* Age was just a number, right? A concept humanity had agreed upon to keep track of the passage of time.

The only reason it was important to a relationship was because it often indicated how long two people might have together and how similar their backgrounds and perspectives were likely to be. Considering that her background and Luc's had happened in different dimesions, they could pretty much assume the "shared experiences" ship had sailed. How else was age important to them?

"Oh, shit, are you going to live forever and never age a day, while I get old and wrinkled and ugly until you find me repulsive and abandon me like a used-up tube of toothpaste?"

Luc let her babble out the question, then nodded. "Absolutely."

"Luc!"

He squeezed her hands. "Hey, my answer wasn't any more ridiculous than your question. Don't be foolish."

"I'm not being foolish. Tell me the truth. Are you? Going to live forever and never age," she added hastily when his expression began to turn angry. "I think that's something I have a right to know."

He made a face. "It's complicated. Like I said, the Fae age differently from humans, and time passes differently in the two worlds. For the moment, let's just say that in Faerie I'll age like any other Fae, but while I'm in *Ithir* I'll age more like a human would. Now can we please stop worrying about nonsense and get back to the problem at hand."

"I wouldn't call it nonsense," Corinne muttered, squeezing his hands back, "but yes, we can get back to Seoc."

"Good." He leaned across the table and brushed her mouth with his.

"It's not that much more pleasant a topic, though. You're certain he couldn't be responsible for Rabbi Aaronson's death?"

"As certain as I can be without having witnessed it myself. I honestly don't think Seoc is capable of that kind of violence."

"I believe you," she reassured him. "If you think Seoc didn't do it, then he didn't do it. But it seems like too big a coincidence that one of the witnesses to Seoc's little magic shows is missing and now another one is dead. It makes more sense if you assume the events are related somehow."

"I agree, but that's my gut talking. I don't see that we have any hard evidence to back up the feeling."

"You're right. We don't." Corinne eased her hands from his and picked up her phone. "Fortunately, I think I know where we might start looking for some."

When Corinne had told Luc that she had contacts who might be able to give them a little more information on Rabbi Aaronson's murder, he'd guessed she was referring to someone on the police force. Reporters were always talking to the police in the novels he read when he visited the mortal world. As it turned out, though, his heartmate must read an entirely different sort of novel. Corinne did have a contact in the police department, but she spoke to him briefly on the phone, then swung by her apartment to pick up a fax he'd sent her before leading Luc back outside and through Manhattan's grid of streets to the East Side and the cool corridors of the city morgue.

The sign in the lobby had caught his attention first:

*Let conversation cease; let laughter flee. This is the place
where death delights in helping the living.*

It was the kind of message that stuck with a man.

And gave him a serious case of the heebie-jeebies.

"You couldn't have asked these people for a fax and gone to visit the police station instead?" He kept his voice low, whether out of respect or unease, he couldn't be certain.

"Everything McMartin had to tell me could be written down," she said, not even bother to glance back at him as she led the way to the building's basement. "Dr. Tortelli can show me things that I'd never understand if I just read about them. I'm a bright girl, but I never did manage to fit in the time for medical school."

Luc understood her reasoning, but that didn't mean he had to like it. Gritting his teeth, he followed her through the starkly lit halls past quiet rooms whose contents he didn't even want to imagine. Like most Fae, he had an instinctive aversion for the dead. It wasn't that no one ever died in Faerie, but it didn't happen with anything like the same regularity. For the Fae, death just wasn't a part of the natural process.

The people of Faerie had been blessed with immortality. Oh, they could be killed—stop any creature's heart or remove its head from its body, and it would have a hard time continuing to breathe—but they never simply died. Old age didn't scare them, because it held no consequences. Their beauty never faded; their bodies never failed. They didn't understand the human concept of fatalism, because they never worried about Fate.

Maybe that was why death frightened the average Fae more than the average human. As a warrior, Luc had encountered the mysterious force more than most of his kind, but he never grew accustomed to it. How was someone supposed to grow accustomed to the destruction of a living soul?

Corinne made no comment on his stiff posture or his uneasy glances, for which he felt grateful. Of course, he had to admit that her forbearance might have owed more to her complete focus on the handful of papers she studied at as she walked and less to her powers of observation. Still, Luc appreciated it.

He steeled himself for something when she finally stopped walking and knocked on a metal door adorned with a small, square window embedded with crosshatched strands of wire. After a brief pause, the door opened and a girl in blue surgical scrubs stepped back to wave them into the room.

"Dr. Tortelli is on her way up. You can wait in here."

Luc fought back the urge to shudder and reluctantly followed Corinne into the large chamber. The girl offered them something to drink, and he felt his stomach revolt. Thankfully, Corinne refused for both of them and the girl left them alone to wait for the medical examiner.

The room approximated Luc's idea of hell—a human hell, since the Fae didn't believe in any such place. It was big and white and cavernous, painfully clean and polished so that every surface gleamed, from the linoleum floors to the stainless-steel tables and counters, to the tiled and painted walls. The fluorescent fixtures bathed everything in an unrelenting grayish light, but they exposed not so much as a single speck of dust. He imagined human hospitals were rarely so scrupulously clean.

No amount of scrubbing, though, could disguise the smell of the place. It stank of antiseptic cleaners, a harsh chemical odor laced with a bitter note of cherries, like cough syrup or cheap hard candies. Under it, Luc could smell the death, a thin miasma of suffering, of blood and waste and urine mingling together with the sweetness of rotten flesh.

He had to brace himself to keep from bolting out of the room.

Corinne appeared unfazed. She leaned against one of the steel autopsy tables, identifiable by the trough surrounding it and the block positioned at one end to elevate the head of the unfortunate body that landed upon it. It didn't seem to bother her that she was standing right beside a place where so many other humans had lain, empty and lifeless. Was it a human trait, to be aware of that kind of tragedy and look past it, beyond it, to matters closer at hand?

"The report McMartin faxed over is a little sketchy," she said aloud, her eyes still glued to the folder she'd grabbed on their way out of her apartment. She'd stuffed the faxed pages inside, but she hadn't shut the thing since they'd stepped into the city-owned building on First Avenue. "Probably because there were no witnesses and the officer who responded to the call about the body was a twenty-eight-year veteran."

"You'd think someone with that much experience would have learned to be thorough."

"Nineteen months to retirement," she disagreed drily. "That much experience has taught him to be halfway to Fort Lauderdale even while he's on shift. I like rookies. The ones who still care tend to give you so many details, you know what side the vic dressed on."

Luc tore his gaze away from a shelf full of implements that looked like props from a particularly gruesome horror film and decided focusing on Corinne's face would be much better for his nerves. Her brow was furrowed as she continued to read.

"You know, I think the ink was still wet on this when McMartin snagged it from the IIC to fax to me. Investigator in charge," she clarified at his blank stare. "It looks like it's smudged in places. The guys says it looks like the victim was approached from behind, but it doesn't say whether he put up much of a fight."

"He didn't."

The voice from the doorway had them turning, Luc with a start and Corinne with a friendly grin.

"Hey, Doc," she greeted the new arrival. "I hear business is pretty good recently."

"Too good." The woman backed into the room pulling a stretcher loaded with a long, black bag zippered tight from top to bottom. Luc swallowed hard and tried not to look at it too closely. "Not including this guy, of course. You'd have missed him if you'd called me twenty minutes later. He never should have come to me to begin with. Next of kin has already started banging down the front doors wanting him back. I can stall them maybe fifteen more minutes, but you're going to have to make do with what I can tell you from just looking at him."

"You don't have an autopsy report?"

"I didn't do an autopsy. Can't."

He saw Corinne scowl, then watched as something occurred to her that made her curse.

"Oh, crap. Jewish law. I should have thought."

The medical examiner nodded. She was a woman of about fifty human years, with sandy-colored hair liberally salted with gray and worn short, possibly as a concession to what looked to be impressively stubborn curls. Her blue scrubs and smock covered a figure that leaned toward the plump and square, but her face was pleasantly freckled and spoke of both intelligence and compassion.

"As soon as I saw his name, I suspected he was Jewish, but when I looked at his ID and personal possessions, I found his cards with the name and address of his synagogue, so I knew I wouldn't be doing any cutting. He never should have come to me. The EMTs were rookies and routed him here without thinking." She waved Corinne to the side of the stretcher opposite her and unzipped the body bag. "I was just going to pack him up and send him home when I got your call, so I took a few minutes to do a visual exam. Don't tell, *capice*?"

"I owe you." Corinne leaned close to the body while Luc tried not to turn visibly green. "Please tell me you found something interesting."

"What's interesting is what I didn't find."

The doctor eased apart the sides of the bag so that they could take a closer look. Luc would have gracefully declined for his part, but his heartmate appeared fascinated.

"No defensive wounds, so like I said, the rabbi didn't put up a fight, which indicates that he either never saw the killer coming, or he knew him and trusted him."

"Him?"

Dr. Tortelli shrugged. "Figure of speech. Easier than saying *him or her* over and over again. But with that said, the cause of death appears to be a single blow to the back of the head with a blunt object. Impact shows a downward trajectory. Since our Dr. Aaronson here isn't exactly a shrimp, whoever struck him would have to be either a player in the WNBA or a man of above-average height." She paused and nodded at Luc, curiosity showing in her shrewd hazel eyes. "Your friend here could have managed it easily."

Corinne glanced over at him with a small smile. "Nah, I can alibi him out."

"Fair enough."

"What else can you tell me?"

"Very little, I'm sorry to say. No evidence of debris under the fingernails, so he didn't even touch the guy with any kind of force; no stray hairs that could have been transferred by a handshake or a how-you-doing hug. Other than the bloody mess at the back of his skull, the rabbi is lean, clean, and pristine."

Corinne grimaced. "Wow, you really meant it

when you said you had very little to tell me, didn't you?"

"I never lie about death."

"Damn, I was hoping for a little more," his heartmate grumbled as she stepped back from the body. He could read the frustration in her expression as well as in her body language.

The doctor nodded her understanding. "Do you mind my asking what made you curious enough about the doctor that you bothered to ask me about his autopsy? I didn't realize you knew him."

"I didn't. His name came up in, uh, a missing persons case I'm looking into," she hedged. "It was a long shot that his murder might have had something to do with it, but stranger things have happened, and this has been a really strange case so far."

Dr. Tortelli looked thoughtful for a moment, then moved the edge of the bag slightly to expose the corpse's left shoulder and upper arm. "Well, if you're looking for strange, this is the only thing that comes to mind."

She pointed as a small spot on the front of the man's shoulder, just above the crease made by his bicep lying against his side. The skin there looked slightly different from the surrounding tissue, slightly paler and smooth, almost shiny in texture.

"See that scar?"

Corinne nodded. Curiosity even moved Luc

enough to peer a little more closely. His feet didn't budge, though. He preferred to keep his distance.

"It looks old, so I didn't bother to connect it to the cause of death or the precipitating attack," the doctor said. "It's bugging me a little bit, though, because I can't tell where it came from."

Corinne looked puzzled. "What do you mean?"

"It doesn't look quite like any other scar tissue I've seen. It's not a knife or a bullet wound; those are easy to spot. It doesn't actually look like any sort of puncture wound. It's the wrong surface texture for a burn, too. Frankly, the closest I can come to describing it is like a skin graft, but that's not quite right, either." She shook her head. "I just can't quite make it out, and I hate things like that. They make me look bad."

As Luc listened to the medical examiner's words, something about them penetrated through his cloak of unease and discomfort. Penetrated far enough that he actually moved a step closer to the dead man to take a look at the small, round spot marring the man's gray-tinged flesh. What he viewed made him stiffen.

Corinne saw it. He knew by the way her gaze shot to his face, searching his eyes for a clue to his thoughts. He gave his head a small shake and shifted back to his previous position. Now was not the time to talk about what he had seen.

Thankfully, Corinne picked up on his cue and stepped back from the stretcher herself to offer her contact a rueful smile. "Well, I appreciate you helping me out, Doc. Especially under the circumstances. But I think it's time we let Dr. Aaronson go back to his family. They'll want to bury him as soon as possible."

Dr. Tortelli rezipped the body bag and nodded. "Your family's done plenty for me over the years, Rinne. You don't owe me for this. But you're right about the burial. His family's been reminding me about it for the last two hours. There's a funeral director upstairs waiting for him even as we speak. I'll make sure he's taken care of."

"I know you will."

Corinne smiled again and touched the older woman's arm briefly and affectionately before turning toward the door. Luc moved to follow. The medical examiner stopped her with a comment.

"If the missing person you're looking for is the one who did this to him," the doctor said, "I hope you find him. And I hope he'll pay for it."

"Don't worry." Luc spoke for the first time since the older woman had wheeled in the corpse, meeting her eyes as he urged Corinne out of the autopsy room. They exchanged a long glance of assessment, then understanding. "We'll make certain he does."

When they reached the entrance of the building and stepped out into the fresh afternoon air, Luc inhaled deeply, savoring as never before the scents of the city, food mingled with trash mingled with humanity mingled with stone and metal and earth. Nothing had ever smelled so good. He couldn't really recall the last time he'd felt as grateful to leave a place—or as glad that he'd been there. For all the misery being in those haunted corridors had caused him, he knew the dead would be delighted they had visited.

Eleven

Corinne barely contained herself until they reached the sidewalk. She gave Luc half a second to draw in a deep breath—one he'd needed desperately, judging by the gray-green tinge to his skin—then pounced. Metaphorically, of course.

"What was it?" she demanded right there on the sidewalk at First and 32nd. "What did you see when you looked at that scar?"

He sighed, but the sound held no impatience, just a bucket-load of relief. A visible release of tension followed closely on its heels.

"The doctor was right about the cause not being any of the things she mentioned," he said, beginning to walk down the street and away from the ME's office. "He wasn't shot, stabbed, burned, or grafted. She was wrong, though, about the mark's age. It was recent; probably as recent as last night."

Corinne swore under her breath. "Then it was related to the attack."

"Almost certainly. I've seen scars like that before, but very rarely. They don't happen to the Fae; only to humans."

"What causes them?"

"A very powerful blast of Fae magic."

She paused to chew on that. It left a bad taste in her mouth. "I thought you said Seoc wasn't capable of hurting anyone."

Luc's jaw clenched. "I didn't believe he was, but clearly I was wrong."

Corinne didn't want to doubt Luc's judgment, and she didn't want him doubting it, either. "Just because the blast was caused by magic doesn't necessarily mean that Seoc is to blame," she said carefully.

He snorted. "So there just happens to be some other person from Faerie with enough power to summon that kind of energy wandering around *Ithir* at the same time as Seoc? No, that kind of magic is specific to the sidhe. The noble race of Faerie. People like me and Seoc and the Queen. Brownies and imps and the other sort of creatures from our world just don't have that kind of ability. It had to have been Seoc."

Corinne took a deep breath and let it out carefully. "Okay, so now we know." She stopped walking and reached out to grab his hand, pulling him to a stop beside her. "Finding out was the first step. It's time to move on to the second."

He nodded curtly. "We have to find Seoc immediately."

"Well, we have four witnesses left. So let's go knock on some doors."

*   *   *

The knocking elicited very little other than a burgeoning headache for Corinne and an increasing sense of urgency for them both. There at been no answer at the apartments of two of the models Ava had told them about. At the third, they found only a disgruntled roommate who bitched at them for waking her up in the middle of the damned night (it was three in the afternoon) and told them that if they saw Leena before she did, they should tell her that if she was late with the rent again, her "ass" would be "grass." A trip to the bartender's place yielded nothing until the super poked his head out to see who was knocking next door and told them that Mark Ingram had moved over the weekend.

"So much for sixty days' notice, right?" the man griped.

"You have his forwarding address?" Corinne asked.

"What, do I look like the postman to you? He paid up, he left. No business of mine where he went."

Corinne gritted her teeth to keep from baring them at the grumpy, unhelpful bastard. "And what if you need to find him again? Say he damaged something moving."

"I still got the number at his job. Pulls the taps at a little place up in Gramercy."

Luc nodded. "Thank you. We'll find him there, then."

The super's snort stopped them before they

reached the exit. "Not at this time of day, you won't. Works nights. Says he likes the money. Personally, I'm gonna like not getting woke up when he slams his door at four A.M. But he never goes on till at least seven. At this hour, he'll be stretched out wherever his new place is sleeping like a corpse. And good luck waking him. Slept through a police raid once. Lady in 3B had her drug-dealing brother staying with her last year. Cops broke three doors yanking his ass out. Bet yer ass her lease ain't gettin' renewed."

"Thank you. You've been very helpful."

"And charming," Corinne muttered as the man closed the door in their faces and went back to his blaring television set. "Damn it. Hank Buckley clearly didn't double-check after he got Ingram's address. There's no telling where he moved to. He could have gone out of state for all we know."

"Not if he's still working his old job."

"Only one way to find out." She had her cell phone in her hand and had already started dialing. She placed it on speaker again so Luc could listen in.

"Landslides, can I help you?"

The voice over the phone was feminine and brusque, but polite, and Corinne held up her finger to Luc to indicate he should be quiet. "Hi, I'm looking for Mark Ingram. Is he working right now?"

"He's not scheduled until seven, which means he'll be here by eight, if the past week is anything to go by," the woman informed them, her tone going cool. "That being the case, I doubt he's going to have time to chat on the phone tonight. Not if he wants to keep his job."

The receiver clicked into silence, and Corinne hung up. "Somehow I doubt she'd appreciate us calling back and asking for his new address."

"Is there another way we could find out?"

There were always ways, Corinne knew, but none of them would be easy. "Nothing quick. I can check with the utility companies, see if he's started service somewhere new. And I know a PI who'd probably do me a favor, but none of that will get us an answer before eight."

"Seven." Luc shrugged when she looked puzzled. "What can I say? I'm an optimist."

She huffed out a laugh. "Well, I'm a realist. Honestly, we'll waste the least amount of time if we just wait until tonight and catch him at work. If we hang out at the bar for a few minutes, he can talk and work at the same time and hopefully not piss off the boss."

"And in the meantime?"

"We regroup."

They headed back to her apartment thoroughly frustrated.

"You're a writer," Luc mused in the elevator up to her floor. "Is there an adjective out there that means an unmitigated disaster, spiraling quickly toward a close approximation of Armageddon?"

"I think *fubar* is the closest you're going to get,"

she said, leading the way to her door and letting them into her living room.

"What language is that from?"

"Military-speak. It's an acronym. It means 'fucked up beyond all recognition.'"

He nodded. "I think that will do to be going on with."

Corinne made a noise of angry frustration and marched to the desk tucked under a window at the rear of the main room. Ignoring the bulk of the mess teetering precariously on every inch of available surface, she grabbed a woefully inadequate stack of papers and photos and carried them back to the sofa. Depositing them on the coffee table, she knelt down between it and the sofa and began to spread everything out until she could lay eyes on every scrap of information all at once. Then, still not satisfied, she yanked her notebook out of her backpack, flipped it open to the pertinent pages, and added that as well.

"Okay," she said, looking over the chaos and wishing there were more of it, "this is everything we have. I've been over it all twice, but there's got to be something I'm missing. I refuse to believe there isn't something in here somewhere that will point us in the right direction. We just have to find it."

Luc sank onto the sofa next to her shoulder and surveyed the scene. "But what exactly is it that we're looking for?"

Corinne bit back a growl. "I don't know yet. Damn it, I'm going to need coffee for this."

She left him sitting in front of the paperwork and stalked into the kitchen to put on a pot of life's blood. If her feet pointed backward, she'd have kicked her own ass. She knew she was missing something. Had she been so blinded by anger with her editor and irritation over finding herself embroiled in Others' business that she had ignored some vital clue? Because she didn't think she could live with that. She didn't think she could stand knowing that if she'd paid closer attention, she might have helped Luc find Seoc before anyone got hurt.

Coffee dripped while she brooded. As soon as she could, she poured a cup and carried it back to the sofa. Settling beside Luc, she sipped as she took another look at the information she had gathered. "You know, there's something that really bothers me about the rabbi's murder."

"You mean aside from the wanton loss of life?" Luc snapped, then apologized when she shot him a quelling look.

"I mean, why was it necessary? If your theory about Hibbish's disappearance is right and Seoc sent him into limbo, why not just send Aaronson there when he got in the way of Seoc's experiments? Why kill him?"

"That assumes the rabbi was killed because he knew about Seoc's experiments—which doesn't make a lot of sense. So far, the witnesses to Seoc's activities have been dismissed as crackpots, am I right?"

"Yes, but you heard Ava. Interest in the story is growing."

Luc nodded. "True enough, but for the moment, Seoc has no reason to fear human discovery. There had to be another reason for the murder."

None occurred to her. "So what was it? Any brilliant theories?"

Rising to pace restlessly, he scrubbed his hand over the back of his neck and scowled. In all, he looked thoroughly disgruntled. "No. And frankly, it's driving me bonkers."

"Join the club." Corinne reached for a couple of sheets of paper and scanned the contents. "Maybe the motive is buried somewhere in the rabbi's statement. Maybe there's something he reported or something about him that set him apart from the other witnesses?"

Interest lightened the man's grim features. "You could be right. Do you have a copy?"

Corinne shuffled through more papers and frowned. She scanned everything laid out on the table, then scanned again. She shook her head. How could she not have something so important?

"I can't find it. I swear Hank told me he gave me all the statements he'd gathered. Why wouldn't Aaronson's be here?"

"What information about his sighting *do* we have?"

She referred back to her notes. "Just that he—" She broke off and read the line over again, to be sure she hadn't imagined it. "Holy shit."

Luc snatched the paper out of her hand. "What? What did you find?"

"Right there." She jabbed a finger halfway down the page. "Hank never gave me his original statement because no one ever recorded it. Rabbi Aaronson was the only one of the eyewitnesses who contacted the police directly about what he'd seen, but they thought he was a total crackpot. Hank sent a PI to verify his report later, and Aaronson said that at first he thought the cops were very professional, listening closely and taking detailed notes, but he'd forgotten to give the officer who took his statement a card. When he went back inside to get one, he saw the cop laughing with a colleague and tossing his statement in the trash. That certainly sets him apart from the others, don't you think?"

A surge of excitement gave Corinne a wave of new energy, but Luc burst her bubble with a shake of his head. He handed the paper back to her.

"I'll admit it's different from the others, but I don't see any reason why it would prompt Seoc to kill him. Seoc has no reason to fear the mortal police. First, to cause him any trouble they'd have to find him, which is unlikely, as we know only too well. Second, he's Fae—he can change his appearance with a snap of his fingers. And even if the police found him *and* recognized him, he has the power to defend himself magically. Discovery couldn't possibly have posed a big enough threat to prompt Seoc to kill."

The logic registered with Corinne, but so did the desire for something—anything!—about this investigation to begin making sense.

"Damn it, just this afternoon you said that Seoc couldn't possibly have killed anyone, but we've both seen that he did! Now you're saying the only motive we can find couldn't possibly have given him motive for it. Will you make up your damned mind?"

She regretted her words the minute she spoke them. Yelled them, actually. Her hand went instinctively to her temple to try to ease the throbbing there. God, her head was killing her. She felt Luc abruptly stand and pace away from her and she sighed. Hell, she nearly whimpered.

"I'm sorry," she said, swallowing back a massive lump of guilt. "You didn't deserve that, and I had no reason to jump down your throat. I'm just—" She swallowed again, but the lump didn't move. "This is just so damned frustrating."

"Believe me, I've noticed."

"I'm sorry," she repeated, catching his gaze and hoping he could read the sincerity in her eyes. Temper had a way of turning her into a brat. She knew it, and she hated it about herself. The last thing she wanted him to think of when he looked at her was a three-year-old in the middle of a tantrum. "I try to pretend I'm not a bitch, but sometimes it just leaks out."

That actually dragged a laugh out of him. "Sweetheart, if that was your idea of being a bitch, I really need to introduce you to the Queen. She's got a thing or twenty to teach you."

"I'll be sure to bring my notebook."

His expression softened and he returned to the sofa. Settling down beside her, he drew her into his arms and cuddled her close. "Hey, forget about it. I didn't notice you being a bitch if you haven't noticed me being an unhelpful killjoy. I feel like I've got this job to do, and so far I haven't managed a single, bloody useful thing."

He surrounded her with warmth and comfort, and she breathed in his scent with pleasure. He smelled like man and forests and subtle spices. "Not true. You made me breakfast. And you bought me coffee, which totally makes up for the whole tea debacle."

She felt a large hand stroke over her hair and heard a distinct rumbling sound.

"Speaking of breakfast," he mused, "I think that was the last time we ate, and it's after three o'clock. Are you hungry?"

Until he mentioned it, she hadn't been, but all of a sudden her stomach woke up and made its displeasure abundantly clear. "Starving," she admitted.

"Then what do you say we go out and get something to eat? We have time to kill until seven. Or eight. And sitting around staring at pieces of paper isn't helping either of our moods."

"I say, pierogi, please. There's a little Ukrainian place a few blocks over. The food is fantastic."

The walk to the restaurant did them good, as did simply getting their minds off the endless treadmill of questions for a while. The meal didn't hurt, either. The pierogi were plump and tender and served with plenty of sautéed onions and gobs of fresh, rich sour cream. Luc ate about a thousand. Corinne counted.

They held hands when they left the small café and began the short trip back to her building. Despite the difference in their heights, they seemed to fit together, naturally matching their strides and laughing together at the sight of the dapper little man on the corner, who bought himself a hot dog from a steam cart and proceeded to eat the empty bun while he fed the meat to the pampered dachshund he had cradled under one arm.

As long as she didn't think too hard about what they ought to be doing, she felt happy, she decided. Something about being with Luc just made everything seem somehow . . . better. She felt at peace, warm. Not just where his hand enveloped hers and not just where the omnipresent sexual awareness hummed between them, but inside herself, perilously close to her heart.

Later, Corinne couldn't have said what caught her attention. She didn't really remember seeing anything unusual, or hearing anything that alarmed her. All she knew was that one moment she was stepping off the curb beside Luc, and the next she was flying through the air and landing hard on the unyielding asphalt with about seven tons of angry warrior pinning her down. She had a vague impression of something small and mean and ominously black, but it didn't make any sense.

And neither did whatever Luc seemed to be shouting at her at the top of his lungs.

"Answer me, damn it!" he bellowed. "Corinne! Corinne, are you hurt?"

She tried to answer, but she had to struggle to draw breath. She nodded vigorously instead. "Wind . . . knocked out . . . ," she gasped, reminding herself to relax. The quicker she did, the faster the tightness in her chest would ease.

Luc scooped her up in his arms and carried her to the sidewalk. He sank down onto the stoop of the nearest building and cradled her in his lap.

"Easy," he murmured, stroking a hand gently over her back. "Easy, sweetheart. Slowly now. Don't struggle. Just let it come back. Easy."

"Geez Louise! Is she okay, man?" Corinne finally got a good lungful of air and opened her eyes just in time to see a scruffy-looking guy in this late twenties jog toward them with wide eyes and an expression of awe. "Did he hit her? At first I thought it looked like a bear had gotten loose in the city, but I bet it was one of those idiot costumed messenger kids. I gotta say, though, I've sure as hell never seen one move that fast. I tried to yell, but he was on top of you before I could even open my mouth. Is your wife going to be okay? You need me to call an ambulance?"

Luc was already moving his hands over her, looking for additional injuries. He looked as grim as death, and twice as menacing.

Corinne offered the stranger a weak smile and shook her head. "I'm fine. I just got the wind knocked out of me. I appreciate the concern, though. We'll just sit here for a minute and catch our breath. You have a good afternoon."

The man looked like he wanted to stay and ask more questions, but Luc raised his head at just that moment, and suddenly the stranger was mumbling something about being late for work and rushing off as if the hounds of hell were nipping at his heels. When Corinne caught sight of Luc's expression, she understood why.

"Okay, I didn't get a good look—because, hey, I was practically knocked unconscious," she said, "but I do know that was no kid on a motorbike that sent me flying. For God's sake, it felt like getting hit by a Mack truck. What the hell was that?"

Luc just shook his head. "Not here. We need to get you inside."

Corinne groaned. "Gee, why do I feel like I've heard that before?"

This time, Luc didn't bother issuing orders or asking directions. He simply picked her up and carried her the remaining three blocks to her building, past a gaggle of teenage girls just out of school, the florist adding water to his rose bouquets, and two of her neighbors on their way upstairs with groceries. When he set her down on the sofa, she still thought he looked about as friendly as Genghis Khan. Which might be why she read a mixed message in the way he began stripping off her clothes.

"Hey," she yelped, smacking at his hands and offering absolutely no impediment to his peeling her shirt over her head and tossing it aside. "Is this like a fetish with you? Every time you get an adrenaline spike, you need to get your dick wet?"

"Just shut up," he growled, unsnapping her pants and pulling them down past her knees. He didn't remove her underwear, though, just pushed the strap of the thong to the side and peered intently at the bare skin of her hip. "I need to see if it marked you."

"Marked me?" Startled and more than a little uneasy, Corinne peered down at her own smooth skin, searching for some invisible brand. "Marked me how? And does this mean you know what that thing was? All I saw was hair and movement and—Christ, I think it had red eyes."

Luc ignored her until he'd flipped her onto her stomach to examine her side and lower back. Finally satisfied, he grabbed a soft throw blanket from the back of the sofa and wrapped it around her before dragging her back into his lap and holding her securely.

"Luc?" she prompted.

He rested his chin on the top of her head. "It was a *barghest.*"

She blinked. "Run that one by me again?"

"A *barghest*."

It sounded like *bar guest* to Corinne, but somehow she didn't think what had run into her was anything quite so innocent.

"Okay, what does that mean?"

He shifted her closer against his chest. "It's a creature from Faerie. Not a very pleasant one, as you've seen."

"Are you telling me that thing was Fae? Because I have to say, if it was, you've got some relatives experimenting with some pretty hinky genetics, buddy."

"Very funny. I've been trying to keep things simple for you when it comes to Faerie, but you have to remember that it's an entire world unto itself. More than one kind of being lives there, and the word *Fae* is a catchall. It just refers to anything that originates in Faerie. It's easy to use it referring to the sidhe, but really it encompasses a lot more."

"The sidhe. You mentioned that word before." She searched her memory. "You said you and Seoc and the Queen were all part of that group."

"Yes. It's a race; or a species, I suppose you could call it. The sidhe are the denizens of Faerie you would look at and equate most closely with humans. We look similar, have similar biologies, even some similarities in culture and civilization."

She positioned her head on his shoulder so she could tilt it back and watch his face as he spoke. "But the sidhe are only one group."

"Correct. There are others, some of whom look similar to humans to varying degrees. Brownies, for instance, could pass for humans in some circumstances. And gnomes are occasionally taken for humans with dwarfism. Even some greater imps can pass, though usually not in daylight. But other creatures could never be mistaken that way."

"For instance?"

"Nightmares and kelpies are an example. They look a bit like horses. And sprites, pixies, and imps. Those are what most closely resemble the Tinker Bell–style 'fairies' that humans are always going on about."

Corinne had begun to get the idea. "And the *barghest*. Did I imagine that looking like some kind of hairy, four-legged pit bull from hell?"

His expression turned grim. "No, you didn't imagine that. They often appear as enormous black dogs."

"Yeah, that sounds about right. But if it's another creature from Faerie, how did it get here in Manhattan? Are those doors still not being guarded?"

"I'm not sure." Luc's hands stroked her arms absently. The lightest touch made her shiver and lean closer. "I am, however, becoming very curious."

"About?"

"When it was discovered that Seoc had snuck out of Faerie and into *Ithir*, everyone assumed that he'd made his way here using one of the doors in the sealed chamber that had been left unguarded."

"Well, how else would he do it? You said the

Queen sealed all the doors except for the ones she controls."

"As much as the Queen might like to think it, she is not infallible." He adjusted her position, dropping his hand to her hip where it cupped and fondled. "The doors have existed for a lot longer than Mab has held the throne—so long that no one knows exactly how they were created. On rare occasions, someone even stumbles over one that has never been discovered before. Or that was hidden very carefully."

Corinne nodded. "Like that one you said was found at the Winter Court. Which is something I don't understand, by the way. Does Faerie have an organized judicial system?"

"Not that kind of court. The royal courts. The sidhe in Faerie are divided into two halves—the Summer Court ruled by Queen Mab, and the Winter Court ruled by her former consort, King Dionnu."

A low whistle met that revelation. "Wow. When they split up, they divided the entire civilization between them? Talk about nasty breakups."

"Mab can hold a grudge."

"I'll say."

"Anyway, doors are occasionally found and used until Mab hears of it and has them sealed as well. It's possible that Seoc left Faerie not through one of the doors Mab controls, but through another entrance entirely."

That made perfect sense. "And if there's a door

in Faerie that no one else knows about, the *barghest* could have come through it. And you implied earlier that the doors don't always work both ways, so maybe whoever comes through it in this direction—"

"Like Seoc."

"—can't use it to return."

"Exactly."

"Then do you think Seoc sent the *barghest* after us?" she asked. "Could that have been what attacked you on the way here yesterday?"

"Yes and no. Yes, I think Seoc must be responsible. Unless you can think of anyone else from Faerie who might want to see you injured." He waited until she shook her head and nodded meaningfully. "But no, it wasn't the *barghest* who came after me yesterday. They're creatures that can't exactly blend into a crown of humans. Other than the black dog, the only form they take is of a goblin."

"A goblin?" She tried to form a mental picture.

"Humanoid, but uglier than sin. Huge nose, claw-like fingers, and ears like a big-eared bat. Think something out of a bad horror film."

"Right. Probably someone would have noticed that. But that means there are at least two people out there trying to get us killed. Unless Seoc could have been there in the crowd yesterday?"

Luc shrugged. "It's possible. I wasn't looking for him, so he could have been there under a glamour that I just didn't catch."

Corinne groaned. "How can this possibly keep getting more complicated?"

"We're just lucky, I guess."

"That's one word for it."

He chuckled and leaned forward until his forehead pressed against hers.

With those amazing green eyes just inches from her own, she felt an entirely new sort of tension creep into her muscles, the kind that had nothing to do with being attacked on the street by a monstrous black dog from the great beyond. Instead, it had to do with the warmth of Luc's breath on her skin, and the weight of his hand on her hip. It had to do with the strength of his arms around her, and the way her heart seemed to adjust its rhythm to beat in time with his.

"I . . . I guess it's better to know," she murmured, her eyes dropping helplessly to his mouth, so tantalizingly close. "I mean, to know what's possible."

He cast her the sort of heavy-lidded glance that made her belly tighten and her mouth water. Of course, the way things were going, she wasn't sure he had any glances that didn't affect her the same way. Was it possible to want someone more with every passing minute?

Was it possible to care about someone this fast?

Luc angled his head until she felt his breath tangle with hers, their lips in perfect alignment, if perhaps a little too far apart for her tastes. His smile was slow, intent, and predatory. "Oh, sweetheart. I can think of any number of things that are possible just now."

Somehow, she didn't think he was talking about Seoc anymore.

She licked her lips, watching his eyes darken as they savored the movement. She wondered if he was picturing himself catching the pink tip of her tongue between his teeth. She also wondered why he didn't go ahead and suit actions to images.

"Possible?" she questioned, her voice barely more than a whisper. Need had closed her throat too much to allow anything else. "Or just . . . appealing."

He continued to tease her, shifting his head back and forth so that his breath teased her like a feathery caress across her lips. It felt like a butterfly kiss, and it made her ache to taste him. She could remember his flavor vividly, sharp and dark and addictively spicy. She wanted more.

"Well, some of the things I'm thinking might be iffy, but I'm willing to work on proving or disproving the theories," he purred. "I will require assistance, though."

Corinne fought the urge to wrestle Luc down onto the carpet and sexually assault him, in blatant defiance of rug burn and stiff muscles and all the other downsides to floor sex. As it was, she could feel her palms itching and her body clenching. Some people might find the news surprising, but she'd never been into overpowering her partner. Maybe she'd been missing something.

Frustration finally made her desperate. Throwing off the enveloping folds of the lap blanket, she twisted in his grasp until she could wrap her arms around him and sink her fingers in the thick, dark silk of his hair. The band he'd used to club back the long strands snapped and went flying. Corinne used her grip on the length of it to drag his mouth to hers.

"Enough teasing," she gasped, sinking her teeth into the flesh of his lower lip and worrying it with fierce delicacy. "What do you say we start exploring those possibilities?"

"I say you still need to buy a bigger bed."

He growled the words against her mouth just before he sealed it with his own, sending the heat between them into a flare-up she was surprised didn't set off her smoke detectors. They kissed deeply, frantically, as they tumbled around on the sofa cushions. Tongues tangled, teeth nipped, lips crushed as if it had been weeks since the last time they'd touched instead of just hours. She couldn't believe any man could make her this frantic, but Luc could.

The instant she touched him, her body began screaming with need, as if he were water and she'd been lost in a desert. She wondered if this was how addicts felt about their fixes, this bone-deep ache to have him, as if she couldn't draw another breath unless he forced the air deep into her lungs.

He tore his mouth from hers and buried it against her breasts, drawing in her scent and laving the soft skin along her neckline with long strokes of his tongue.

"Lady, I can't believe I need you so badly," he groaned. "What have you done to me that I need you this much?"

Corinne moaned, the only reply she could make. It almost frightened her to hear him speak her own thoughts out loud, but she found it vaguely comforting as well. Hearing that, at least she knew she wasn't in this situation all by herself. If he felt about her as strongly as she felt about him, at least she didn't have to worry about an imbalance of power.

What had started with a slow burn of need quickly erupted into a flashfire of desperate lust. She tore at his clothing until fabric ripped and garments went sailing across the room. She thought she heard a crash as Luc's jeans flew into some unsuspecting object, but she couldn't have cared less. She was too busy savoring the heat of his bare skin pressing against her own.

She stroked hr hands over warm bone and muscle, murmuring her approval. His body fascinated her, hard and hot to the touch, but so supple and so vibrantly alive. She could have touched him for hours.

Luc, though, didn't appear to have that kind of patience. His own hands remembered everything they'd learned about her the night before and unerringly sought out all the soft, secret places that made her head spin and her breath catch and her legs weaken. He exploited the knowledge ruthlessly, driving her deeper and deeper into the flames.

Well, two could play at that game. Squirming out of his grip, she bent her head and trailed her lips across his broad chest, following the center crease like a road map to his own personal vulnerability.

When she took him in her mouth, he groaned something obscene.

She smiled and let her teeth and tongue play over sensitive flesh. The way he responded enthralled her. Every touch, every movement, every change in pressure or direction caused his entire body to tauten or flex, to shift or writhe. She felt like a puppeteer moving invisible strings and making her partner dance.

But there was, apparently, a limit to his self-control. He reached it in seconds, his hands shifting from their death grip on her hair to curl around her arms and drag her back up his body until her racing heart pressed up against his and their mouths mated once again like two halves of a magical whole.

She realized the truth of that on an elemental level as he laced their fingers together and gave himself up to the kiss, seeming content to taste her forever. When they made love, it didn't matter who was Fae and who was human, who had powers and who didn't. When they came together, Corinne possessed as much magic as Luc, because being with him made her magical. Together they generated the kind of power that couldn't be contained in just one physical body. It was too much—it must have been stronger than even the Faerie Queen herself, on her best day.

Corinne pulled away and pressed her lips against his throat, his cheeks, his chin. Joy filled her, the joy of being in the perfect place with the perfect man for the perfect moment. When she returned her mouth to his, that joy radiated from her and infused the kiss. Slowly, tenderly, their tongues tangled, no longer frantic or wild, but hungry and wanting and reverent, as if Luc, too, understood the epiphany she had just experienced. She opened her eyes as they kissed and found him watching her. Their gazes locked as he drew her over him and adjusted their bodies until they slid into place like pieces of a puzzle.

Despite the position, Corinne didn't ride him; she worshipped him. Sinking slowly down over him, she whispered with her body of his strength and virility, his courage and intelligence. With her body she compared him to a god, and he responded in kind.

Grasping her hips in his hands, he held her tightly against him as they rocked slowly together, not thrusting or withdrawing, but gently rocking like the ocean waves, his body worshipping her in return. Silently, he compared her to a goddess, showing her the ripe promise of her form, the depth of her tender heart. He showed her the capacity of her body to receive, and the capacity of her heart to give.

They stared into each other's eyes for hours, days, lifetimes, all the while joined together, body to body and heart to heart, in a union both elemental and sacred.

Corinne found herself fighting back tears, and she shook her head in denial. She didn't want anything to mean this much, especially not sex, but she was afraid she was already much too late. This was more than sex, more than lovemaking. Somehow, when she wasn't paying attention, it had become communion, and she feared she'd never be the same again.

In the end, their climax came upon them together, building like the wave their motions mimicked, drawing them under with a powerful force, then lifting them again to the surface and washing them ashore, clean and new and reborn.

Twelve

Some people apparently had no respect for rebirth.

At first Corinne thought the pounding was in her head, but when it was accompanied by a shout, she sat bolt upright on the sofa and stared at her front door. It practically vibrated under the force of the fist that pounded against it. Before she could react, Luc shifted her to the side, slid off the sofa, and appeared at the door between one breath and the next. In his hand he held a lethal-looking silver dagger, and he put his shoulder against the door before he said a word.

"Who is it?" he demanded, voice low and rough and wary.

"Luc, damn it, open the door before I open it myself. It's Fergus."

Corinne frowned. "Who?"

"Just put on some clothes," Luc instructed. "Wear my T-shirt."

She pulled the too-large shirt on over her head and was reaching down to grab his jeans for him when he opened the door. "Luc!"

"Luc, it's about time. I have news."

Corinne watched, horrified, as Luc opened her front door—stark naked—to admit an enormous, auburn-haired man wearing worn blue jeans, a slate-colored T-shirt, and a four-foot broadsword. And his name, apparently, was Fergus.

"What are you doing here?" Luc demanded, apparently oblivious to the fact that he was still bare-assed and probably reeking of sex. Corinne blushed crimson and threw his jeans at his head, half wishing they were made of stone. Though from what she'd learned over the last couple of days, granite would shatter on impact with something as hard as Luc's head. He looked at her a little oddly, but obligingly pulled on his jeans.

"Rafe told me where you would be." Fergus stepped into the apartment, closing the door behind him and ignoring Corinne completely. She wasn't sure if she was insulted or relieved. "The Queen sent me after you."

Luc cursed, stalking back toward the sofa to grab his socks and boots. He sat to pull them on. "For Lady's sake, I've been here two days. What's her bloody royal rush?"

Fergus looked incredulous. "Have you ever known her to be patient before?"

"Fine, but we don't have anything concrete to report to her, so you'll have to tell her you've wasted your trip."

The red-haired Fae winced. "Have mercy, Luc.

You can't send me back entirely empty-handed. She'll crucify me."

Luc hesitated for an instant, then nodded. "Fine, but at the moment all I have to give you are theories and the questions we've just started asking. So far, the answers haven't been as easy to find."

Corinne listened while Luc briefly—very briefly—summarized their work over the last twenty-four hours. Fergus seemed to take it like a blow to the gonads. He even turned a little pale.

"Then the situation is more serious than I thought," the lieutenant murmured.

Luc frowned. "How do you mean?"

Corinne watched while the other man collected himself. "Mab was prompted to send me by a new development at home—a ripple at the Woodland Door."

Fascinated, Corinne watched as Luc looked up from concealing his dagger in his boot and gave his friend a disbelieving stare. "That's impossible."

"So the Queen thought, but apparently we're all mistaken."

"What's the Woodland Door, and why was it rippling? And who the hell are you, by the way?"

Both men turned to Corinne with a look of surprise. They'd probably forgotten she was there. She glared up at them, wishing she were wearing something other than Luc's enormous T-shirt, even if it did cover her from neck to knees. She'd curled her legs up against her chest so she could pull the hem all the way down to her ankles. It still left her lacking a certain amount of dignity.

Fergus spoke first, after raising his eyebrows and giving her an appraising once-over. "This one is not your usual type, friend. A little . . . ordinary, don't you think?"

"She's extraordinary enough to make you eat your teeth if you talk about her like that again," she growled, eyes narrowing in a violent glare. She decided quickly that she really didn't like Fergus.

Luc put his arm around her and hugged her to his side, sending Fergus a glare of his own. "Corinne, this is Fergus of Eithdne. He serves as my lieutenant, when he's not making an ass of himself. And sometimes when he is." Fergus didn't even blink at the insult. He was too busy watching them curiously. "Fergus, this is Corinne D'Alessandro."

Fergus looked from Corinne to Luc and back again. "She's human."

He said it the way he might've said *She's a woolly mammoth*—with total disbelief, as if checking to make sure Luc hadn't missed the pertinent facts.

"She's also not deaf, you Fae freak," she growled, "so you might want to try being civil. Or don't you guys have manners where you come from?"

Fergus stiffened and rested his hand on the hilt of his sword.

Corinne laughed. "Oh, right. I tell you when you're being a raving jerk and you reach for the sword. What happens if I call you an asshole? Do you have a hand grenade in your pocket?"

She might have laughed at the way the interloper's jaw dropped if she hadn't been hoping to see it rot off.

He looked at Luc. "She can't possibly see my sword. I charmed it before I left Rafe's. It's under illusion."

"Not a very good one, I guess, because I can see it as clear as day," she informed him before Luc could open his mouth. "I can also see right through you, to what an enormous jerk you are."

Fergus frowned. "Can you see this?"

He waved his hand around for a second before he opened his closed fist to reveal a perfectly formed flower resting in the palm of his hand. Corinne frowned. "Yeah, it's an orchid. So what?"

The Fae ignored her question and turned to Luc.

"That's impossible," he said in the sort of tone that brooked no argument. "There's only one reason she would be able to see through the masking glamour on my sword, but not notice anything odd about a simple creation spell. That reason, however, is clearly a ludicrous bit of nonsense. She's human. She can't possibly be your hea—"

"She doesn't know what she is, Fergus, and I don't have time to explain it to her," Luc interrupted, giving his friend a meaningful stare. "So why don't you let it go for now and tell me what you know about the door."

The other Fae nodded briefly and took a seat on the edge of an armchair. "Right. Mab sent me because she detected—"

"Um, hello?" Corinne interrupted, struggling very hard to resist grabbing them both by their hair and ramming their heads together as hard as she could. Maybe it would knock some sense into one or the other. "Person here who doesn't know what the hell you're talking about. What is the Woodland Door?"

Fergus glared at her, so she glared right back, but Luc hurried to answer her question before they came to blows. "Remember the doors we've been talking about for the last day and a half? The Woodland Door is one of those. It's been sealed for centuries, but at one time it led from a forest here on this island to a forest in Faerie. That's how it got its name."

"A forest in Manhattan?"

"Well, it used to be in a forest. Now there's no telling where it is, though I'm guessing in an area that's at least lightly wooded. It has an affinity for trees."

She groaned. "Of course it does."

"Central Park, maybe?" he guessed.

Corinne had recently learned that Central Park was practically a hotbed of Other activity. Between Faerie doors and werewolf pack meetings, she didn't think she'd ever be able to set foot in the place again. She almost longed for the days when the weirdest things going on in there were protest rallies and creative flashers.

"Can I go on now?"

She rolled her eyes at Fergus's petulant tone, but Luc just nodded.

"Fine. So as I was saying . . ." He paused to glare at Corinne. She smiled sweetly, just because she knew it would piss him off. "Last night, after you had left, we stationed extra guards in the Chamber of Doors. Everything seemed normal until around midnight, when Connor and Ewen said they felt a disturbance in the air. They alerted me, and I sent for the Queen."

"What did she find?" Luc asked.

"At first nothing, and she was less than pleased. I thought she was going to banish all three of us to bogle duty for a century or more. But then it happened again, and this time we all felt it. An Undoing charm."

"That shouldn't do a thing, though. Mab made sure her seals couldn't be undone by something that simple."

"I know," Fergus nodded, "but then we felt a Passing charm cast, and that's when the Queen got nervous."

Luc scowled. "That would still never be enough to open a sealed door."

"No, but if what you suspect is true, it might be enough to force a hidden door to reveal itself. After the ripples stopped at the Woodland Door, something pushed at the Hearthstone Door as well."

Luc's only response was a curse, and this time even Corinne thought she understood what he had to swear about. If she understood correctly, what Fergus had just told them was that Seoc had very nearly discovered the location of the hidden door between Faerie and *Ithir*. Once that happened, nothing would stop him from wreaking all the havoc Luc had described on an unsuspecting Manhattan.

"Okay, I admit that sounds like it sucks," she ventured, wrapping her arms around her knees. "But it's not like he's already done the deed. We still have time to beat him to it, right? I mean, if he's trying every door he finds in turn, he'll get to the right one eventually. We just need to get there first."

"If it were that easy," Fergus snapped, "don't you think we would already be there?"

Corinne jerked back, feeling like she'd been slapped. She had never been one to count solely on first impressions, but so far all her impressions of Fergus told her he was a creep. She snarled, "Listen, freak boy—"

"Stop it," Luc growled. "I don't have time to listen to you two squabble." Fergus subsided under a Captain-of-the-Guard glare, and Corinne shut up when Luc turned a similar expression on her. "Of course that is the intention, Corinne, but locating a hidden Faerie door isn't the easiest thing to do."

She blinked. "Well, duh. If it were, I sure as hell hope we'd have accomplished something more useful by now."

"Useful? A human? How droll."

"Fergus. Shut. Up." Luc spared a glare at the other Fae before turning back to Corinne. "Faerie doors don't work like physical doors. A Faerie door isn't a door at all. It works entirely differently, because it isn't usually fixed to any one spot. Mab fixed the doors on the Faerie side because she always wanted to see who came into or left her realm, but on this side she wanted to make them difficult to find, so she charmed them to open in random locations unless she specifically requested otherwise."

Corinne shook her head. "Do I detect a hint of paranoia? Still, I suppose we're lucky she was so worried, since it's kept Seoc from finding the right door yet."

"Yes, but he's had a lot more time to look than we have now," Luc said, getting to his feet with a grim expression. "If we want to get to the door first, we need to find out from the Queen where it is."

"And how do we do that?" Corinne asked. "I don't suppose she's got a cell phone."

He shook his head. "We don't need a phone to contact her. Before we do, I want to talk to the head of the Council. I have a feeling we're going to need all the help we can get if we plan to spring a trap for Seoc."

"How can Rafe help us?"

Luc shot her a look of surprise. "As head of the Council, he'll have a direct link to communicate with Mab. He can put us in touch with her faster than trying to reach her ourselves."

"A direct link? What is he, some sort of official ambassador?"

"Someone has to maintain diplomatic ties between the worlds. On *Ithir*, it's the responsibility of the head of the Council."

"Right. Great. Looks like we go talk to Rafe then. Just give me five minutes."

"What for?"

She was already heading for the bedroom. "So I can get dressed."

She heard him sigh. "All right. I'm going to call Rafe and tell him we're on our way."

"What makes you think we plan to take a human along with us?"

Even if she'd been deaf, Corinne couldn't have missed the sarcastic, arrogant tone in Fergus's voice.

"Because if you don't, I'll just follow you," she explained. "And then I'll get all pissy. When I get pissy, I'll bitch about you to Reggie and Missy. In turn, they'll bitch about you to Misha and Graham, and then there'll be this whole big interdimensional incident just because you got your shorts in a knot." She stopped in the hallway door and looked over her shoulder at him. "So do you really want to go there? I kinda thought we were pressed for time."

She stalked back into her bedroom to the sound of Luc's chuckle and Fergus's curses in a language she didn't recognize. It was just as well. They would probably just have pissed her off even more. And she was already planning to stash a metric buttload of aspirin in her backpack to take with her. Judging by the size of the headache Fergus had given her, that might spare him from her wrath for about an hour. Two, if he'd learn to keep his mouth shut.

It amazed her that one Fae—namely Fergus—could be so obnoxious and set her teeth on edge in a nanosecond, while another—that would be Luc—could give her that scary, happy, glowing feeling in her chest. She must have lost her mind.

As she pulled a pair of comfortable worn jeans out of her dresser drawer, she heard Fergus yell something impatient and rude from her living room. Eyes narrowing, she decided to make it two metric buttloads of aspirin. Just in case.

Thirteen

Five minutes, Corinne decided as she climbed out of the cab she and her two enormous companions had squeezed into for the trip to Rafe's Upper East Side home. That's all she needed, just five minutes of peace, of uninterrupted privacy where she could sit down, take a deep breath, and try to figure out just what the hell was going on and when exactly she'd gotten on this ride that wouldn't stop. Was it really so much to ask?

Apparently.

Reggie and Missy were waiting for her when she, Luc and Fergus arrived at Rafe's front door. They'd barely gotten the damned thing closed behind them before her friends pounced. Corinne looked to Luc for rescue, but the damned man was already huddled with her traitorous friends' traitorous husbands.

"All right, Rinne, spill it," Reggie demanded, crossing her arms over her chest and fixing her friend with an expectant stare. "What in blazes in going on?"

"Yeah. Why did Graham and Dmitri drag us all

the way over here mumbling something about dip-lomatic ties, interdimensional incidents, and the end of the world as we know it?"

Missy mustered up an intimidating glare, but the effect paled a bit when she began rubbing her hand over her swollen belly. She was currently three months' pregnant and, ridiculously enough, half-way to term. She looked at least six months along, which was just one of the results of getting knocked up by a werewolf, apparently.

"It's a really long story." Corinne tried to ease her way past them and closer to Luc. Even if the fink hadn't come to her rescue, he'd make an aw-fully big obstacle to hide behind, if she could move quick enough.

"Not a chance," Reggie snapped. "Even if you could move faster than Missy, which I doubt, you sure as hell wouldn't be faster than me. So stay put and start talking."

"Damn it, Reg!" Corinne stopped sidling to-ward Luc and threw up her hands. "You know how much I hate it when you do that! I don't care how cool you think it is, stay the hell out of my mind!"

"I'm not in your mind, you idiot." Reggie straightened up haughtily and looked offended. "I don't need to read you when you're broadcasting so loud, a deaf dog could hear you. You should be glad I didn't bring up what else you're broadcast-ing."

"You don't need to," Missy put in, her face taking on an arch expression. "I can smell it. Our dearest friend has been getting down and dirty with the man in black over there. And—" She paused, and Corinne tried not to notice that she was inhaling delicately. "—the man in black is not quite human."

"Corinne!" Reggie gasped, fighting back a smile. "I thought you only wanted to get involved with human men. I thought you said Others weren't your type."

"She's clearly been fibbing."

Blushing scarlet, Corinne was all ready to turn around and head right back out the door when Luc called her name.

He turned away from the men's huddle and held his hand out to her. "Come here. I think this will all be a lot easier if we explain to everyone at once." He turned back to Rafe and raised his eyebrows. "Think we can move into the living room and sit down?"

Trying desperately to act casual, Corinne ignored the stares of her friends and Luc's outstretched hand as she crossed to his side. He didn't get offended, just wrapped the hand around her instead, resting his palm possessively on her hip. She pretended not to notice, but she couldn't help seeing the way Rafe's dark eyebrows shot up, and his normal expression of lazy amusement took on a decided note of curiosity.

"By all means," the suave werecat said, gesturing for the others to precede him through the double doors that led to his living room. "Let's make ourselves comfortable. Can I offer anyone a drink?"

"Sure."

"Yes."

"Absolutely."

"Hell, yeah."

Rafe chuckled. "I'll just open the bar, shall I? That way we can all help ourselves."

They made an odd little party as they filed into Rafe's immaculately decorated living room. The damned thing was about twice the size of Corinne's entire apartment. Was it, like, a rule that all the Others in Manhattan had to be obscenely rich?

Rafe settled himself behind the bar and began setting decanters and bottles onto the inlaid top, while Fergus took about three steps into the room and leaned his shoulder against the fireplace mantel. He seemed determined to be a pill.

Reggie and Missy tried to herd Corinne toward the sofa, but Luc actually came in handy and steered her to a love seat, taking the place beside her and draping his arm casually over her shoulders. She saw Reggie start to protest, but Misha hooked an arm around his wife's waist and sank down on a retro-looking curved armchair, pulling her onto his lap. When Reggie opened her mouth to protest, he shook his head and gave her a quelling look.

Graham just led Missy to where he wanted her to sit, helped ease her down into the chair, and sat on the floor at her feet with one knee drawn up to his chest and his arm draped over it. It looked like a casual pose, but Corinne saw he had Missy completely hemmed in and gave a sigh of relief. Luc noticed and flashed her an amused look.

"Champagne, I think." Rafe's voice rumbled through the tense silence, and Corinne looked over to see him holding aloft a black glass bottle. "Would anyone care to join me?"

"You think we have something to celebrate? You should know this matter is too grave not to be taken seriously."

"I take many things seriously, Fergus," Rafe replied, bracing the bottle against his thigh as he eased the cork from the top. "However, I fail to see how all hope is lost."

"Then maybe you don't really have a grasp on the situation. Would you like me to explain?"

Corinne felt her eyes widen. "I know red hair is supposed to indicate a quick temper," she muttered to Luc, "but I had no idea it also equated to rudeness and criminal stupidity."

"Watch it, Emily Post," he murmured back.

The man made more pop references than she did half the time, and wondering how he'd become so conversant in human culture threatened to drive her crazy. She reminded herself to ask him about it later. Right now she wanted to watch the fireworks.

"I hardly think I need any explanations from you, Fergus, nor is this the time for us to listen to you throw a tantrum," Rafe purred. Not the way a cat being stroked purrs, but the way a leopard feasting on the entrails of his kill does. "However, if you feel the need to question my understanding, I would be happy to discuss it with you. Later. Alone."

Corinne shuddered and decided to be very sure she wasn't around for later.

"Can we get down to business?" Luc asked, cutting through the tension and drawing all eyes off Rafe and Fergus and onto him and Corinne. She fought the urge to squirm.

"I think that is a marvelous idea." Dmitri shifted Reggie on his lap and spoke over the top of her auburn head. "Perhaps you could fill us in on what is happening, Luc. Rafe already told us of the reason for this most recent visit of yours to our world, but I suspect something important has happened if both you and Fergus felt the need to call us all together here."

"The calling-together was Rafe's idea, but I'll admit it was a good one. From what Fergus told me, I have a feeling it's going to take all of us to wrap up this mess." Luc reached out a hand to accept the glass of champagne Rafe handed to him and passed it to Corinne. "And we don't have a lot of time."

Across the room, Graham sighed and rested his right hand on Missy's distended belly. "Then I suggest you make with the storytelling, buddy."

Corinne watched and listened and sipped champagne as Luc filled the others in on the saga of

Seoc, Hibbish, Rabbi Aaronson, and the Faerie doors. Everyone but Fergus listened intently, their faces growing grimmer as the tale came out. No one seemed pleased to hear about what was going on, and Corinne found herself feeling almost sorry for Seoc. She certainly wouldn't want these five men—well, these four men and a sorry-assed excuse for an ill-mannered Fae—to add her to their fecal rosters. Just the thought made her shiver.

Luc must have noticed, because he tightened his arm around her and began to rub his hand up and down her arm, as if chafing some warmth into her. She grimaced when she saw both Reggie and Missy make note of the motion and exchange *Aha!* glances. Maybe if she climbed over so she was sitting directly behind Luc, they'd forget she was there.

When Luc finally stopped speaking, Dmitri grunted. "I can see why you were concerned, *brahtok*. The Queen's nephew is breaking at least five clauses from the concordance between our peoples. I think Rafael would agree that the Others are as anxious as you are to see him stopped and returned to Faerie."

Rafe nodded over the rim of his champagne flute. "Of course. We will be happy to do all we can to help you."

Luc turned his gaze to Dmitri. "Will it involve more this time than giving me your phone number and wishing me luck?"

Dmitri chuckled. "If more is required, of course it will." He cast a knowing glance at the arm Luc still had snugged around Corinne's shoulders. "But I believe you have managed to discover quite a bit all on your own. Do you disagree?"

Luc smiled lazily in return. "No, I don't suppose I do. Remind me to thank you later, *brahtok*."

"Excuse me," Corinne snapped, looking from one self-satisfied male face to the other, "but I'm sitting right here, and I'm not brain-dead. Do you think you could refrain from talking about me as if I were an object? At least while I'm in the room to hear you?"

Luc brushed his lips against her temple, and she could feel his suppressed laughter. "Maybe. It'll be tough, but I'll make the effort."

A strange squeaking noise made them both turn to look at Reggie. She sat in Dmitri's lap, struggling to get to her feet, but he held her easily with his arms wrapped around her waist.

"That's it!" Reggie cried, grabbing her husband's wrists and attempting to pull his hands off her. "I want to know what you've done to Corinne! Have you cast some sort of weird Fae love spell on her? Have you?"

Dmitri tried to hush her, but he was having trouble speaking over his laughter. Reggie ignored him.

"What makes you think I had to use magic to make her love me?" Luc asked. "I think I may be insulted."

"Oh, no, you'll know when you've been insulted," Missy growled from the other side of the room, "because I'm about to insult you big time. What kind of dirty, rotten, manipulative, rat-faced bastard plays with someone's emotions like that? You ought to be ashamed of yourself! Graham, let me go! I want to hit him. Hard."

Corinne groaned and tried to squirm out from under Luc's arm, but he was having none of it. "Would you all stop it? You, too, Mr. Grabby Hands." She glared at Luc before turning back to her primary targets. "And you, my supposed friends who went and got involved with figments of the collective human imagination long before I ever met the guy you want to punish, who the hell do you think you are? If I want to fall in love with a three-toed tree sloth, I'd like to see you try to stop me."

Breathing hard, she jerked back and felt her eyes widen. Had she just shouted that she was in love with Luc? Had she?

"We don't care who you fall in love with," Missy said. "Though the tree sloth thing might take some getting used to. But we do care when you have a spell cast on you by some unscrupulous Fae Lothario."

"For your information, there is no magic involved here," she retorted. "Luc couldn't use magic to make me love him if he tried. He's already told me his illusions don't work on me. So there."

She realized that the *so there* might come across as a little childish, but when faced with the choice between saying it and sticking her tongue out, she went with the verbal jab and patted herself on the back for her restraint.

She also braced herself for another volley of arguments, but it never came. Instead, every eye in the room turned to stare at her and Luc, and every jaw—except Fergus's—dropped to the floor. Her friends were dumbstruck, and Corinne had no idea what was wrong with them. She looked from face to face, reading in each the exact same expression of stunned disbelief. Finally, she crossed her arms over her chest and gave a distinct harrumph.

"What?" she demanded.

Luc froze and wondered what the best way was to convey to everyone in the room that the first person to inform Corinne she was his heartmate would die a slow, gruesome, and painful death at his hands. Did that need to be in writing?

"Corinne, are you serious? Do you understand what you just said?"

Missy was the first to recover from the initial shock of Corinne's revelation, and Luc fought back a wave of regret. He hated to harm Graham's unborn cub, but figured his friend would see the necessity. He braced himself to leap off the sofa and tackle her.

"If that's true, then you're Luc's—"

"Missy, honey," Graham cut in, "I don't think it's polite to question Corinne about her feelings for Luc. That's between the two of them."

"But, Graham, you heard what she said," Reggie protested. "And she clearly has no idea of the significance—"

"Whether or not this is true, it is none of your business, *dushka*." Dmitri's voice was stern but loving. "It is not your place to have this discussion with Corinne."

Luc sent his friends grateful looks, but apparently his heartmate actually wanted him to have to kill her friends.

"No, let them talk," she said, arms crossed over her chest, her kissable mouth turned down in a scowl. He recognized that expression better than her smile, he mused. "My friends can say anything they want to me. I can tell them myself that they're full of crap."

"But Corinne, you don't understand about Luc," Reggie said. "He's not like other men. He's not like humans."

"Oh, and you're one to talk, Mrs. Fang." Corinne cast an apologetic look at Dmitri, who just grinned. "You're the one who started all of this. We all led perfectly normal lives until you decided to bump uglies with a guy on a liquid diet."

"Rinne, he's clouded your mind!"

Corinne laughed, even though Luc didn't think she sounded all that amused. "Am I the only one who finds this scene strangely familiar, only with different cast members in the leading roles? You gonna wave a cross at me, Reg? Or maybe some—"

She paused, frowning, and looked at Luc. "What

do you use against Fae, anyway? I know there was something in all those stories."

"Cold iron," he murmured, trying not to laugh.

"Right." She turned back to Reggie. "Maybe some cold iron then. Don't be such a hypocrite."

"Reggie is not trying to be a hypocrite, and neither am I," Missy said in her I'm-the-moderator-here voice. "We're just concerned about you."

Luc broke in at that point. He just couldn't take the chance of this going on any longer. "You have no need to be concerned. I will do everything in my power to take care of Corinne. You have my word."

His loving heartmate thumped him across the chest. "What about if I want to take care of you? I'm not some helpless porcelain doll, you know."

Luc winced and rubbed the spot where her fist had landed. "Yes, I know. It was a figure of speech. Regina, Melissa, I swear to you, I will tell Corinne everything, and I will allow her just as many choices as I can. You have my word on it. But now isn't the time. We need to find Seoc and protect the Faerie door before it's too late."

He watched while the two women looked at him, at Corinne, at their husbands, and back at him.

"All right," Reggie said, without sounding all that pleased about it. "We'll give you until Seoc is back in Fae hands, but not a minute more. And we expect you to be completely honest, and to respect her wishes. Is that clear?"

Luc looked at the petite, fledgling vampire and the delicate human Luna and almost laughed, but then he looked at the eight-hundred-year-old vampire and the alpha Lupine who were their mates, and nodded respectfully. "It's clear. And again, you have my word on it."

He heard Corinne snarl next to him and looked down into her irritated eyes. He had the nearly overwhelming urge to kiss the tip of her wrinkled nose, but figured unless he wanted to risk losing his tongue, he'd better refrain.

"I have no idea what's going on here," she growled, "but I'm pretty damned sure it's pissing me off."

He couldn't help grinning. "I'll explain everything later, but right now we have work to do."

Fourteen

Once everyone stopped trying to run Corinne's love life for her, they were actually able to get to the reason they had all met up at Rafe's house—to develop a plan for trapping Seoc and getting him safely back to Faerie.

"I take it jumping out of the woods or wherever with a big net isn't going to cut it, huh?" Missy's mouth twisted into a grimace as she rubbed her belly and sipped from the champagne glass full of milk that Rafe had handed her.

"Not exactly," Luc said. "Seoc is intelligent enough to be hard to catch at the best of times, but he knows that if he's caught this time, the Queen is not going to be nearly so lenient as in the past."

"Yeah. Because it's better to catch him now, when he's trying to end the world, than it would have been, oh, say, the last billion times he's caused trouble and gotten no more than a slap on the wrist." Corinne ignored Luc's horrified expression. "Either way, though, I doubt the net is going to be all that effective. Because I'm guessing even these guys don't have, like, a magic net."

"No magic nets." Rafe actually let her down politely, which was more than she could say for Fergus's dismissive snort. "But I believe we make up for in numbers what we would otherwise lack in . . . nets."

Luc nodded. "As long as I can count on you all for support, I'm not worried. The trick is going to be finding the door and getting to it before he does." He looked hopefully at Rafe and Dmitri. "I don't suppose that particular bit of intelligence is something passed down from Council head to Council head?"

"I wish that it were, *brahtok,* but if any of the others had such knowledge, they never passed it on to me." Dmitri shrugged. "I doubt anyone did know, however. Mab is not the sort who would trust such knowledge to an outsider."

"Yeah," Luc said. "The problem is that she didn't trust it to any insiders, either."

"Um, wasn't that the question we were going to ask the Queen?" Corinne interrupted. She only saw four male faces grimace, because she didn't bother looking at Fergus.

"I was hoping we wouldn't have to," Luc said with a sigh. "I have a feeling she's going to be a little . . . cranky."

"Why? Because she didn't bother to provide you with vital information before you came here? Or because it's been twenty-four whole hours and you haven't managed to accomplish your mission?"

Luc just looked at her. "No. Because she's the Queen."

"It might be better if you waited outside."

Corinne looked at Luc as if he'd lost his mind and reached past him for the doorknob to Rafe's library. The host had offered to let them use the private space for their talk with the Faerie Queen. "Thanks, but I want to see this."

He grabbed her hand. "No, really," he repeated, slowly and deliberately. "It would be better."

"I don't particularly care. I'm not planning to interfere, but I want to hear this conversation. Are you telling me I can't come with you?"

"Would it do any good if I did?"

"Not a bloody bit."

"And that's why I would never try to tell you anything of the sort. But I am trying to let you know it might be better—"

He looked at her expression, sighed, and opened the library door. "Fine. But don't say I didn't warn you."

She rolled her eyes. "I'll sign a waiver."

"If only I believed that."

She ignored him and strode into the library ahead of him, waiting while he closed and locked the door. She expected to see him batten down the hatches and don Kevlar, with the way he'd been acting. "So what do we have to do?"

His eyebrows shot up and she thought he turned a little paler. "We don't have to do anything. I will take care of everything. You will sit quietly and try not to look directly at the Queen."

She scoffed. "Why? Will the sight of her turn me to stone, or drive me mad, or something?"

"No!" He looked appalled. "I just don't want you to make her mad."

"Hey!"

He ignored her protest, took her by the shoulders, and pushed her down into a leather club chair, placing her hands on the arms and warning her sternly to keep them there. She considered boxing his ears instead, but he refused to let go.

"Now," he said, putting his face right up to hers and looking at her the way her third-grade teacher, Sister Mary Agnes, had when Corinne had gotten into trouble. "This is going to be a delicate sort of situation. Since you're not familiar with the protocols of the Faerie court, or how the Queen expects to be addressed, I will do all of the talking. *All* of the talking. Understand?"

She glared at him. Seething.

"You will sit very still, keep your eyes on the floor or the fireplace mantel, and stay absolutely silent. Understand?"

She bared her teeth at him. If they hadn't been clenched so tightly, she might have sunk them into something vital. Like his jugular. And here she thought only folks like Graham got the urge to rip out throats with their teeth. That was before she met Luc.

"Oh, I understand," she said, very, very softly.

"I understand that you'd better be very careful not to turn your back on me anytime soon, Lucifer. God knows you obviously can't trust me to control myself."

"Right." He nodded. "So long as we understand each other."

She watched through narrowed eyes and a strange red fog while he straightened up and took two steps away from her chair, facing the large cabinet against the wall. Opening the door, he revealed an elaborate panel of stained glass carefully mounted in a wooden frame.

Corinne wasn't precisely sure what she had expected to see, but she knew this wasn't it. Maybe she'd been prepared for him to recite a few lines of bad poetry, or chalk arcane symbols on the floor, or sacrifice a chicken, or something. Hell, even a little chanting and a stick or two of incense would have been nice, but somehow she'd been expecting magic to look a little bit more . . . well . . . magical.

This way, all she got to see was Luc make a weird gesture with his right hand before the panes of brightly colored glass began to shine and turn liquid, rippling like the surface of a pond. Then all at once the picture in the glass disappeared and Corinne found herself looking at the face of the most beautiful woman she had ever seen.

Eyes the deep, stormy green of a cold-water ocean seemed to glow in a face that had the complexion of a bowl of vanilla cream. Her sharp,

angular, and yet wholly feminine bone structure
could make an angel jealous. Her brows were thin,
dark, and arching, and her eyelashes were long
and thick. Her red-gold hair, worn long and loose,
shone like a halo around her. Corinne felt her jaw
drop and wondered if there weren't another reason why Luc had told her not to look directly at
the Queen.

When she spoke, the Queen's voice was musical
and her words rang from her mouth like the chim-
ing of a bell. "Hello, my Lucifer. I did not expect
to have you call me this eve. Have you word of my
nephew?"

Corinne watched as the man who had refused
to concede anything to her without a fight bowed
neatly from the waist and addressed the vision with
deferential courtesy.

"My Queen, I have discovered some things
about Seoc, but I'm afraid it is not heartening
news."

"Yes, well, I expected as much."

The Queen's airy, dismissive tone made Corinne's
eyes widen and made Luc straighten his already
military posture. "You expected it, my Queen?"

Mab nodded. "Why, yes. I assumed that if Seoc
were really ignoring my summons, he must be doing something worth angering me. So naturally,
I assumed he was attempting to open the door."

"And you didn't tell me?"

Even after only knowing him for a day, Corinne
could tell that this slow, deep, controlled tone of

voice meant Luc was about one step from committing a violent act. She watched curiously, wondering if perhaps it was a really good thing that he was only speaking to a vision of the Queen, and not in her physical presence. She assumed that the Fae still frowned on regicide.

"You are my finest warrior. I assumed you would find out soon enough, my Lucifer, as I see you have." The Queen seemed to turn her head and her lips curved in a bewitching smile. "Ah. I see you have indeed found something to please you, my Lucifer. As I said you would."

"Me?"

Corinne heard the squeak, but it took a few seconds to realize it had come from her own lips. She honestly hadn't meant to speak, but the Queen's comment had caught her off guard.

"Corinne . . ." Luc's voice was a growl, and she shot him an apologetic look.

"Do not scold her, my Lucifer. I was indeed speaking of her, and I would speak to her now. I had hoped you would bring her to me."

Oookay. Corinne could practically hear the theme from the *Twilight Zone* playing in the background, but she sat up straighter in her chair and eyed the Queen warily.

"Tell me, child, what is your name?"

"Corinne. D'Alessandro."

"Ah. Lovely." The Queen smiled. "And what do you think of my Lucifer, young Corinne?"

Young Corinne? For Pete's sake, she hadn't been

referred to that way since this past Thanksgiving, when her great-aunt Corinne had died and she had finally moved up to the "big people's table" for dinner. She saw Luc watching her, a look of horrified panic on his face, and kept her thoughts to herself. "I think he's . . . very dedicated."

"Yes, he is. And though he dedicates himself to few things, he is unswervingly loyal to them."

Not knowing what else to do, Corinne gave a murmur of agreement.

"But what I really wanted to know, Corinne, is what you think of Lucifer as a heartmate."

"A what?" She heard Luc's groan even over her question.

"A heartmate. Surely you've given some thought as to how well he suits you? Not that you can refuse to have him, of course, but I am curious to know how a human would feel to be bound so to one of our kind."

"Bound? How he *suits* me? *Can't refuse him?*" Her voice rose an octave with each question. She was about to leap out of her chair and issue a very blunt demand that the Queen of Faerie explain just what the hell she was talking about when Luc stepped forward and put a hand on her shoulder to press her down into her chair. She wanted to know what the hell was going on, damn it.

"My Queen," he began, his voice carefully controlled and only a tiny bit more forceful than usual, "I am sure Corinne is honored by your attention, but I am afraid that Seoc's actions leave us short on time. We need your help if we're going to bring him back soon and safely."

Mab looked back toward Luc and frowned. If she weren't the Faerie Queen and a powerful magical force, Corinne might have come to hate her for being able to do that and still look gorgeous. Scary, but gorgeous.

"Do not speak to me as if I do not grasp the situation, my Lucifer. I am well aware of all that is at stake, as I am well aware that I ordered you to take care of it."

Corinne could actually hear Luc gritting his teeth.

"I am doing my best, my Queen, but I am afraid Seoc had too long to plan his attack before we became aware of it. I fear that if you cannot provide us with the information we need, I will be too late to stop him from opening the door permanently."

"That would leave me very displeased."

"I know."

Corinne watched as the Faerie Queen and the Captain of her Guard eyed each other warily from across the worlds. Any second now she expected to hear a haunting whistle and see a tumbleweed blow past. Finally, Mab spoke.

"The door," she snapped. "I can tell you where it is, but it will be up to you to reach it before Seoc. And I can tell you that I feel he is very close. By moonrise tomorrow, it will be too late to stop him."

"Then we'll get to him before that."

"Very well." Mab pursed her lips, looked from Luc to Corinne and back again. "You should consider yourself very lucky I cannot take back the gift I have given you, Lucifer, for I begin to doubt whether you truly deserve it."

"It is already mine," he growled, "and you are the least of the dangers I would risk to keep it."

Corinne thought she saw a smile tease the corners of the Queen's mouth, but then the woman in the vision lifted her chin and schooled her face into a haughty mask. "Remember you said that, my Lucifer, for I know that I will. The door waits for now at the Old Stone Gate. I expect you to find it before my nephew does."

While Corinne stared in fascination, the Queen turned her back on them and the vision shimmered before smoothing out, until nothing but quiet, colored glass remained where it had been. Blinking rapidly to adjust her eyes, Corinne wished she knew a technique to adjust her brain as well, but she had a feeling it was already much too late for that. Still feeling a bit dazed, she followed Luc out of the room.

Fergus and Rafe were waiting outside the door, putting the kibosh on any chance Corinne might have had to ask Luc the questions that spun through her mind. The foremost of which happened to be something like, *What the hell?*

"So?" Rafe drawled, not bothering to straighten from his lazy slouch against the wall.

Fergus put things a bit more bluntly. "Where's the door?"

Corinne smirked and waved. "And here I thought you'd never ask. Bye now! Don't remember to write!"

Luc growled.

"Oh, fine." Corinne crossed her arms peevishly. "He can be uncivil all by himself then, and I'll just take it like a good little martyr."

Rafe stepped forward, putting an arm around Corinne's shoulders and leading her back down the hall to the living room. She could hear Luc's growls get louder even over the chuckling purr Rafe was making. Could none of these men behave even halfway normally?

"Just ignore him," Rafe said. "He'll get over himself soon enough."

"Fergus or Luc?"

He hummed. "Both, I imagine."

"Yeah, that'd be great," she said, "but we still have the tiny problem of having to work together until we find Seoc."

"But that won't be a problem on either count." The problem with not looking at Fergus was that she could still hear him. "Now that we know where the door is, we can just go there and wait for him, and since we don't need a human getting in the way, you can go home and we'll work just fine without you."

Corinne turned just in time to see Luc yank the other Fae to a stop by the braid. "The next time you speak that way to her, I'm going to break something. Probably your pretty nose," he growled. "So stop. Now."

Fergus whined. "She started it."

"And she has now stopped." He raised an eyebrow at Corinne. "Haven't you?"

Ooh. So she got to play the moral superiority angle without actually having to be superior? Fabulous! "Absolutely. My lips are sealed."

"Good. Keep them sealed. Both of you." He released Fergus's braid, stepped forward, peeled Rafe's arm off Corinne's shoulder, and replaced it with his own. "Let's get back to the others. I only want to go through this once."

"Sounds like more than enough for me," she mumbled.

She didn't say another word while he dragged her back into the living room and pushed her down onto the love seat. She even refrained from commenting during his retelling of the conversation with Mab. She was very proud of herself.

When he finished, Graham was frowning. "The Old Stone Gate? Is that supposed to be here in Manhattan? Because I've never heard of it."

"I have." Dmitri shifted Reggie in his lap and leaned forward. "I thought it was an old legend, and I cannot say I don't still think it is. It is supposed to be a hidden gate, more powerful than anything the Fae wanted known about, here in the city in an old wooded grove. I heard that more than the Fae used it at one time, to travel between farther-flung places than Faerie and *Ithir*."

"But it can't still be standing, can it?" Reggie asked. "I mean, Manhattan hasn't exactly remained unchanged for centuries or anything. It must have been torn down or built over or something, right?"

Missy chimed in. "Yeah. It would have to be long gone, wouldn't it? There are no real woods left here. Even Central Park was landscaped and planted to be the way it looks now. You'd have to go off the island to get a grove that's been around long enough for the Fae to consider it old."

"Not true," Graham said, an expression of slow understanding beginning to light his face. "There is one place on the island that contains original woodland."

"Inwood Hill Park." Corinne spoke the epiphany aloud. "It's where Peter What's-His-Face supposedly bought the island from the Indians for a pile of souvenirs, at the northernmost tip of the island." She frowned. "But I don't remember any old stone gates up there. It's all hiking trails and stuff. A gate wouldn't have remained hidden for long from all the joggers and dog walkers. I mean, it's not as busy as Central Park, but it's hardly desolate, either."

Rafe shook his head. "It wouldn't need to be. If the Fae considered it a hidden gate, then likely it wouldn't be recognized as anything at all to anyone else. It could be nothing more than a crevice in some rock."

"Well, there's plenty of rock up there, so I suppose anything is possible."

Luc nodded. "That's likely where we'll need to be then."

Fifteen

Fergus wanted to head to Inwood immediately, because he was apparently a big fan of the abject-failure scenario. Corinne almost bit through her tongue keeping that observation in check, but she really was trying to be good, so she kept silent and let Luc explain that tomorrow would be a better bet.

"The moon will be new. He'll need that extra help if he's going to undo Mab's seals. He's too smart to try tonight, only to end up failing."

When she later asked him to explain that without making her brain hurt, he summed it up as, "Magic. If you're trying to get rid of magic things—in this case, the seals on the door—it's easier when the moon is new. You want to create things, it's better when the moon is full."

She didn't pretend she really understood that, but at least he'd used simple words, so she just nodded and moved on.

She really wanted to move on to her apartment, her bed, and her very own REM sleep cycle. She got as far as standing up from the love seat before Luc grabbed her. "Where are you going?"

She sighed. "Home. To bed. I don't know about you, but it's been a long day and I'm exhausted. You just said we wouldn't be able to go to the park until sundown tomorrow, so I'm going to spend every available hour between now and then unconscious."

He tugged her hand, trying to get her to sit back down. "Okay, but I can't leave until I go over a few more things with Fergus and Rafe and the others."

"That's nice." She pulled her hand away. "But since I'm sure you don't need me around for the strategy stuff, I *can* go. And I plan to. Witness me leaving."

He snatched up her hand again and yanked, sending her tumbling down onto his lap in a heap. "No. I'll go with you, but you have to give me a few more minutes to make arrangements for tomorrow."

"Luc, what are you doing? Let me up!" She tried really hard to pretend she didn't notice the roomful of people watching her with avid curiosity, but the heat in her cheeks told her about how well that worked.

"No." He tightened his arms and frowned down at her. "I don't want you to leave without me. If you give me fifteen more minutes, I'll be done here, and we can go home together."

She blinked. "Did I invite you home with me?"

"Did you think you would have to?"

"Perhaps we could meet in the morning to talk," Dmitri offered through a smile that Corinne felt she was better off ignoring. "Since you had so little sleep last night. That way you need not waste fifteen minutes of, ah . . . sleeping time."

Reggie punched her husband in the ribs, not that he so much as flinched. "Misha, don't help him. He doesn't need it. Corinne is the one we should be trying to rescue."

"I don't need to be rescued."

"She doesn't need to be rescued."

They spoke both at once and Corinne rolled her eyes, pushing off Luc's lap to stand in front of him and face her interfering friends. "Look, it's not that I don't appreciate your concern," she said, "but I really don't need an intervention."

Reggie scowled. "I got an intervention."

"You got bit by a vampire. No one is going to be sucking my blood and turning me into a creature of the night."

"That doesn't mean we're not right to be concerned," Missy said, sounding as sweet and stern as when she told her class of five-year-olds to settle down for nap time.

"Like I was concerned when my best friend told me she was marrying a werewolf and having a cub? And let's see if I remember how said friend reacted to my concern . . ." Corinne blinked innocently for a second before she held up a finger in mock realization. "Oh, yeah! She told me to mind my own damned business and to make sure the baby gift was unisex."

At least Missy had the grace to blush. Reggie just charged ahead. Or at least, she tried to. "Rinne, you don't under—"

That's as far as she got before Dmitri put one hand over her mouth and flashed Corinne a grin. "Since I can guarantee my charming love is about three seconds from sinking her fangs into my hand, I suggest you take advantage of the silence to leave while you can." Reggie's eyes narrowed and her jaw clenched, and Dmitri's grin turned into a wince. "There, you see? Go away and have a good night."

Luc chuckled and stood, wrapping one arm about Corinne's waist and steering her toward the door. "We will. Let's all meet back here tomorrow afternoon around three. We can decide how to best deal with Seoc's capture then."

Rafe nodded and rose to walk them to the front door. "Of course. My home is at your disposal. And just because I love you, I will even keep our friend Fergus for the night. It would upset our plans if we had to spend all evening trying to stop Corinne from killing him."

They took a cab back to Corinne's, and she didn't even bother to pull away when he laced their fingers together and held their joined hands against his thigh. Instead, she actually leaned her head against his shoulder and watched the city roll past the windows.

Several minutes passed in silence while she sat with her cheek pillowed on his chest and his cheek resting against her hair. Finally she stirred, tilting her head until she could see his face. "Do you have a plan for tomorrow night?"

"I don't think it requires a better mousetrap, just stealth and speed," he said, snuggling her closer against him. "With the Lupines, Rafe, and Dmitri and Reggie on our side, we'll have that in abundance."

"So we just hide near the gate until he shows, and then jump him?"

He smiled at the incredulity in her voice. "You expected something a bit more elaborate?"

"I guess. It just seems so . . ." She shrugged. "Anticlimactic."

He chuckled. "A good many things are."

And then again, a good many things aren't, she thought and pressed her legs together against the involuntary ripple in her core. She seemed to have developed a reflex action, with the thought *Luc* and *climax* leading to the thought within a thousand synapses or so.

She fell silent again and stayed that way until they paid the cabdriver and headed up to her apartment. When she unlocked the door and led him inside, she felt almost like she'd been stuck by déjà vu, but this time when Luc shut the door behind them he reached for her immediately.

His lips settled on hers like rain, and she soaked him up as quickly as the desert floor. In fact, she was about half a second from drowning when the niggling in the back of her mind turned into a pounding and she pulled away on a groan.

"Wait," she said, bracing her hands against his chest to keep him farther than lip-length away from her. "You and I have some talking to do."

Luc groaned against her throat as he laved it with his oh-so-clever tongue. "We can talk later."

"Right," she scoffed. "Like we're really going to have the energy to talk after we screw each other into a couple of senseless puddles of goo. I can see that happening."

"I have no problem with goo," he muttered, scraping his teeth against her collarbone. "That sounds fine to me. Let's aim for goo."

"No." She pushed him firmly away and squirmed out of his arms, walking around the back of the sofa to keep some sort of barrier between them. If he touched her again, she knew darned well the only things coming out of her mouth would be cries for more. "I said I wanted to talk."

He groaned and let his arms drop to his sides. But he didn't look happy about it. "Fine," he said. "Just do me a favor and try and talk fast, okay?"

"Fine. I've really only got one question for you." She crossed her arms and braced herself. "What is a heartmate?"

She saw Luc tense, heard him swear, and then watched while he collapsed into an armchair and closed his eyes on a sigh.

"Luc?"

He didn't say anything, but she saw him rubbing his hands over his face, so she knew he was still conscious.

"Luc," she prodded, "answer me. Tell me what the Queen meant when she called you my heartmate."

He shook his head. "Corinne, that's . . . I really . . . it's just too much to go into right now. It's complicated."

"So simplify it for me."

She watched his face carefully, noticed the wary expression in his eyes when he finally opened them to look up at her. "Baby—"

"Don't baby me. Tell me what the Queen was talking about." When he continued to hesitate, she sighed and sat down on the arm of his chair. He looked so wary and tired and vulnerable that she couldn't manage to keep up the über-bitch routine. She stroked a hand over his tousled hair. "Look at it this way. You might as well tell me now, when I'm all tired and ready for bed. If you wait until I'm alert, I'll just have that much more energy for being mad at you."

"You have a point." He took her free hand in his and brushed a kiss over her fingertips. "But you don't really need me to tell you what you already know. It's a sort of self-explanatory term."

She slid off the arm of the chair and into his lap. "Then it's the same sort of thing as when Graham calls Missy his mate. It's like a . . . like a . . . wife?"

He rested his cheek against the top of her head

and wrapped his arms around her, cuddling her close. "In a way. The Fae don't have any formal marriage ceremonies. Couples stay together because they want to stay together. If they change their minds, they go their separate ways."

"Does that mean you might change your mind about us?"

She heard the smile in his voice. "Never. I can't. To have a mate in Faerie is one thing, but to have a heartmate is entirely different. A mate is a companion you choose and discard as it suits the both of you. A heartmate is the other part of your spirit. Fate chooses for you, and the bonds last forever. It doesn't happen for all Fae, but when it does, it's seen as a blessing from the goddess Anu."

She was silent for a few minutes, listening to the echo of his heart beating beneath her ear and his words swirling in her mind. "Forever, huh?"

He nodded.

"And you're sure that's what's happened to us. It's not just the companion thing?"

Corinne heard the note of vulnerability in her voice and winced. She didn't want to turn into the weepy, clingy, needy type, but damn, this was hard. It tied her thoughts in a tangle and her stomach in knots and her heart in a butterfly net. She tried to at least keep her head down so he couldn't read her expression, but he touched his knuckles to her chin and gently raised it until he could look into her eyes.

"I'm more than sure," he said, his green eyes

deep and solemn and potent. "A heartmate can see through glamours to the truth that lies beneath so that deception can never interfere with Love's Truth. The minute you saw through my human disguise, I knew you were my heartmate. Not even the gods can change that now."

She held his gaze for the span of a dozen heartbeats before she felt her mouth begin to curve in an irrepressible smile. "All right, then," she said, laying her head back against his chest. "I'll take your word for it. For now."

He chuckled. "And what will it take before you're fully convinced?"

"Not much. Only a decade or two."

Sixteen

Again, Corinne woke to the feel of teeth delicately nibbling at her skin, but this time it was accompanied by the sweet, sleepy feel of a warm, familiar body joining with hers. She gave a drowsy moan and arched her back to deepen the contact. Strong, callused hands slid around her body to cup her breasts and knead gently.

"Good morning." Luc's raspy morning voice rumbled against her ear, the vibrations traveling all the way down to where their bodies were linked and making her contract around him in pleasure.

"Mm." It was the only answer she could manage.

Instead of struggling to speak, she reached up behind her and buried her fingers in his hair, pulling the long strands forward until they blanketed both of them, covering them in a thick, silken sheet that smelled of woodland and spice and strong, vibrant male. She heard Luc's purr, and his hands shifted. One continued to cup her breast, teasing her nipples alternately with soft caresses and gentle pinches. The other hand slid down her torso, over her ribs, and down to rest on her belly.

His fingers spread wide, spanning the space between her hip bones and pressing her back against him as he began to move his hips in a deep, lazy rhythm.

Corinne hummed and let her head fall back against his shoulder as she surrendered herself totally to his loving. She let his hand guide her hips, rocking her bottom against his pelvis with sleepy pleasure.

"So sweet," he whispered, his breath another caress against the curve of her ear. "So precious to me. Heartmate. We have all the time in the worlds, and nothing in *Ithir* or in Faerie can compare to the feel of you next to me, or the smell of your warm, soft skin."

His words sent shivers racing through her and she shifted in an attempt to get closer to him. She reached one hand back, curling her fingers around his firm behind to urge him to a quicker rhythm.

"Sweet girl." He licked the soft hollow just behind her ear and smiled into the curve of her neck when she shivered in response. "You make the most adorable little noises while you're sleeping, did you know that? But I think I like the ones you make when you're awake even better."

She parted her thighs, curling one closer to her chest and draping her top leg over his. The position sent him stroking so deep, she had to fight for breath. She'd gone from dreaming to needing so fast, she thought her head was going to drift right off her shoulders. He was driving her crazy.

She tried to press her hips harder against him, but they were already so close that not even the dew on their skin could separate them. She whimpered and pressed her head hard against his shoulder. "Luc," she whispered. "I need you."

He stroked deeply. "You have me."

Shudder. "I want you."

He shifted his hips just a fraction, but it was enough to send him sliding against a sweet, special spot deep inside her. "You have me."

She came with a quiet gasp and a rolling wave of pleasure, her body clenching around his, dragging him with her into the whirlpool.

"I love you," he whispered into the quiet of aftermath.

She smiled sleepily. "You have me."

The second time Corinne woke that morning wasn't nearly as pleasant. Instead of Luc making love to her, she heard a heavy fist pounding on her front door.

"Shit. Fergus."

Luc, already out of bed and pulling on his jeans, looked at her curiously. "What makes you think it's Fergus?"

She gave him a sour look. "I have a doorbell. Who else would be rude enough to ignore it?"

Luc laughed, tugged his T-shirt into place, and leaned down to kiss her. "Go ahead and get dressed. I'll answer the door. And if it's Fergus, I'll make him promise to mind his manners."

"Good luck," she snorted.

He patted her ass affectionately before heading into the living room to answer the door. Corinne sighed and dragged herself out of bed, feeling a little stiff, a moderate amount sore, and a whole lot content. She and Luc hadn't actually managed all that much sleep last night, but they'd managed to stay energized despite it. In fact, she couldn't wait to take care of Seoc so they could come back here and burn off the rest of that energy in a more satisfying manner than chasing naughty Fae.

She felt her mouth curve in a cream-licking smile. There was only one naughty Fae she wanted to waste her time on, and he fell into a whole different category of naughtiness.

She heard the sound of her door opening, and Fergus's voice followed by the even deeper rumble of Luc's before she shut the bedroom door. She used the bathroom quickly, then pulled out underwear, a black T-shirt, and her beat-up old camouflage cargo pants and began to dress. The trousers were slightly ridiculous in a civilian context, but they were enormously comfortable and made her feel like kicking ass, which she thought might come in handy, given their planned activities for the day. They also had a plethora of pockets so she wouldn't have to bring her backpack or a purse to the park. Something about taking a purse to a stakeout just seemed wrong to her.

Once dressed, she pulled on socks and laced up her black Doc Marten boots—perfect for hiking—

and began to load her pockets. Since she couldn't hear anything from the other room, she figured the men were being macho together and discussing strategy or something, so she took the time to get everything she thought she'd need now.

She grabbed tissues and ChapStick first, then her cell phone, a mini flashlight, and her keys. She was about to head for the other room when she remembered Fergus, so she grabbed her bottle of aspirin. Figuring the rattle might drive her almost as crazy as he did, she emptied a huge handful into her palm and dropped them into a clean pocket. Better lint-covered tablets than a breakdown mid-stakeout.

Finally ready, she opened the bedroom door and found herself face-to-face with Fergus. She raised an eyebrow. "Do you have a problem? I'm all ready to go, and that couldn't have taken me more than five minutes, so save your bitching." She frowned. "Where's Luc?"

The Fae didn't say a word, but something about his silence made Corinne look down, and that's when she saw the knife clutched in Fergus's hand. The sharp, glittering, blood-soaked knife. Her eyes flew wide open, and she opened her mouth to scream, but she never managed a sound. She saw a fist coming toward her, and then she didn't see anything else for quite a while.

She came to swinging, which just earned her a hard slap and a warning growl. Fergus loomed over her, his handsome face twisted in a snarl before he dropped her to the ground with a thud.

Corinne felt the air whoosh out of her lungs as she landed on a conveniently placed root that threatened to give her an impromptu appendectomy. She rolled to the side with a moan. "What the hell is going on?"

Fergus didn't bother to answer. He was too busy consulting an ancient-looking map and then glancing down at an object in his palm that seemed to be glowing a sickly green color. Corinne opened her mouth to repeat her question—only louder and with stronger language—but she changed her mind. Better to take a look at her surroundings and figure out where she was before she started asking him what was going on.

She was definitely outdoors—the tree root that had dug into her side could attest to that—and judging by what little she could see of the surroundings in the deepening gloom of twilight, she was in a hilly wooded area with her hands tied in front of her and a whole lot of New York spread out below her. Making an educated guess, she decided she was in Inwood Hill Park, and Fergus was a lousy, no-good son of a bitch.

With that four-foot sword strapped to his back.

"It wasn't Seoc trying to open the Faerie door at all," she said suddenly as realization flashed through her. Her voice sounded unusually loud in the quiet surroundings. "It was you. Luc was on a wild goose chase looking for the Queen's nephew while you were off testing the old doorways to see if any of them still worked. You little shit."

Fergus looked up from his map to sneer at her. "Is this where I'm supposed to tell you the details of my dastardly plan while you saw through the ropes binding you with a carefully concealed dagger? I hate to disappoint you, human, but I'm not that stupid, and you don't have a dagger. I searched you before we ever left your apartment. I even took away your keys. So shut up and let me work."

Corinne snorted. "Right. Sure. Let me make this as easy for you as possible, 'cause that's my main goal whenever someone kidnaps me."

He stared down at her with contempt, his lip curled in a malicious smile. "If I were in your position, and I had seen my heartmate's blood staining the blade of the enemy's dagger, I think I'd reevaluate my main goal."

Corinne stilled, her mind flashing to that moment when she'd opened the door to find Luc out of sight and Fergus standing in front of her with a knife and an evil intent. She waited for the sickening wave of grief to wash over her, and blinked when none did. After she and Luc had talked last night about heartmates and the bonds they shared, she expected his death to devastate her. So that meant one of two things: either Luc had been lying about being heartmates, or he wasn't really dead. Since even the Queen of Faerie had gone with the heartmate scenario, she decided she would, too.

Luc was still alive, and if she knew him even a

little, she guessed he would soon be making Fergus very, very sorry for his betrayal. In the meantime, she needed to stay alive and find a way out of this situation. Just in case.

"If you were going to kill me, you damned sure would have done it by now." She used her elbows to push into a sitting position, making it seem like more work than it was so she could get her hands into her pocket for a second. She didn't need a knife or her keys to make things tough for this jerk. "Which means you need me around for something. So forgive me for not kissing your ass."

"Unlike the mighty Lucifer, I realize a human isn't worthy to kiss my ass," he snapped. "And don't delude yourself. You're only here in case your friends show up before I get the door open. Once I'm done with that, I'm done with you."

She stiffened. This guy needed a class in Remedial Bad Guy 101. Telling a hostage you planned to kill her when you got what you wanted took away all her incentive to cooperate and made her that much more likely to fight every step of the way. But hey, Corinne wasn't going to lose her advantage by telling him that.

She scoffed at him instead. "What? Didn't you take care of them, too, before you dragged me up here? Some criminal mastermind you are."

He ignored her taunt, holding the glowing green thing—which she could now see looked like some kind of stone—aloft and pointing it in different directions like a compass. When he faced the hill in front of them, even Corinne could see the stone glowing brighter.

"We're close," Fergus muttered, "but we have to get up higher. Come on."

He grabbed Corinne by her arms and hauled her to her feet, shoving her along in front of him as he marched up the hill. She clenched her bound hands into fists and every few feet moved her middle finger to allow a white, buffered aspirin tablet to fall unnoticed to the ground. Hey, Hansel and Gretel had bread crumbs, she had aspirin. Folkloric German urchins didn't get her kind of headaches.

They hiked over the rough terrain, which was harder than it sounded, especially given the fading light and the fact that one of them had her hands bound in front of her, but Fergus just watched the stone in his hand and pressed forward.

Corinne kept her eyes open for any chance to escape, but still bound, still walking in front of him, and still waiting to get a chance to stop him for opening the door, the chance didn't come. If she was lucky, the cavalry would ride to the rescue and she wouldn't end up having to run for her life. She liked that scenario.

Since the plan had been to meet up at Rafe's place at three, and—judging by the advancing state of dusk—it was likely closer to eight, she knew Rafe, Dmitri, Graham, and her friends would already know something had gone wrong. If they bothered to check her apartment, they'd probably find Luc—and they'd damned well better take good care of him—and then they'd be after her. Provided any of them had used their supernatural mojo for a good cause this time, they'd have been on her trail by seven at the latest. They couldn't be very far behind Corinne and Fergus, so she just crossed her fingers, kept dropping her aspirin trail, and hoped they'd hurry the hell up.

Seventeen

Luc didn't just wake up swinging; he awoke swinging, swearing, and strangling an unsuspecting Graham. That didn't last long, since Missy immediately shouted something nasty and leapt forward to plant her foot on his arm. Graham used the opportunity to wrench himself out of the enraged Fae's grip.

"Calm down before we decide to leave you to bleed to death," Rafe said, speaking calmly over the sound of Missy's furious chatter and Dmitri's low chuckle. "Save the righteous rage for the one who tried to gut you."

"Where's Corinne?"

"Gone." Graham rubbed his hand over his bruised neck. "Presumably with the one who tried to gut you. But there's no blood or evidence she's been hurt."

"Fergus." Luc spat the name like a bitter taste from his mouth. He relaxed a little, though, because now that he took the time to breathe, he could feel that she was still alive. He would know if his heart-mate had been taken from him permanently.

Rafe nodded. "I could smell him here, but I don't claim to understand what happened."

"I've got my theories," Luc growled as he pushed himself to his feet.

"Hey," Reggie scolded, rushing to press a thick gauze pad to a sullenly bleeding wound in his side. "What the hell do you think you're doing? You're wounded, here!"

He tried to brush her away, but she clung like a barnacle, and with Dmitri watching closely he couldn't exactly put his back into it. "Don't worry about it. I'll be fine. We need to go find Corinne."

"Fat lot of good you'll do her. What are you going to do to rescue her from Fergus? Bleed all over him?"

He started to protest, but by then Missy had assured herself of Graham's safety and climbed on board with Reggie. "You've got to take care of these wounds before you go anywhere, or you're not going to be much good to Rinne or anybody else," she scolded. "These stab wounds look awful."

Luc scowled. "They'd look worse if he'd been smart enough to use iron, but these are from silver. They'll heal fast enough. We need to go now, though. He's already killed once. He won't hesitate to hurt Corinne."

"He's already hurt you." Reggie pushed hard enough against his wound to make the damned thing throb uncomfortably. "And I, for one, don't want to be the one to explain to Corinne that we let you run off untended, and you bled to death before we could catch up with her. She gets mean when she's angry."

"Yeah, I noticed that."

"Then do us a favor and sit down and shut up long enough for us to bandage you up. Then you can go after Corinne, okay?" Missy didn't wait for his reply but headed back toward the bathroom.

"Bring lots of adhesive tape!" Reggie shouted after her before turning back to Luc. "Right. Now that shirt has to go. Strip."

Luc's eyes widened and shot to Dmitri's face. The vampire looked somehow amused and jealous all at once.

"Why don't you tell us about these theories you have regarding Fergus, my friend," Dmitri suggested, crossing his arms over his chest and keeping an eagle eye on his tiny wife as she and Missy began mopping up Fae blood. "It will distract me so I do not give in to the urge to give you a few new wounds myself for having my wife's hands on you."

Luc could sympathize. He spread his arms wide to give the women access to his wounds. "I'm kicking myself that I never suspected," he said, "but now I realize Fergus was the problem all along, not Seoc. It never did sit right with me to think that Seoc had killed that rabbi. He's just not the violent type. Fergus, though, is a different story."

"You mean you came here for nothing? Seoc was never wandering unattended through the city?"

"No, the Queen's nephew is irresponsible and annoying, and I don't doubt he was the Fae all those witnesses reported seeing, but it was never him trying to open the doors. That was Fergus."

"But why would he do that?" Graham asked. "Doesn't he have as much to lose as any of the Fae if the doors open? At least with Seoc, I could see it as a revenge-against-his-controlling-aunt thing."

"I haven't decided on a why yet," Luc said, "but I think I've nailed the how. Fergus was the guard on duty the night Seoc slipped into *Ithir,* and I think that not only did Fergus know about it, he helped, knowing that Seoc would provide the perfect distraction while Fergus went looking for the door. It wouldn't be hard for a guard to slip through fairly regularly on his shifts without anyone suspecting. He had access, and no one would question the loyalty of the Queen's guardsmen."

"The perfect cover." Dmitri scowled, and Luc just hoped it was at the idea of Fergus's betrayal, and not the fact that Reggie was currently pressed up against his chest while she passed the roll of adhesive tape behind his back.

"Exactly," he continued, figuring distracting the vampire with his theories couldn't hurt. "It probably wasn't even all that tough. All he had to do was nose around while Seoc provided a red herring; he could even use his place on the Guard to keep up-to-date on how close we were to finding Seoc. And yesterday, we gave him everything he needed to find the door." His mouth twisted in disgust. "We practically handed the location to right to him."

Reggie ripped off the last bit of tape and pressed

it against his skin before stepping back and handing him a clean T-shirt. "True, but he doesn't know any more than we do. We'll get to him before anything happens."

Graham nodded and handed Luc the duffel bag he'd left at Vircolac. They must have brought it with them when they came looking for him. "Regina is right. We know where he went, and we know what he's planning. He's an idiot if he thinks we won't find him and stop him."

"True," Luc growled. "He is an idiot, but he's the idiot who has my heartmate."

Corinne cursed as she stumbled on another root. The sun had well and truly set, making the going over the rocky, uphill terrain slow and treacherous. She'd already skinned both her knees and lost the rest of her aspirin in one big pile a few stumbles ago. Still, maybe there was enough of a trail for Luc to find her.

She never doubted for a minute that he was on his way. She just hoped he managed to get to her before Fergus succeeded in opening the Faerie door. She was still struggling to get accustomed to the fact that she was sleeping with a Fae; she definitely didn't want to see what would come traipsing through into *Ithir* if Fergus got his way.

"You know, I don't want to make you play out the villain cliché," she said as she scrambled over a fallen tree trunk, " 'cause mainly I just want you to drop dead, but I'm having trouble with the why of this whole scenario. Why the hell would you want to open the door? You've got as much to lose as any Fae if humans start pouring into Faerie, right?"

"Humans are so simple-minded," he scoffed. "I couldn't care less if Faerie teems with your detestable little species, so long as that faithless bitch is dethroned and I rise in her place."

Corinne paused to look back at him. "Oh, shit," she breathed. "You're not just an asshole, you're a megalomaniacal lunatic, too. Oh, man, this so sucks."

He drew back his hand and hit her so casually, she never saw it coming. One minute he was looking at her with his characteristic sneer, the next she was picking herself up out of the dirt, wiping the trickle of blood away from her mouth. "Watch what you say, human. I still have the option of killing you slowly if you piss me off."

"Is there really any way I can *not* piss you off?"

He paused for a moment. "No, I don't think so."

She wiped her bloody fingers on her shorts and watched him consult his glow-rock. "How much farther?"

He ignored her.

"I can change that to *Are we there yet?* but I was trying to be nice."

"We're nearly on top of it." He didn't even bother to look at her. "Now shut up and keep moving."

She moved, but she also plotted. They were making too much noise for her to hear if anyone was following them yet. Well, to be honest, she was making too much noise. Fergus seemed to move silently, though how anyone could walk over dead leaves and twigs and loose rocks without making a sound was beyond her, even if he wasn't human. Since she couldn't tell if Luc had caught up to them, she tried to slow him down.

"Okay, fine," she huffed, "I get the power goal. That's understandable, but if you're the one who's been causing all this trouble, where has Seoc really gone? Was he the one who sent Hibbish to limbo and killed the rabbi, or was that you?"

He laughed coldly. "The only one in limbo is Seoc himself. All the humans are dead. I didn't want them telling the story of two Fae wandering through their city. Having spotted Seoc was a convenient cover, but spotting me was too much to let go." His mouth twisted in a sneer. "No one was supposed to find the rabbi, but I didn't have time to dispose of him like the others. He cried out when I struck him, and I could hear someone running toward the sound. I had to leave him out in the open. It was my one mistake."

Corinne felt her stomach turn at the callous way he related the news, as if their deaths meant nothing to him. Clearly they did mean nothing.

"Oh, I think you've made more than one," she growled, "but that's the one I'll see you pay for, you miserable little prick."

"They were human and, therefore, expendable."

"Who isn't expendable in your fucked-up universe?"

His grin flashed, unrepentant and soulless. "Just me. I'll even see Mab dead eventually. After I'm done with her."

The tone he used to speak of the Queen dripped with bile and a sick kind of desire. It made Corinne's stomach heave, but the longer she kept him talking, the longer she gave Luc to find them.

"What, you think you're going to screw the Queen of the Faeries?" she scoffed, deliberately taunting him. "I doubt she gets off on insanity *or* disloyalty. I imagine she'd rather spread her legs for that *barghest* you sent after us."

"An impulse, one that almost worked out better than I had anticipated. But it wouldn't be the first time the Queen spread whatever I asked her to. I've had that bitch in ways you can't even imagine. She took me as her favorite more than a century ago, and she made promises to me that I'm going to see she fulfills."

He must have seen the shock on her face, because he chuckled deeply. "Oh, I'm sure she made quite an impression on you earlier, human. Wearing her crown and her all-knowing, all-loving expression. She likes to make people fear her almost as much as she likes to make people love her. It's just too bad she's not capable of returning the emotion."

"Oh, my God," she said, shaking her head and staring at him in disbelief. "You're about to destroy all of Faerie because you're pissed off that the woman you were seeing dumped your psycho ass. And you have the nerve to look down on humans as if we're less evolved!"

He struck her again and this time she saw stars for a minute before the world righted itself. She knew she was right, though, and she wondered what Luc would say when he learned he'd been betrayed by his friend over a bruised ego.

"I've heard enough from you," he snarled. "From now on, you can keep your mouth shut. We're so close, I could probably kill you and still get the door open before anyone found us, so don't push me."

Fergus grabbed her by the arm and shoved her forward, ignoring her pained hiss. When she stumbled yet again, he hauled her to her feet and pushed her faster. He had her nearly running up to the crest of the hill, struggling frantically to keep her balance. Her breath came in shallow pants by the time he dragged her to a halt and shoved her down against the base of a tree trunk.

"Stay there."

He wasn't stupid enough to turn his back on her—sadly enough—but he had clearly tuned her out before she even hit the ground. Corinne propped herself up against the tree and eyed him warily. His glow-rock had turned a bright blue-green color, the same shade as in all the ads for the Caribbean. That seemed to be the cue he was looking for, because he pocketed it and began to examine the rock formations and almost-caves that covered the rocky hilltop.

He was muttering something under his breath, and she really hoped it wasn't the spell that would open the door. "Now would be a really good time for the cavalry," she mumbled.

"Shut up!" he snarled. "Keep quiet, or I'll knock you out again."

She didn't doubt it, and since she really needed to be conscious in case the cavalry didn't arrive, she fell silent and watched him search. She thought about trying to distract him by talking or running, but refrained. Better to gather her energy and wait for an opportunity to tackle him to keep him from magicking the door open.

She watched as Fergus began to run his hands along a crevice in the rock and stiffened when he crowed in triumph.

"Finally!" He stepped back and turned his head to send Corinne a particularly nasty smile. "Just a few more minutes, and then I can take care of you as well."

He faced the rock, spread his arms, and began to chant in the same language she'd heard Luc swear in after she'd pissed him off particularly badly. She swore herself. This was it. There was no sign of Luc or the others, yet, and their time had just run out. Even as she struggled to her feet, she saw something begin to happen.

The crevice Fergus had explored began to glow, the same sort of turquoise color as the rock the Fae had used to lead them there. It began as a fine line of light and slowly expanded until it was as tall as the Fae and nearly an inch wide. Corinne knew that in a moment it would be big enough for someone or something to pass through.

When that happened, it would be too late for Luc and the others to rescue her. It would be too late for everyone.

"Oh, well," she muttered under her breath, gathering herself for a leap. "If you want something done right . . ."

She pushed off, but she never landed. At least, not on Fergus.

She heard a growl and almost simultaneously saw a blurry figure launch itself from the trees. She grunted as it hurtled past her, shouldering her roughly to the side before it continued forward and slammed full-length into Fergus. Both figures toppled to the earth and rolled around. For several seconds they struggled, the air thick with rage and curses, before a hoarse shout dragged their attention to the woods.

Luc and Dmitri emerged, running full-tilt toward Fergus, with Reggie and Missy hurrying along behind, held in check only by one of Rafe's hands on each of their shoulders. In one fist, Luc carried an enormous sword that gleamed dully in the dim light that bled into the park from the city below. The other was clenched and looked positively eager to pound something.

Corinne's eyes flew over her heartmate, but she couldn't even see an injury. Even though Fergus's knife had been covered in blood, he must not have done any permanent damage. Relief threatened to bring her to her knees. Except she was already there, where she'd landed after the impact of her savior's weight against her shoulder had sent her sprawling. She hadn't landed very far from the pair, though. In fact, she barely realized just how close she was in time to scramble out of the way before the combatants rolled right into her.

The figure wrestling with Fergus spun away, and now Corinne could see that the one who had originally attacked Fergus had dark fur tipped with silver along the spine, and was definitely not human. It was a wolf.

Graham.

The werewolf pulled away from Fergus to let Luc get a chance at him. Even Dmitri seemed to know to hang back; this battle belonged to the Fae warrior and not to his friends, no matter how well meaning. Instead, Graham placed himself between Fergus and Corinne and growled at her when she tried to go to Luc.

"Fergus." Luc's voice was a low, feral snarl that sounded almost like it was coming from Graham's throat. He halted a few feet from the other Fae and watched as the traitor climbed slowly to his feet. "You should have forgotten about the door and kept running, because the moment you touched my heartmate, you sealed your own fate."

"So dramatic," Fergus sneered, "but tell me, Captain, how are you feeling? I hope you didn't mind the inconvenience of my knife sliding between your ribs, because I have the urge to repeat the experience."

"Too bad you won't get to fulfill it. I'll give you a choice, Fergus of Eithdne. You can surrender to me and consent to be taken in irons back to our Queen, or you can die, here and now, for crimes against Queen Mab and all of Faerie. You choose."

Corinne stood so close, she could hear the sound of Fergus's sword hissing as he pulled it from its scabbard. Even if she had been farther away, though, she doubted she would have been able to avoid what happened next.

He moved so fast, she almost didn't see him strike, feinting toward Luc and then spinning around Graham's unsuspecting form to grab Corinne by the hair. He pulled her across the ground until she knelt in front of him. His hand gripped her hair tightly, bracing her against his thigh while he held his sword in his other hand.

"I think you should choose." Fergus raised his blade and pointed the tip at her throat. "Either you finish opening that door and let me pass through, or I slit your heartmate's throat and see if she bleeds any faster than you do."

Luc gave a roar of rage and threw himself forward, only to catch himself in mid-stride as Fergus's sword nicked Corinne's skin, sending a tiny trickle of blood to slide down her throat.

"Be very careful, my friend," Fergus sneered. "I'm not feeling charitable toward the human to begin with, so it would be no hardship for me to watch her die. In fact, I might just enjoy it."

Luc growled impotently, but he stilled and met Fergus's gaze with rage burning in his own.

"Very good. Now open the door."

Corinne met Luc's gaze and saw the frustration there. His concern touched her, but it also pissed her off, because she knew right then that he was going to give in to Fergus's demands and open the Faerie door himself. To save her.

She wanted to scream in frustration. Among Graham, Dmitri, and Luc, they had enough power to mash Fergus into tiny bits, but because he had a sword to her throat, all three stood there paralyzed. Even Reggie and Missy looked too intimidated to move. Damn it, they had to get over this little phobia of seeing her die.

"Don't do it, Luc," she said, her voice trembling. Not with fear but with anger.

Her heartmate spoke in an unsteady voice himself. "I can't let him hurt you."

"This is touching," Fergus interrupted. "Repulsive, but touching. However, it's also quite futile. I don't know how I can simplify this for you any more. Either open the door, or the human dies. Choose."

Luc swore and turned toward the glowing sliver of doorway. Corinne screamed.

"Don't you dare!" She didn't care about the fist in her hair or the blade at her throat or anything else. What mattered was that Luc couldn't throw away everything he stood for because some lunatic with a superiority complex was holding a knife on her.

"Shut up!" Fergus shouted, loosening his grip in her hair so he could cuff her against the side of the head.

Idiot. That was all she needed.

She threw herself backward, screaming as she felt a large clump of her hair stay behind in Fergus's hand. The force of her movement sent her slamming into the ground harder than when she'd been dropped earlier, knocking some of the wind out of her. Her head landed a glancing blow against a rock, making her vision fuzz and blur.

She couldn't see what happened next, but she sure as hell heard it. Roaring echoed in her ears, and she couldn't tell if it came from Luc or Fergus, or the Others, or even all of them at once.

She knew the cheering she heard definitely came from Reggie and Missy.

She heard the sounds of a brawl, but her eyes had closed against the blinding pain in her head, and she couldn't pry them open. Nausea roiled in her stomach and she curled instinctively into a fetal position, gagging helplessly. She couldn't work up the strength to protest when she felt two pairs of small hands hook under her arms and drag her out of the way of the struggle.

They needn't have bothered. With odds of four

against one, Fergus didn't last long. Before they had even stopped moving, silence descended on the hilltop.

Well, silence punctuated by the sickening sound of a fist thumping violently against flesh and bone.

"Luc. Luc, stop!" she heard. "He's unconscious. Stop before you kill him."

Rafe. The voice of reason.

"Why should I? He touched my mate."

"But she's safe now. And do you want to have to explain his death to the Queen?"

A brief silence. Corinne struggled to breathe through her mouth and ride out the pain. At least the nausea seemed to be fading.

"Trust me," she gritted out, "we'll have plenty to tell Mab without adding that to the list."

The effort of the short speech exhausted her. She felt as if she'd been trampled by a herd of elephants. And she suspected they'd been wearing high heels.

She heard a vague grumbling, then more silence until she was lifted and settled in a hard lap, cuddled close in muscular arms.

"I'm so sorry, baby." She felt his lips moving against her forehead as he pressed his cheek to her hair. "I love you so much. I'm so sorry he touched you. I should have been quicker."

"Fine." Her voice cracked and squeaked this time, but she figured she'd managed enough to get her point across. She was fine. Or she would be. Eventually.

She needed to say something else, though. She parted her lips and gathered her strength. "Love, too."

Not real clear, but he was a bright guy. Sometimes. He'd figure it out.

His arms tightened convulsively around her and she knew he had.

She pressed her face against his chest and whimpered one, critically important word. "Aspirin?"

Then she blacked out, safe in her heartmate's arms.

Epilogue

She got Tylenol with codeine.

After the doctors checked to make sure she didn't have a concussion, they prescribed the good stuff and released her to Luc's tender loving care. He had to fight Reggie and Missy for the privilege.

"Are you okay? Does your head hurt?"

Corinne sighed. "No more than it did the last time you asked. Five seconds ago."

She cracked an eye open to see Luc's beloved face hovering just inches above hers. Instead of bringing her back to her apartment, he had taken her to Vircolac, to a room Graham provided and stocked more completely than your average private hospital suite. She thought there might even be a bedpan under the night table.

She would be more comfortable, the Alpha had informed them, with twenty-four-hour room service.

"Isn't that what Luc is for?" she had asked.

Her heartmate had been incredibly solicitous, so much so that it was beginning to drive her the littlest bit crazy. She was all for being adored, but

not when the man seemed afraid to handle her like
anything other than spun glass.

"Do you want a glass of water? You can't have
another pill for an hour, but I could do a charm if
your head hurts too much to wait."

"I'm fine. Stop hovering." She glared at him.
With love, of course. "Either go away or get into
bed with me, because I'm about one second away
from forgetting about the doctor's orders and taking my own damned self home."

He got into bed with her.

"Sorry," he said, sounding sheepish and adorable. "You just scared the hell out of me when you
passed out."

"I scared myself a little," she muttered, snuggling against his chest and feeling his arms close
very gently around her. That made her feel more at
home than returning to her apartment possibly
could have. "But I'm fine now. The doctor even
said, no permanent damage. I'll be good as new in a
couple of weeks. I just have to take it easy and reduce the number of times I get attacked to less than
three in a forty-eight-hour period."

He didn't appear to appreciate her attempts at
humor. "I still wish Rafe had let me kill him."

She grinned. "But then I'd have gotten jealous
that I didn't get a lick at him."

The grin faded when she looked up and saw the
rawness of the emotions etched on his worried
face.

"I'm glad Rafe stopped you," she told him seriously. "Mab was upset enough by what he'd done, especially given that their relationship had been so close. I think she felt a little guilty that her ending things could have spurred him to put her entire realm in jeopardy. But I think things would have been even worse for her if you had killed him."

He sighed against her hair. "She was upset. She never guessed one of her favorites would betray her."

"That wasn't why she was so upset. Or at least not all of it."

He looked his question.

"She obviously sees the members of the Guard as her children. She just saw one of her sons turn against the others. That would nearly kill most mothers, I think."

"Okay, you can't tell me they were lovers one minute and then refer to him as her son the next." He gave an exaggerated shudder. "Even in Faerie some things are still taboo. Not to mention creepy."

She smacked him lightly. "You know what I mean."

He kissed her forehead. "Sometimes."

"Anyway, at least she got Seoc back safely."

Luc chuckled. "Yeah, and he'll be using his innocence to get out of trouble for centuries."

"Hey, I would, too, if I'd been so falsely accused."

He laughed. And snuggled her just the slightest bit closer. "She demanded to be invited, you know."

Corinne frowned at him. "Mab? What did she want to be invited to?"

He smiled slightly. "Our wedding."

She paused meaningfully. "Are we getting married?"

"Well, since we'll be living together here in *Ithir* and I plan to stay with you till the end of our days, I thought we could."

Corinne tried to ignore the fluttering in her stomach and the aching fullness of her heart. "But you said Fae didn't get married."

"You aren't Fae," he said simply.

"You know, now might be a good time to keep your promise and explain to me how it is that in fifty years I'm not going to look like your great-aunt Ida."

"Well that's easy," he said with a grin. "I'm not going to look this way in fifty years."

She frowned. "How do you figure that?"

"Aging is only partially genetic for the sidhe. Most of the eternal-youth thing has to do with living in Faerie. No one there really ages past adulthood. As long as I'm living in *Ithir,* I'll age almost like a human. And if we want to slow things down once in a while, we can always go to Faerie for a visit. Mab says we're welcome in the palace anytime."

Corinne digested that. "I suppose that could work. But are you sure about getting married?"

"I thought it would make you happy."

It would make her ecstatic, she realized, but she didn't intend to let him skip all the steps between meeting and marriage. She wanted all that good stuff, too.

"It will," she admitted, "but we're not going to do it yet."

She felt him stiffen. "Why not?"

"Because I want to date first." She pulled back to smile up at him. "Look at it this way. You know I'll say yes to your proposal eventually, which takes the pressure off, but you still get all the fun of trying to persuade me."

He laughed softly. "Ah, I understand. In that case, rest up, sweetheart. You're going to need your strength for my brand of persuasion."

"I can't wait."

They lay together in silence for a few minutes, and Corinne felt the drowsiness caused by the drugs and the events of the past couple of days start to take over. She could hear his heart beating steadily beneath her ear, and knew there was no place she'd rather be than in his arms. She couldn't wait for the future.

She didn't realize she'd drifted off to sleep, but when she woke again, Luc was gone and the clock told her she had been out for almost three hours. She rolled over and winced at the pain in her head.

"Here. Have some medicine."

She accepted the pill Missy pushed into her hand and swallowed it with a sip of water from the glass that was pressed against her lips. When she dropped her head back and opened her eyes gingerly, she saw Missy and Reggie sitting on opposite sides of her bed. "Where's Luc?"

Missy grinned. "Graham, Rafe, and Dmitri pried him away from you long enough to feed him. He was starting to turn a little gray."

"We think they plan to get him drunk, too. Just to celebrate."

Corinne scowled and looked around, her gaze screeching to a stop when she saw Ava watching her from the foot of the bed. "What?" she asked. "No Danice?"

"We couldn't get ahold of her," Reggie said. "She and Mac are away at their mysterious 'weekend house.' But I left a message on her machine at home, and with her secretary and her paralegal. And Daphanie stopped by earlier, but she was on her way out of town with Asher. She's exhibiting at some kind of craft show down south this weekend."

Corinne rolled her eyes, then winced at the pain it caused. "Did you send out notices or something? It's not like I'm on death's door or anything."

"Oh, we know," Ava drawled. "But we thought the whole gang deserved a chance to grill you on Tall, Dark, and Faerie."

"Fae," she corrected.

"Whatever. So spill it. Tell us all about him."

"Buy the movie."

"I'm not into porn flicks, darling. I prefer to read the book, but that takes so long, and you can summarize for me."

There would never be a book. If she had her way, Corinne's article on summertime mass hysteria in Manhattan would be the last time she ever mentioned a non-human being in her life. From now on she'd just focus on loving one.

"Can't you get a life of your own instead of prying into mine?" she demanded.

"Why should I?"

Corinne looked helplessly to Reggie and then to Missy for help. They just grinned at her.

"Don't look at us," Reggie said. "She did this to us, too."

"It's like a rite of passage," Missy added. "We all have to go through it eventually."

Corinne scowled. "That's ridiculous. She has no right to pry like this."

Ava arched a slim, dark brow. "Why do you think I waited until you were exhausted and vulnerable and too weak to fight back? Now spill."

Corinne knew when she'd been beaten, but that didn't stop her from scowling furiously at the object of her displeasure.

"Fine," she growled. "Until Luc escapes and comes to rescue me—which is becoming a distressingly familiar scenario—I'll satisfy your prurient curiosity. But just remember this. One day soon, it'll be your turn to answer questions about your love life."

Ava laughed. "Corinne, darling, the day I fall in love is the day I'll answer any question any one of you wants to ask me."

Corinne felt her mouth curve into a wicked grin, and saw the same expression mirrored on Reggie's and Missy's faces. Oh, boy, she could hardly wait.

"Ha! You said it, and I've got witnesses," she purred. "I want you to remember that promise, Av, because we are going to take great pleasure in holding you to it. One of these days you're going to get yours. And believe me when I tell you that love has a nasty habit of ignoring what you want, and giving you exactly what you need."

That's just what it had done for her.